CROSSROADS

WRAK-AYYA: THE AGE OF SHADOWS BOOK 13

LEIGH ROBERTS

DRAGON WINGS PRESS

CONTENTS

Editing by Joy Sephton www.justeemagine.biz
Cover design by Cherie Fox www.cheriefox.com

ISBN: 978-1-951528-36-2 (ebook)
ISBN: 978-1-951528-37-9 (paperback)

Dedication

*For those of you who have stood at their own crossroads
in life and wondered...*

What If?

CHAPTER 1

Across the verdant hills and valleys of Etera, a lone figure was making its way toward the People's territory. The Sassen watchers, placed by agreement at the High Council meeting, were covering the areas farthest out. The Sassen were more well suited to longer stays than the Akassa watchers and could cover the long distance back to Kht'shWea very quickly if necessary.

The Sassen watcher squinted, trying to make out who or what it was. He could tell it was not one of the Brothers, but it didn't seem quite like one of their own kind either. The coloring was also wrong, and that further confused him. He remained at his post, waiting until he could get a better idea of who it was coming toward him.

The figure had been traveling a long time. He kept putting one foot in front of the other, churning up the fallen leaves. There were plenty of food and water sources along the way, but it was still difficult going. He had been given general instructions with some landmarks, but he had not been able to pick up a magnetic trail that would easily have taken him where he was going. He was heading in the right direction, he was fairly certain, but he would have preferred to have some specific detail to reassure him.

He was tired of his own company, and while he was unsure of what to expect, he was looking forward to meeting these others. He had never met strangers, but he had no fear of them and was only hoping they would let him tell his story and would believe it.

Finally, as he came up over a high crest, he could see a great winding river far off in the distance. He let out a long breath that he watched escaping upward in the cold air. At last he knew he had been traveling in the right direction.

Over the next few days, the rest of the Sassen Guardians gave birth to their offling, and altogether, there were six females and six males. Each Guardian wondered privately if the evenly matched genders was part of the Order of Functions—that there would be six pairs of the first generation of naturally-born Sassen Guardians. Pan had explained that the offling would be able to pair with whoever they wanted, but they would still have to be wise. They would need the help of Bidzel and Yuma'qia to plan for their offling and the generations ahead, and there could be a whole colony of Sassen Guardians one day.

But there was only one Akassa Guardian—the Promised One.

Acise and Oh'Dar were still settling into their quarters. Acise had been to Kthama many times, so it was not foreign to her. She was used to being around the People, and their towering size no longer intimidated her, though she could not yet overlook it.

In a woven basket in his private corner, Oh'Dar stored the letters he had written while on trial for his life. He couldn't bring himself to destroy them as he had poured his heart into each one, thinking he would never see his friends and family again. The couple had decided to stay in their quarters for the most part for the first few days, unpacking and arranging, though they did visit Ben and Miss Vivian, who could not get enough of seeing little I'Layah.

"How is your leg feeling, Ben?" Oh'Dar asked.

"The crutches you made help, though I have to

be careful with them on the rock floors. It aches sometimes, but Nadiwani helps me with that." Ben repositioned his outstretched leg, trying to get more comfortable. "Oooff. Have you given any more thought to the idea of Ned Webb coming here to live?"

Oh'Dar let out a long breath. "I talked to my parents about it. I truly do not know what to do. "

"We made the adjustment, and he is much younger than we are. Perhaps the Overseer would have some insight? Would she not have to agree to it first anyway?"

"Yes, she would. And I know it is not my place to decide what is right for his life; I just do not want to misstep, and I fear he is too young to be making such a big decision. The People can never be discovered by the Waschini.

"But I should talk to the Overseer. I must also return to Wilde Edge at some point because I have to file the papers that Newell Storis drew up."

"You bluffed the constable then," Miss Vivian said, twirling I'Layah's locks between her fingers.

"Yes. Luckily he did not think it strange that I signed them in front of him, as signing is not the same as recording them. It was too important a responsibility to ask the Sheriff to undertake, and besides, I didn't want to remind the constable that it wasn't yet legal by asking the Sheriff to do it. Which means I will see the Webbs, and no doubt Ned will bring the topic up again. I saw the fire in his eyes. I don't think he is going to forget about wanting to come here to live."

Acaraho agreed with Oh'Dar that they would talk to the Overseer, who was still at the High Rocks, about Ned Webb wanting to come live among them. They found Urilla Wuti in the Leader's Quarters, standing next to Adia, who was seated holding the bundled-up twins.

"We have a situation to discuss with you if you have time. Adia already knows about it."

"Go ahead," Urilla Wuti said, finding a comfortable place to sit.

Acaraho explained about Ned Webb and how, despite their best attempts to keep as much of Kthama from Ned's awareness as possible, the fact remained that Ned knew he was somewhere other than another Brothers' village. And that though they went to so much trouble to keep everything secret, this had also made it obvious that there was a mystery being concealed.

"You must be in favor of it, to some extent, to have brought it to me?" Urilla Wuti said.

Acaraho looked at Oh'Dar, who then spoke.

"He is a fine young male, mature beyond his years, sensitive, and intelligent. He would be able to learn Ben's work and help us in moving forward, perhaps in ways we cannot imagine. He would be an

asset to us. If you could see the passion in his eyes—
I do not believe he is going to forget about it."

"Ben and your grandmother are both getting on
in years," Urilla Wuti said. "It would definitely be
beneficial to have someone for Ben to pass his
knowledge on to. But, before he makes such a final
decision, Ned Webb needs to experience what a huge
life change this would be. For his sake and for ours,
we need some assurance that he truly can adjust to
such a change."

Urilla Wuti explained what she was thinking, and
they agreed with her plan, working out the details
then and there. Acaraho said he would seek the
cooperation of the others who would be involved. If
everyone agreed, then Oh'Dar would tell Ned the
conditions under which he would be allowed to
come.

Oh'Dar, Ben, and Miss Vivian were living among
the People. They had lost the stigma of being
Outsiders, so the idea of another joining them was
not deemed a violation of Sacred Law as it had been
when Adia rescued Oh'Dar so many years ago. The
First Laws were immutable, but the Second Laws
were meant to adapt and grow as their situations
changed. Years before, the High Council had allowed
Healers and Helpers to pair and have offspring.
Sometimes, what had been beneficial before was no
longer in the People's best interests.

CHAPTER 2

Once again, Oh'Dar was on his way to Wilde Edge. He stopped at the Brothers' village to pick up Storm and to tell Chief Is'Taqa and Honovi that he and Acise had settled in, that she had lots of care and was in good hands, and that he had to take care of some pressing business in Wilde Edge so would be gone for a few weeks. Honovi said she would visit Acise and I'Layah to keep them company while he was gone.

Storm acted as if he knew the way by now. The crisp fall air made travel easy, with no oppressive summer heat to bear up under. Oh'Dar had his Waschini clothes in his saddle bags, including the hated Waschini boots that pinched and bound his feet.

As he rode, Oh'Dar rehearsed his conversation with Ned. He wasn't sure what he wanted the young man to decide. On the one hand, it would be nice to have another Waschini among the People, and Ned would also be company for his grandparents. But it would mean that Nora, Matthew, and Grace—and Grace's husband—would lose a family member. He wondered what he would choose if he were in Ned's place. When he left home to find his Waschini family, Oh'Dar had known he could always return. But for Ned, that would be an impossibility.

Ned had never stopped thinking about his and Grace's experience with Oh'Dar's grandparents. Whenever they were alone, he brought it up again.

"Ned, please stop talking about it," Grace said, her eyes teary as they sat on the porch swing together. "You can't truly be thinking of leaving us. Besides, Grayson didn't seem encouraging about it. He said they would have to get permission." She pushed her feet against the floor, sending the swing rocking back and forth.

"Permission from whom? See Gracie, even that. Even that little detail tells me something. It tells me that there is some hierarchy of authority. And the cave system— It is not just some dirty, overgrown hole in the side of a mountain like one might find. If you think about it, the floors we walked on were smooth. We didn't trip, weren't warned to step over this or step over that. Whatever it was, a lot of work had been done on it. It was not—natural. At least, it was not in its natural state. But who would have the ability or time to do that? It must have taken ages."

When the swing stopped, Grace slid closer to her brother and turned to face him. "It's all you talk about now. What about Alicia? I thought you liked her?"

"Alicia Baxter? Well, yes, I do."

"She would make a fine wife. And the Baxters are good at having babies; you could have lots of children!"

"Wait," Ned chuckled. "I am not ready to make a decision as big as marrying someone."

"But you're ready to make an even bigger decision to leave everything you know behind, forever?"

Ned put his arm around his sister. "Gracie, I know you don't want me to go. And I probably won't be able to. But I wish I could make you understand. It's not that I want to leave you or Mama or Papa. I wish we could all go together. Wouldn't that be something?"

Grace looked up at her brother and shook her head, "No. No, it wouldn't. I love my life here with Newell. And it's just starting. In the next year or two, we will have a baby, and I'll quit helping him out with his business and stay home and raise him or her. Those are the kind of things I think about, not exploring some dark, mysterious caves inhabited by who knows what!"

It broke Ned's heart that Grace couldn't understand. He didn't want her to think he didn't love her, didn't love them all. He just couldn't get it out of his mind. It was as if the mystery of it had gotten into his blood, and he couldn't drain it out.

Ned pulled her closer, so her head was resting on his shoulder. "How I wish I could make you understand."

Storm lifted his nose and snorted as if he knew they were getting close. It seemed a bit of a waste to be riding such an expensive animal back and forth across the country, but Oh'Dar and Storm had a bond, and he couldn't imagine making the trip on another horse. Storm was built for speed and stamina, and to Oh'Dar, there was no equal.

As they neared Millgrove, Oh'Dar slowed Storm to let him cool down.

It seemed someone else remembered Storm, as no sooner had he turned the horse down the lane that led to the Webbs' house, but Oh'Dar heard Buster's familiar bark and saw his little shape tearing around the corner from behind the Webbs' barn, fallen leaves kicking up behind his little heels.

Oh'Dar dismounted, caught Buster up in his arms, and paused a moment. But the familiar sight of Grace bursting out of the front entrance announcing, "Grayson is here!" never came. She was living with Storis now. Change was inevitable, and though

Oh'Dar was happy for them both, he grieved the loss of the joyous greeting.

But Nora Webb did come out, wiping her hands on a kitchen cloth as Mrs. Thomas often had, then smoothing the out-of-place hair away from her face. "Oh, Grayson. How wonderful. Ned and Grace will be so glad to hear you've come back. You are staying with us, I hope?"

"I would be happy to; thank you so much." Oh'Dar tied Storm's reins to the hitching post. "Let me take my bags inside if you don't mind, then I'll take Storm to the barn and tend to him."

"Of course," Nora said, stepping out of the way. "Just leave them inside the door if you wish." Oh'Dar put Buster down, pulled his saddlebags off the huge black horse, and carried them inside. "Is Ned back there?" he asked.

"No, he's over at the Baxters'. I think he is cultivating a friendship with one of the Baxter girls."

Within a moment, Oh'Dar was back out and headed with Storm to the barn. *That might be the end of all this.* It would be just as well if that was the case. He would hate to see Ned make the biggest mistake of his life.

The warmth of the barn was comforting, and the heat from the animals' bodies mingled with the smell of straw and hay. Storm was happy to follow him in, nuzzling first Rebel and then Shining Rose as he headed past them to his usual stall.

"It feels like a second home, doesn't it?" Oh'Dar

said as he gave Storm fresh water and hay. Then he removed the saddle and other tack and thoroughly combed and brushed the horse. He checked Storm's hooves, and after cleaning the equipment, was finally ready to go back to the house.

When he got there, Ned was just back from the Baxters and greeted him warmly. "I didn't expect to see you so soon. But I'm glad you're here. Grace will want to know, and it's on your head if you don't tell her right away," Ned joked.

"I will, first thing tomorrow morning, I promise. Right now, I just want to clean up, spend some time with you all, and then get a good night's rest."

Later, they enjoyed one of Nora's hearty meals. There was always more than enough to eat, and Oh'Dar went a bit overboard. "I have to say, I agree with my grandmother. I miss butter!" Then, a heavily-buttered biscuit held in his hand mid-trip to his mouth, he glanced up at the three of them looking back at him.

"Oh, of course," Ned said. "The Brothers don't keep cows or goats, do they?"

"Well, I have no idea about all of them, but those I do know don't." Oh'Dar put the biscuit down on his plate. "Though I think my grandmother wishes she had some. It's funny you should mention that; I've often thought of taking some home, but for one reason or another, it's never worked out."

Nora and Matthew Webb had learned long ago not to pry. They were curious about his growing up years, but as it was none of their business, they left it to him to share what he wanted, when he wanted to.

"Buster is a father," Nora said, changing the subject. Oh'Dar looked down at Buster in his familiar place under the kitchen table. "Alicia Baxter came visiting Ned about two months ago with her dog, Winnie. And now there are seven little Busters in their barn in a big wooden box Mr. Baxter built."

"They're all male?" Oh'Dar asked.

"Oh, I don't know what they are. I am sure they are not all, though."

Oh'Dar looked back down at Buster and gave him a butterless corner from his biscuit, "Congratulations, Buster," he said, and Buster wagged his tail furiously as he gulped down the treat.

Oh'Dar wanted to ask if Ned and Alicia were serious but waited to see if it came up. If not, he was sure Grace would fill him in the next day.

With dinner finished, Oh'Dar excused himself. He said he would be awake early the next morning as he had business to conduct in town with Newell.

Grace and Newell had quickly fixed up their two-story house, and now it was filled with homey and cozy furnishings. In the living room was an uphol-stered couch in a beautiful soft floral print, with matching oil lamps on sofa tables at each end. They had kept the butter-colored interior walls and the ivory curtains. Her kitchen was filled with new cooking pots and pans in addition to those hanging from the overhead rack that had been left by the previous owners.

The walkway was lined with flowers, suffering now with the cooler weather. A bird feeder hung in the front yard, something her father thought imprac-tical as the birds could fend for themselves. But she enjoyed watching them from the front porch and would put into it whatever cuttings and scraps she had left over that Ned had said would not harm them.

Grace was torn. She looked forward to their first child but also hoped she would not become pregnant right away. She wanted time to be alone with her husband, though she did have her eye on one of Alicia Baxter's adorable puppies.

The next morning, intending to pick up some supplies on the way back, Oh'Dar had borrowed the Webbs' wagon to go into town. He walked up the few steps to Newell's new office and knocked.

"Grayson! I wondered when you would show up. Good to see you."

Oh'Dar pulled the packet of papers out of his jacket pocket and handed them over.

"I'll get these recorded right away. Grace is at home. She took the day off because it's such beautiful weather; she wanted to stay home and make something special for dinner. She loves homemaking and is so happy fixing our little place up. You must come over for dinner tonight; she will be so glad to see you."

"Oh, no, I don't want to intrude. Especially if she is making something special. Is there an occasion?"

"Oh, it isn't like that. She just enjoys making an extra effort now and then. She would be mad if she knew you were in town and I didn't invite you to dinner."

Then Oh'Dar explained what had happened when the constable showed up with the Sheriff.

"I would have loved to have seen the look on the constable's face when you told him to get the hell off your land!"

Oh'Dar laughed. "I did enjoy it, I will admit. But luckily, he didn't realize that signing the papers in front of him didn't mean they had been recorded. He was angry and not thinking straight, I suppose. Have you had any more trouble out of Snide Tucker?"

"As far as I know, he accepted the arrangement and is long gone."

"It was a wise way to resolve the problem. But I have to wonder, is Tucker himself smart enough to honor his side of it?"

Grace's face broke out into the widest grin when she opened the door and saw Grayson standing on the porch next to her husband.

"I wondered why in the heavens you were knocking at your own door," she laughed.

"I wanted to surprise you."

"Oh, Grayson, it is so good to see you. How long are you staying?"

"I had some paperwork to bring back to your husband. I am staying just long enough to get some supplies, and then I'll head back."

Over dinner, Oh'Dar told them all about his baby daughter and how enamored his grandparents were with her. And he thanked Grace over and over for the courage she and Ned had shown in coming to the Brothers' village and bringing back Miss Vivian's letter to the Judge.

"Have you talked to Ned?" Grace asked.

Oh'Dar knew what she was alluding to, but since he had asked her not to tell Storis about where they had been taken to see Ben and Miss Vivian, he assumed she had kept quiet about it.

"Just last night, briefly. By the time I got to your parents' house and had dinner, I pretty much fell into bed. I am sure there will be plenty of opportunities to spend time with him before I go back." Oh'Dar caught the worry that fleetingly passed over Grace's features.

"I have to say, you are as good a cook as your mother!" Oh'Dar smiled, changing the subject. He had savored every bite.

"Indeed she is, and as you can see, I have put on some weight since we were married!" Storis laughed.

On the spur of the moment, Oh'Dar asked, "Do you know if anyone has any goats for sale? A pair or two for me to take back at some stage?"

Grace laughed out loud, then quickly covered her mouth. "Oh, I know what that is for. Your grandmother loved her butter!"

"Yes, well, she isn't the only one," Oh'Dar answered. "I'm afraid I also miss it!"

"I'll ask around, and you might also ask Matthew if he knows of any," Storis said.

Oh'Dar took another bite, swallowed, wiped his mouth with his napkin, then said very casually, "Did I hear correctly that Ned is courting someone?"

"Oh, Alicia Baxter," said Grace. "No, it hasn't gone that far. He sees her now and then. But they did spend quite a bit of time together last summer before all this happened with your grandparents."

CHAPTER 3

On the way back to the Webbs' house, Oh'Dar decided he wouldn't bring up the topic of Ned's earlier desire to move to Kthama if Ned didn't. Though Oh'Dar had been sure from the excitement in Ned's eyes that he would not get over it, perhaps this Alicia Baxter had changed his mind.

Oh'Dar was in the barn tending to Storm when Ned found him.

"We haven't had a chance to talk since you've been back. Is now alright?"

Oh'Dar looked around, then went back to brushing down the black stallion, "Give me a minute. I'm almost done here."

He finished the last few brush strokes, and finally satisfied, cleaned the brush and comb and put them up, then swiped the hair and straw off his pants and gave Ned his full attention.

"He seems to like Shining Rose and Rebel," Ned said.

"I believe he does, too. Has your father decided what to do with them?"

"No. Not yet. But that isn't what I want to talk to you about. And if not now, I don't know when we might have another chance."

Oh'Dar sat on a stack of hay bales.

"I haven't stopped thinking about what happened, and I still want to go back with you. I haven't changed my mind."

"What about Alicia Baxter?" Oh'Dar asked.

"Oh. Did Grace tell you about her?"

"Not in any detail."

"I like Alicia, but I'm not going to let any girl stand in the way of something this big."

"Don't underestimate the power of finding the right wife, Ned. It can change your life in ways you can't even imagine."

"I didn't mean it like that. Alicia would be a fine choice—if that's what I wanted. But I have been touched by a mystery and it won't let me go. Please tell me there's a chance I can go back with you?"

Oh'Dar shook his head and picked a piece of hay out of the bale. He twirled it around in his fingers. "Look at what's around you, Ned. You probably never think about the things you see every day. This barn, the clothes you wear. Even something as simple as this piece of hay. Imagine never seeing one again. The general store. Imagine all the things around you that you take for granted, most of them gone. Everything looks different, smells different, sounds different. The pieces of your life that form the foundation of who you believe you are, your place in the world, gone. Even words can't portray the impact."

"I know you're thinking I haven't thought about all that. But I have. You're underestimating me and my ability to know what I want out of life."

"I could well be. I admit that. Have you talked to your parents about it?"

"No. No use upsetting them if there is no chance of it happening. Are you saying there is?"

Oh'Dar stood up, throwing down the piece of hay. His mind returned to the conversation between his parents and Urilla Wuti.

"There is too much risk to bring him directly here, Oh'Dar," said Urilla Wuti. *"No doubt your grandparents had to make huge adjustments?"*

"Yes. They were not used to living with so much less ease than they were used to. They had to adapt in many ways that I cannot adequately explain."

The Overseer closed her eyes a moment before speaking again. "A testing period," she said. "A testing period that will determine if he can make the adjustment to such a primitive lifestyle compared to how he has lived his life to now. Your grandparents are spared much of it, but he will not be. He will be expected to hunt, provide for himself, learn the patterns of the night sky, and navigate in the forests surrounding Kthama without the help of tracing the magnetic lines. Just as you did, Oh'Dar.

"If he passes that," Urilla Wuti continued, "if he has the determination to adjust to that much of a change, then we could introduce him to ourselves."

Acaraho said, "He could stay with the Brothers. They could teach him much of that. I would say it will take at least several months. Or however long it takes for the novelty to wear off."

"Yes," Adia agreed, "but it must be a village that is not strongly associated with us, so it cannot be Chief Is'Taqa's. That leaves Chief Kotori. They have just recently joined our brotherhood. Khon'Tor could ask him, and if the Chief agrees, that would be the ideal village."

"Yes, there's a chance."

Ned clasped his hands together. "Thank you! Thank you, Grayson!"

"Wait, you must hear me out. There are stipulations. Stipulations for all our sakes."

"Whatever they are, I agree."

Oh'Dar couldn't help but smile. He admired Ned's spunk and pioneering spirit. "How about I explain them to you first. We are talking about a very natural lifestyle. No hot water, no running water. No woodstove to fire up and cook on. Much of the food isn't even cooked. You eat what you can hunt and prepare. It's often too hot out, or too cold and you have to stay bundled up. There are no soft mattresses and fine linens. No hot baths. No barn dances, no general store with little packages of licorice."

"I've already figured that out," Ned said.

Oh'Dar sighed. "I am sure you have. Very well,

then. Here is the offer. You would have to stay in one of the local villages for several months. During that time, you will be trained in their ways of how to hunt, trap, preserve. How to use the local plants and roots for medicinals. Emergency medical care using the materials at hand—"

"I can handle that; I have been studying with Mr. Clement after all," Ned interrupted.

"Let me finish. You won't know the language. Someone there will teach you, but you have to take it upon yourself, push yourself, to learn it."

"But there is that woman there, Honovi, and your wife—"

"Yes, but you cannot live the rest of your life communicating only with a handful of people. Besides, you will not be staying in our village. There is another, a way off."

Ned's eyes widened slightly at this point. "I see."

"In time, if you pass the test and want to continue, you will learn more complicated skills, like how to read the night sky, the forest, the behavior of the birds and animals, and how to forecast the weather coming in. Yes, I know this is not all foreign to you, but your knowledge is a just a small representation of what you have yet to learn."

"And if I don't pass the test?" Ned asked.

"If you don't pass the test, believe me, you will be glad to come home to Wilde Edge. This is for the best, Ned, trust me. It isn't meant to make it hard on you; it is meant to protect you from making the wrong life-changing decision, one that can't be undone."

"I can do it."

Oh'Dar caught himself before reacting. Ned's confidence was inspiring but also troubling. Was he taking it seriously enough?

"You have a life ahead of you here. You could marry, maybe not Alicia Baxter, but someone. There, you won't easily find a wife."

"Why wouldn't I? You did!" Ned countered.

Oh'Dar raised his eyebrows. Ned was right, and his reply answered a concern in Oh'Dar's mind about Ned's view of the equality of white people and the Brothers.

"Alright, yes, that is true. But it won't be easy. Our people are making it difficult for the locals everywhere. As a white man, you will have a stigma to live down. And—" he hesitated "—you will never see your parents again, or Grace."

"I accept everything you have said, except that last statement doesn't make sense."

"My grandparents knew when they left Shadow Ridge that they could never return to this life or see anyone they knew here."

"Yes, but that's different. They were supposed to be dead. We could make up a plausible story, perhaps that I went far away to be an animal doctor in another city. That way, I could come back now and then. You do it; why couldn't I?"

Ned's answer gave Oh'Dar pause. *Maybe I'm so*

worried about his making a mistake that I am not seeing both sides fairly. But it really wouldn't be up to Oh'Dar; the High Council would have to agree to any return visit.

"That's a fair point, Ned. But there are other opinions that would play a role in that decision."

"Other opinions?" Ned asked.

"Yes. I don't want to go into that now, though."

"That is very intriguing. What happens when I pass the test?"

"We'll face that when—and if—you do."

Ned's face fell.

"If you think I am being discouraging, yes, I am. Please understand; I know the world you will be entering. And you have to trust me when I say you cannot possibly imagine the impact it will have on you. I do. I have to do my best to make sure you are ready for it." Oh'Dar paused a moment. "Think about it, Ned."

"How long do I have to decide?"

"Only a day or so, and then I need to return while there are still easy findings for Storm to eat on the return trip. I would need to know before I go. If it's yes, I will make arrangements to come back for you in the spring. And if you decide you really want this, you first have to tell your parents."

"That," Ned said, "will be the hardest part of all. Trust me."

Mr. Webb had a lead on some goats and took Oh'Dar over to meet the farmer. After some conversation, they made a deal for Oh'Dar to get two pairs on his next trip to Wilde Edge, most likely the next spring. He didn't know whether to tell his grandmother and Ben or just let it be a surprise. Of course, he might be bringing back an even bigger surprise if Ned decided to return with him and was able to pass the test the Overseer had set up for him.

Ned had some soul-searching to do. He knew he could not tell his parents until he was rock solid that it was his choice, so he went to his best friend and confidant, his sister. He had talked with her about it many times, but now it was decision time.

Grace listened as patiently as she could. "I'm trying to be objective, but it's hard; I would miss you so much. You can't imagine it, I guess."

"No more than I would miss you. But I'm sure I would come back to visit like Grayson does. So it wouldn't be forever."

"I am being selfish, I know. Because it wouldn't be like seeing you every day or watching our children grow up together. And Mama and Papa—"

Ned hung his head, then looked back up at Grace. "I know. Perhaps it is just me who is being selfish."

Grace's heart softened at seeing the defeat in her

brother's eyes where a moment before there had been excitement. "Ultimately, it's your life. You are old enough to make that decision. I suppose every parent hopes their children will stay close, but all don't. And our parents still have the Baxter boys to help with the farm; it isn't as if you were going to take it over. Still, it won't be the same around here."

Then she had an extra thought. "What about Buster? I can imagine him grieving himself to death if you disappear."

"I remember seeing a tame wolf in that village. If they keep wolves as pets, why not dogs?"

Grace chuckled, "Well, if you get to take him, just make sure no one eats him!" And their laughter broke the tension.

Ned embraced his sister. "I love you, Grace. I couldn't imagine going the rest of my life without seeing you and Mama and Papa. Will you help me when it is time to tell them?"

Grace nodded into his shoulder, not wanting to leave the comfort of his hug.

Since Ned had decided to tell their parents, Grace was free to tell her husband.

"What?" Storis said. "Is he serious?" A pang of something like jealousy shot through him.

"Yes. He hasn't been able to stop thinking about it since we were there."

Storis became quiet, lost in thought for a while. "I can understand it. I have wondered to myself, where do they actually live? Neither Grayson nor his grand-parents live with the locals; that is obvious. I am glad to hear he could come back, that is if he can come up with a plausible story for disappearing. Certainly can't use the sudden death scenario again."

"I imagine he won't be able to talk about it, though, when he does return. So it will always remain a huge mystery. It's a shame, really."

CHAPTER 4

Not everyone was content to accept it as a mystery, though. Despite Constable Riggs's last encounter at the local village and despite knowing he could not legally go back, the constable was still looking for a way to cause trouble for them. Sheriff Boone had told him about the arrangement with Snide Tucker—that he would leave the territory and never bother them again. But Tucker had struck the constable as being very much like himself and therefore not likely to let it all go that easily.

He asked around Shadow Ridge and found out that Tucker was still hanging around.

"I heard about your arrangement with the Morgans," the constable said, sitting down next to Tucker at the bar. "I thought you would be long gone."

"I meant to be. Having trouble finding the right

horse, though," Tucker said. Riggs wasn't fooled; it had nothing to do with finding the right horse. He had been right. Tucker still wanted revenge, which was why he hadn't yet left the territory.

"Since you're still here, I have a proposition for you. But we would need about four other men."

"So whatever you have in mind would take six of us?"

"Yes. And we would all need to be armed."

"I don't really want any more trouble with the law," Tucker said.

"I would deputize you, so you would be under my orders," the constable said.

"What is it about?"

"There are mixed-race women and children at the Morgans' local village. I have permission from the Governor to remove them." Riggs kept his face straight to mask the lie.

"The *Morgans'* local village?" Tucker sniggered.

"Best way to single out which one I mean."

"I knew what you meant." Tucker slammed his glass down for a refill and nodded at the bartender. "As I said, I don't have a horse," he stated, glancing back at Riggs.

"I'll take care of that. I did it before. Just find four men, but make sure they have horses and weapons. I can't cover everything."

"Won't be a problem."

"We'll be gone for at least two weeks, accounting for travel. I'd like to leave as soon as possible."

"What's in it for me? And them? Ain't gonna risk our lives for free if that's what you're thinking."

"I'll make it well worth everyone's while. Trust me."

Tucker didn't trust the constable, but it didn't really matter. He was bitter that Newell Storis had gotten off and that he had married Grace Webb. Also that his plan to see Grayson Morgan the Third hang had been foiled. A wiser and humbler man, one without unbridled passion, would have cut his losses and learned to live with defeat. But Snide Tucker was none of those, either.

The constable seemed surprised when Tucker showed up at his room at the inn within a few days.

"I've got your men. When do we leave?"

"Tomorrow morning?"

Tucker nodded and walked away, saying, "Meet you at first light at the stables."

None of the men were talkers, so the trip was made in relative silence. Tucker had made it enough times now that he knew all the places for resting the horses, the best places to hunt. It was still fall, and enough grasses were left to feed the horses along the way, though they did take some grain with them. One of the men drove a wagon Riggs had provided, and the rest were on horseback.

Riggs had said he had no expectation of arriving unseen as he knew that there were scouts in the area.

However, none of them knew that the scouts were not the locals alone.

❁

Notar's watchers had dispersed throughout the territories surrounding the villages that had accepted Haan's offer of help, and they were the first to see the five Waschini riders and the wagon. The lookouts recognized that the Waschini were carrying similar weapons to the one described as used to murder one of Notar's males, Nit.

The watchers immediately carried the news back to Kht'shWea.

❁

Acaraho, Haan, and their High Protectors sat in council. "Neither of our peoples can reveal them-selves to the Waschini," said Haan.

"And Oh'Dar is not here to handle them," Acaraho said, "not that I want to put him in harm's way. What we can do is send a group to surround the village, remaining hidden and staying alert, and we can pray for wisdom and guidance. I don't know what the answer is, but we cannot let harm come to Chief Is'Taqa's people."

"I will send some of my males," stated Haan.

"They can cloak themselves with no chance of being seen."

Chief Is'Taqa's scouts notified him that the Waschini were coming. The Chief remembered Oh'Dar saying that they were not allowed back, so that they were ignoring their own laws told him to prepare for trouble.

Just as the Chief was ordering the women and children inside, the Waschini rode into the village. The one whom Chief Is'Taqa recognized as the constable dismounted first. Two of the other men dismounted with him, while two remained on horse-back and the last stayed with the wagon.

As much as he hated to, with his life-walker at the High Rocks visiting Acise, Is'Taqa was forced to call Snana over to translate. Pajackok was standing with him.

"You are not welcome here," the Chief said.

"Doesn't matter if we are or not. We're here on official business. I have the authority of the Governor, far higher than your authority here, to remove this woman," and the constable pointed at Snana. "And any others of mixed blood."

Is'Taqa saw Snana involuntarily glancing over her shoulder at Noshoba, who stood not far behind.

The constable followed Snana's gaze, walked over to Noshoba, and stared down at him. "This is your brother, isn't it? And where is your husband? And that wife of Grayson Morgan's? And their child? I know she just had it. They are also coming with us."

Chief Is'Taqa stepped forward and placed his spear between Noshoba and the constable. "You will not take our people. You have no authority here."

The constable pulled out and raised a pistol. The Chief's eyes went immediately to the weapon, as did everyone else's.

Tension filled the air. As one of the men started toward Noshoba, the boy's pet wolf, Waki, now grown, snarled and darted out from behind, lunging at the man, his jaws snapping. The man pulled his pistol and took aim, but Pajackok sprang forward and pushed his arm upward, and the gun fired harmlessly into the sky.

As the sound of the shot shattered the air, chaos ensued. The braves rushed the armed men, trying to force their weapons out of their hands. Chief Is'Taqa brutally punched the constable directly in the face, knocking him to the ground. The Waschini's pistol flew out of his hand, and the Chief kicked it away. Seeing that the constable and their men were losing the fight, Tucker started firing rounds in the air to frighten everyone. The struggle stopped, and the Waschini were in control again, their firearms once more aimed at Chief Is'Taqa and his people.

For thousands of years, the forest's silence had been unbroken by the calls of the Mothoc. And for thousands of years thereafter, the Sassen had kept the Rah-hora and left the Brothers' care to the Akassa.

But no more.

Earth-shattering howls split the air. It was unlike anything the Waschini had ever heard. Neither had any of the Brothers living at the time, but they knew what must be causing it. A chorus of deep-throated voices, almost human but not. Resonant and resounding, the growing sound seemed to flash off the hillsides and echo back. When one round started up, another joined in, and it encircled them. It was clear that whatever was making the noise had them surrounded.

The Waschini stopped, stunned. The howling continued, seeming to draw closer. And while it seemed it could not get any louder, it did until, without time to think, the men had to drop their weapons to cover their ears. The constable looked around at the Brothers, all of whom were now standing with placid faces as if nothing untoward was happening. The women and children had left their shelters. Whatever this was, it wasn't scaring them, which frightened him and his men all the more.

Suddenly, the constable's men made a dash for their horses, which were bucking wildly, only controlled by the two left with them and the man from the wagon. The constable and Tucker were right behind them, and within moments, all were mounted and riding away as fast as they could, the wagon wheels wobbling with the great speed.

They rode away as hard as they could, but they could still hear the horrific noise in the background. Only fear of exhausting the horses beyond recovery made them eventually come to a stop.

Once a considerable distance away, those on horseback pulled up in a circle, talking loudly as their horses pawed the ground.

"What the hell was that? What were those things?" one of them shouted.

"Some type of demons, no doubt!" another exclaimed. "We heard that the forest was haunted. Been talk of it ever since those men were arrested for killing that Morgan couple more than two decades back. They said they didn't look for the baby because something made a noise at the treeline! Had to be the same thing!"

Of course, it wasn't. What had scared the men who murdered Oh'Dar's parents wasn't the Sassen but Adia approaching through the underbrush.

Tucker yelled, "I'm done with you and your schemes, Riggs! You're on your own from now on. Whatever back there caused that sound, I never want to run into one! Nor hear that ever again. The hair is still standing up on my neck and arms."

"And did you see the locals?" another man said. "None of them were afraid of it."

"No one will believe us, that's for sure. And I

don't feel like being a laughingstock wherever I go. Word of these things has a way of traveling," yet another said.

"Alright," Riggs agreed. "I can see we're done here. Let's head back." He did his best to hide his shaking hands.

When the Waschini had ridden off, Chief Is'Taqa looked at Pajackok and his daughter, waiting for the Sassen to quit howling. When they had, he said, "I do not think those Waschini will be back."

"That was—I do not know what the word is," said Snana.

"I think what frightened them equally was that we were not frightened," said Pajackok.

"I agree," said Chief Is'Taqa.

It was a long time since his people had heard the call of the Sasquatch, though never so many howls raised in unison and in so many numbers, but it was unmistakable, and his people had recognized it when they heard it. Though the Sassen were the protectors of the Brothers, and even the children knew they had nothing to fear from them, what had just taken place would become legend.

The Chief called out, "You are brave, my people. Together with our brothers, the Sassen, we have defeated those who would do us harm. Today is a great day. Let us celebrate together tonight."

"Someone needs to tell Acaraho what happened," said Pajackok.

"I am sure their watchers were among the Sassen, and someone is already on the way."

Acaraho and Haan listened patiently. While no one was harmed and neither Snana nor Noshoba had been abducted, they realized the Sassen's solution had created another problem. The Waschini, at least a handful of them, now knew something unknown was living in the woods surrounding Is'Taqa's village.

CHAPTER 5

All day, Ned was sick to his stomach. He had decided this was the day to talk to his parents. He made sure that Grace and Newell had been invited to dinner, as he was counting on at least Grace's support.

With the napkins back on the table, before his mother and sister could get up to start clearing it, Ned spoke up.

"If we could still sit here a while, please, I have something I want to tell you." Ned swallowed and dared a glance over at Grace.

"Of course; what's on your mind, son?" Mr. Webb asked.

"You raised Grace and me to think for ourselves, to accept responsibility for our actions and decisions in life. And so I have come to a decision, perhaps the biggest one of my life." Ned saw his mother look at his father. *Oh no.* They thought he was going to ask to court Alicia Baxter.

"Before I tell you what it is, please don't blame Grayson. If anything, Grayson has tried to discourage me from it."

Now his mother's smile became a deep frown that creased her forehead.

"I guess what you're going to tell us is not what I expected," his mother said.

"No, Mama. There is no way you could be expecting this, I am sorry to say. Ever since Grace and I went to meet Grayson's grandparents and brought back that letter, I haven't been able to stop thinking about their lives. How much they have changed. How they gave up everything they knew to follow a dream. It has taken hold of me deeply. And it won't let go."

Mr. Webb was looking puzzled.

"I know you will think I am crazy, and I know it will come as a shock, but I want to go and live with Grayson and his grandparents."

His mother looked at his father, "Did you know about this?"

"No, not at all."

"Grace?" she looked at his sister.

Grace pushed her chair away from the table a bit. "Honestly, Mama, it's all he has talked about since. He is not exaggerating. Yes, we have talked about it together, and I, like Grayson, have done my best to help him see all sides of it. It's a big decision."

"Certainly not the one I thought you were going to announce," his mother said, a bit sadly.

"I know it is not what you want for me. You want me to get married, raise a family, and live a normal life. Maybe you even thought I was going to say I wanted to ask Alicia Baxter to marry me. And I thought that was what I wanted, too. Until this happened. And now, the thought of an ordinary life sounds—suffocating."

"Ned," Grace said.

"No, I'm sorry. That's not right or fair. No one could have had better parents or a better upbringing than Grace and I. But a normal life; it just isn't for me. Ben and Miss Vivian shaking their lives up like this affected me and got me thinking about my own future. And I realized I was jealous of them. And then I thought, well, I am a lot younger than they were when they decided, maybe I should wait. But that is also part of it. I don't want to wait until my life is nearly over to live how I want. And if I don't make a change soon, I will never leave Wilde Edge. I know it."

Mrs. Webb turned her head away, and Mr. Webb reached over and grasped her hand. Then he looked at Ned.

"If it helps, I can perhaps come back and visit like Grayson does. I just need to have a good cover story for leaving."

Mr. Webb looked at Oh'Dar, who said, "I want you to know I did not entice Ned to leave. If anything, I did my best to discourage him. And, if it helps, there will be a trial period. Ned will have to learn to function in a very basic lifestyle. He has to experience it day-to-day, so if this is some type of idealized fantasy, it will come apart pretty quickly."

"So he would come back after that?" Mrs. Webb asked.

"Yes. If he doesn't succeed, or if he changes his mind after seeing what it is really like. And there will be no shame, either way, however it turns out," Oh'Dar explained, glancing over at Ned from time to time as he spoke.

Mrs. Webb finally turned back to Ned, and he could see tears in her eyes.

"The last thing your father or I want to do is stand in your way," she said. "If this really is what you want—"

Ned glanced over at Storis, whose lips were tightly pressed together. He had no doubt decided to stay out of it, not having been in the family very long.

"When would you—leave?" his mother asked.

"I need to go within a few days," said Grayson. "I need to get back to my wife and daughter. I will leave enough funds for Ned to buy a horse and supplies and any clothing he needs to take with him for extreme weather. I won't be back until the weather breaks again, so that means around springtime."

"What if I left with you this time? I can get ready," Ned said.

"Oh Ned, really?" his father asked. "Your mother—"

"I'll be alright. I'll manage if that's what he wants," and Mrs. Webb squeezed her husband's hand tightly. Then she spoke briskly, "Well, these dishes aren't going to wash themselves. Grace, please give me a hand?"

The women got up and started clearing the table while Ned and the other men stepped into the sitting room.

"Papa, I swear, this wasn't Grayson's doing. I can't say it enough; please don't blame him."

"I understand, son. You apparently had a life-changing experience, followed by an epiphany about what you wanted out of your life."

"An epiphany?"

"A burst of inspiration. Almost a mystical insight or realization. A thought that becomes a turning point. That leaves us changed forever. In a way, you are lucky; most people never experience a moment like that."

Ned smiled at his father, gratitude filling his heart for his father's support.

"I will help your mother. And so will Grace. To help her through it, I'll make sure we get together more frequently after you leave. In time, she will adjust. I hope we will see you again. Knowing that would make it easier."

"For what it's worth, Ned would be a big help to Ben," Oh'Dar said. "The work he is doing is very important, and Ben is having trouble getting around since he had a fall."

"I need a good cover story," put in Ned. "I think it will work if I say I am leaving to study elsewhere."

"Don't forget, it will have to fool Mr. Clement, too," Mr. Webb said.

"That's true. Do we have any distant relatives far enough away to make it inconvenient to come back often?" Ned asked.

Oh'Dar grinned. "No, but a friend of yours does; he has grandparents who live far away and are getting older. They may need someone to run their farm."

Ned nodded. "That will work. And it is somewhat related to the truth, which feels better to me. Let's go with that. I will also have to let Alicia know. I owe her that much, even though we weren't that serious."

"Wait until just before we leave, if you don't mind," Grayson suggested. "It leaves less time for questions."

The next few days seemed to drag. Ned was busy getting ready, and to his credit, he put in a lot of time thinking about what Oh'Dar had told him to expect. He finally came up with a list of things he thought would be good to take with him and asked Oh'Dar for his approval. Knowing what to take was half of it; the rest of it was quieting the nervousness that stayed with him day and night. Part excitement, part fear of the unknown, part the reality of what he was doing.

He met with Alicia the day before he left. They were sitting outside on her porch swing that afternoon, their jackets keeping them warm enough in the cooling fall weather. A blanket covered their legs.

Ned explained that even though they had not really gotten serious with each other, he realized there might have been potential, and he wanted to let her know he was going to leave town and why.

"Well, I am sorry to hear that. Oh, I don't mean it that way. I wish you luck, really, and I'm sure your friends are grateful for your help. But is there any chance you won't be gone that long?"

"No," Ned said, having promised himself he would be strong and not leave her any hope if it seemed she was looking for it. "I will be gone quite a while. It is best to plan on it being that way. I'm sorry."

Alicia smiled and said she understood. Then she asked, "What about Buster? Oh, I don't suppose he is going with you; he would just be in the way."

Her point was well made, and though Ned had wanted to take Buster, he now realized it wouldn't work. He was disappointed, but in the back of his mind, he had known the adjustment would be too much for the little dog.

"No, I don't suppose I can. Are you keeping any of his puppies?"

"Yes. Papa says I can keep one. Two, maybe, if I

tell him one of them is for you when you return! Would you like that? And would you want a girl or a boy?"

Ned couldn't disappoint her; it was the first time she had really smiled since he told her he was leaving. Maybe this was something that would ease her sadness, having something to take care of.

"I would like that. Maybe a female. And if your parents say no, maybe Grace would take her for me?" Ned did like the idea of someday taking a little Buster back with him.

"I will miss you. Please be safe." Then she leaned over, gave him a peck on his cheek, got up with her blanket, and quickly left.

Ned saw himself out and took the long way around to have more time alone. He tried to make himself feel better on the walk home. He would be leaving tomorrow, and he was afraid, but not of leaving his present life. What he feared was always feeling guilty about leaving.

Ned had worked hard getting everything put together, checked, and double-checked. He and Oh'Dar had gotten Storm and one of the Webb horses ready and now brought them out of the barn. Mr. and Mrs. Webb, Grace, and Newell were there, ready to send them off.

As Mrs. Thomas had always done long ago for

Oh'Dar, Mrs. Webb had prepared a basket for the trip. Fresh biscuits, butter, jellies, dried strips of meat, and cider. It wouldn't last the whole journey, but it would give them a good start.

Ned shook Newell's hand and gave his sister a long hug. When they pulled apart, he could see tears in Grace's eyes.

"Be careful," she said. "Oh, I wish you could write."

Then his father embraced him and gave him a couple of strong pats on his back. "Don't worry about things here. We'll be fine."

Ned nodded and steeled his jaw. His mother was next. He could hardly bring himself to look at her.

"Mama," he managed to get out before his voice broke.

"You'll be back before you know it," his mother said. "And with some stories you can tell us, I hope." Ned nodded in her embrace.

Mrs. Webb let him go and stepped back. "I know you're in good hands."

She turned to give Oh'Dar a hug.

"I'll take care of him. I promise," he said. At their feet, Buster looked up, wagging his tail, oblivious to what was going on.

"Oh, I am going to miss him so much," Ned said. "And all of you, of course."

"On that note," Grayson laughed, "we'd better be off. The days are shorter, and we'll lose a fair amount of travel time because of it.

Grace bent down and picked up Buster. She lifted his little paw and made him wave goodbye, which just about destroyed any remaining composure Ned had. He snapped the reins and cantered off, leaving his family standing together in front of the homestead.

For a long time, neither man talked. Each was dealing with his own feelings about how their lives had just now been changed—maybe forever.

CHAPTER 6

Yar, the Sassen watcher who had spotted the lone figure, had reached Kht'shWea and went directly to Haan. "Adik'Tar, someone approaches."

"Who? From where?"

"A way off still, but definitely intentionally heading our way."

"Tell me exactly what you saw."

"A single figure, walking determinedly."

"Are you talking about an animal?"

"No. No, from the shape and how it walked, this is one of us."

Haan's thoughts went immediately to the thought of another Sassen establishment somewhere. After all, there had been Notar's community. If so, this was good news. They could always use more Sassen bloodlines.

"How many days away?" Haan asked.

"I would say two by now, given how long it took me to get here."

Haan called for his High Protector, Qirrik, and explained what was going on. "Send another male with him," Haan ordered. Then to Yar, he said, "That way you can rotate and not chance losing sight of him, or her, whatever it is."

After the three watchers had left, Haan told Acaraho what Yar had reported.

Yar had a moment of panic when he could not find the figure again, worried that he had lost track of him. But they finally spotted him along the banks of the Great River.

"If he follows the Great River, it will lead him here," said the male with Yar.

"You sleep; I will watch for now. I am too excited to sleep, anyway."

Within a couple of days, the figure was close to the Brothers' village, and Haan sent out extra sentries to make sure it did not bother any of the Brothers.

He could hear voices. What sounded like offling, only higher pitched. Happy, cheerful, as if they were playing a game together. It made him smile but also made him miss home terribly.

He found a secluded area close enough to see who was making the noise and cloaked himself for good measure. They were unattractive tiny things, really. Nothing but skin and very little hair. He knew who they must be. The Others. They had been described enough to everyone back home, though they had not been seen by anyone except the eldest members. He spent a whole day watching them. Those his kind was sworn to protect.

He watched them huddled around the fires they built at night and wondered how they survived, as insignificant as they appeared. Having seen them in person, he realized now why they were given to his people as wards, to look over and protect. They had pointy features, sinewy spindly arms and legs. Their fingers looked as if they could snap off at any moment. They must need a great deal of protection.

But he also witnessed the kindness between them, not only mothers to their children but adult to adult. He heard them chanting around the fires. They were thanking and worshiping the Great Spirit. In the end, he left, being assured that these were good people and knowing that if the need arose, he would play his own part in protecting them.

The next morning he continued his journey. He had been told to look for what might remain of an old oak tree, though he doubted anything could remain of it by now. But to his surprise, it was still there. How could that be? How could any part of it have survived for thousands of years? But there it was, and at least enough of it to know what it had once been. Its massive trunk still remained, and he imagined the spread and depth of its roots reaching into the heart of Etera. Those parts of the trunk that had rotted away lay on the ground. He didn't know how any of it had been preserved this long but was reassured that it had. Coupled with the large meadow that spread out past it, the combination assured him that he was where he needed to be. He crossed the meadow, his heart starting to beat more rapidly. He was close, so close.

Yar had returned to Kht'shWea to give his report. "There is no doubt where he is headed." "We all agree, and the others are still following him, though they are being very careful not to show themselves. But he doesn't seem to be paying attention. He is fixated on his destination."

"Where is he going?" Haan hid his impatience at having to ask the obvious question. The stranger's appearance and indiscernible intent were eating at his nerves. As far as Yar's statement that his people had not been noticed, he was not so sure about that.

"Kayerm."

The figure stepped up onto a ridge and looked down. He was sure this was it. It was barely noticeable, being covered by vines and foliage, but it was there if one knew what to look for. An entrance into the side of a mountain, just as he had heard them speak of it. It was nightfall, so he squatted down to observe.

He waited. He scanned the area as it got darker. No evening fires were set anywhere. Maybe they didn't do that. But there was no one coming in or out, either. Surely they would not all be asleep this early? It made no sense. Looking for some activity, he waited all night as the stars traced their patterns across the black night sky. The only movement was a lone wolf going in and out of the entrance a few times.

At first light, he approached the entrance. There was no sign of footprints anywhere. The wolf's prints were the only disturbance in the soil. There were no signs of any recent fires; nothing. He stepped inside and waited for his eyes to adjust. His heart fell. There was no one living here. It was empty. The people he had come to find were gone. But where? Had they left? Had they died off? He sat down and put his head in his hands. *All this way. For nothing?*

After a while, he got up and explored the tunnels, which spread out in two main directions. Where there had been no signs outside, there were inside. It had definitely been inhabited once. And not all that long ago. So, where had they gone?

Wanting the emotional comfort of a fire, he gathered up kindling and branches and made one of his own. As the flames licked the sky, he pondered his situation. Not knowing what else to do, he did the only thing that comforted him when he was at a loss. He praised the Great Spirit.

"It was the ancient language of The Fathers-Of-Us-All," Yar explained. "He praised the Great Spirit, asking for wisdom and comfort. He said he had come so far, and now there was no one here. He asked for help in finding us."

"He specifically said us?"

"He said, the Sassen and his people."

Haan stopped. "Tell me about him again."

"We were able to get a good look at him. He is not Sassen. He is much larger than us. And his coat, it is silver-white. At least part of it. Like the Guardian, Pan. Could there be more than one Guardian?"

"There is only one Mothoc Guardian of Etera. It is said the birth of a second heralds the death of the existing one. There is only one explanation. He is Mothoc. And no doubt he has come from the rebel

camp the Guardian spoke of. I must see Acaraho."
He summoned his High Protector and First Guard to
accompany him.

Acaraho immediately called together Commander
Awan, First Guard Thetis, Adia, and the Overseer,
who was still there helping Adia after her recent
birthing.

Their faces were stern as they listened to Haan
describe what his watchers had seen.

"We need Pan," Adia and Urilla Wuti said almost
in unison.

From where she was, sitting in deep meditation, Pan
suddenly sat upright. *I must go to Kthama.*

As they stepped outside to talk a little more before
Haan left, Adia suddenly pointed past them and let
out a gasp.

The Guardian was standing on the main path
to Kthama's entrance waiting for them to
notice her.

"We are relieved to see you, Guardian. However
you knew to come, thank you," Haan said. "Some-

one, someone who must be a Mothoc, has traveled to Kayerm."

Pan had advised Acaraho and his watchers to stay away while she went with Haan and his males to Kayerm.

Her heart stopped when she saw the figure come out of Kayerm's entrance. It was definitely one of her kind. But the markings— No, it couldn't possibly be. She pulled herself together and started walking down the ridge toward whoever it was.

The figure looked up and turned. He dropped the foodstuffs in his hands and froze. Pan could see a look of astonishment cover his face. He stayed still, unmoving, as she approached him. She stopped when she was several arm-lengths away.

"I am Pan, Guardian of Etera." She studied his face.

"I am Moart'Tor."

Pan's stomach clenched. *Tor.*

"Where are you from, and how is it you came here?"

"To Kayerm? My people lived here long ago. I am the son of Dak'Tor, son of Moc'Tor and E'ranale, and kin to Straf'Tor from the time of The Fathers-of-Us-All."

My brother's son. My brother's son. He was as tall as she was and physically no doubt stronger. She had seen that he had much of her brother's coloring, silver-white hair covering the top of his head and down his shoulders though not as far down his back as Dak'Tor's. His coloring had briefly led her to think he was Dak'Tor.

His eyes seemed to bore into hers as if searching for something. What she could now see of his silver-white coloring sparkled in the morning sun, in some areas appearing almost translucent.

"And where is your father, Dak'Tor?"

"He is back where I have come from. It is said you visited once, beseeching us to return to the other Mothoc community."

All the questions Pan had about why he had come here were only compounded.

"Why have you come to Kayerm?"

"I sought to find my people. Our people. The Sassen and the Mothoc. I came to seek sanctuary. But they are no longer here. Do you know what happened to them?"

"Sanctuary? From what and whom?"

"I do not belong with them. Our Leader believes that the Akassa and Sassen are abominations and should be destroyed. Though our numbers are few and certainly would cause no real threat, I could not stay there. I had to leave. I had hoped to find a new family here," and he motioned behind him.

Pan had to choose her words very carefully lest she reveal too much. Her brother lived at the rebel camp, so that must be where this stranger was from.

And what about the crystal? She wanted to ask about it, but it was possible her brother had never revealed its existence.

"The Sassen no longer live here. Neither do the Mothoc," she said, stating the obvious and buying time.

"Can you take me to where they are?"

"In time, perhaps." She eyed him further.

"I understand."

"If you want my help, you must stay here. There are plenty of resources, and you will have no problem finding them. But do not leave the immediate area. You can understand that I must get to know you."

"You think I am lying about why I am here?"

"It is a possibility."

"You are right to be cautious. Again, I understand."

"Good. I will return in a day or so. I will bring you some additional food, items that are out of season now but which will supplement your diet. It has been a tiring journey, I am sure, even for one of your vigor."

"More emotional than physical. I was not exactly sure I was on the right path. Kayerm is difficult to find with no clear magnetic streams to follow."

He has not mentioned Kthama. Yet surely he knows it exists. That was not a good sign. Pan could feel that he was not being fully transparent. He was trying to learn as much as he could without giving up much information himself.

"Until then," she said.

Haan and his males were waiting for her back down over the ridge, and she held up her hand for silence as soon as they saw her. Pan then did as Wrollonan'Tor had taught her. She pinched the fabric of their realm together, closing the distance between Kayerm and Kthama, and in the next moment, they were back at the High Rocks.

"He is a Mothoc. More than that, he is my brother's son," Pan said. "He said his name is Moart'Tor."

Acaraho, Adia, Urilla Wuti, and Haan listened patiently.

No one had known that Pan had a brother, so they were caught off guard. But then, so little was known about her.

"He says he is here looking for sanctuary from the rebel band I told you about earlier."

"You do not believe him," Acaraho said.

"Not all of it. Not about asking for sanctuary. The rebels know of the Promised One. They know he is the key to opening the Wrak-Ashwea."

"Do you think they know he has been born?" Adia said, the alarm in her voice apparent.

"No. Your son is not old enough to draw sufficient power from the Vortex to alert anyone that he has arrived. But I am, which could potentially lead him to the High Rocks, so I will not stay here. I will go to Kayerm and stay with Moart'Tor. When and if I think it is time, we will introduce him to your people, Haan."

"As for An'Kru," Pan said, looking at Adia and then to Acaraho, "Moart'Tor has promised to stay at Kayerm until he earns our trust. However, he still presents a risk. The most prudent course is to send your mate and your offspring elsewhere. Perhaps to the Far High Hills."

Acaraho looked at Adia for her response.

Urilla Wuti spoke up, "I agree. I will go with them; it is time I get back. My niece Iella will help you care for your offspring, Adia. What about the female Sassen Guardians and their offspring?"

"I suggest you speak with them, Haan," Pan suggested. "Find out what they prefer. If they would feel less nervous with their new offling at the Far High Hills, send them there as well. As for the males, part of their sacred duty is the protection of Kthama and Kht'shWea. We must take this one step at a time. He is powerful. Not as powerful as I am or as the six Sassen Guardians are when working together. But an altercation is the last thing we want. Every drop of Akassa, Mothoc, and Sassen blood is crucial to Etera's survival."

CHAPTER 7

After Pan and Haan had left, Adia turned to Acaraho to answer the question that had been on his face a moment before. "I do not want to leave. But as the Guardian thinks it is best, I will not second-guess her wisdom."

Then she said to Urilla Wuti, "I need to tell Nimida I am leaving. We have not spoken in a while, but I cannot leave without letting her know. No matter how she feels about me, I would not feel right otherwise."

"Have you talked to her since—"

"No. I have let her have her privacy; it is a lot to ask anyone to process. And I still feel so guilty. That I should have kept her. That I should have found a way," Adia lamented.

"Adia," Urilla Wuti said, moving closer so the younger Healer would be forced to look at her. "You are letting your emotions cloud your thinking. The

High Council would not have let you, you know that. I took her somewhere safe, and she was loved and happy. It was not until her mother died that problems arose."

"She said her father was—difficult."

"There is no family alive that does not have some friction at some time."

"I fear she will never forgive me."

"She may not," Urilla Wuti admitted. "Or she may yet have life experiences that will help her realize that there is not always a perfect answer. But what else do you think you could have done?"

"I could have taken them both and gone—somewhere. Raised them myself. Moved to another community; oh, I do not know!"

Acaraho came over and pulled Adia into his embrace. "She needs time, Saraste'. And Urilla Wuti is right; there is a chance she will never forgive you. We all have to make the best choices available at the time. I believe with all my heart that is what you did. But whether Nimida ever forgives you, you must forgive yourself."

"I do not know if I can," Adia said into his warm broad chest, feeling his arms circle around her. She felt warm and protected, as she always did in his embrace.

"You need to think this through," Urilla Wuti said. "You feel you should have taken them to another community. The High Council's reach would have found you there. And living out in the world on your own, scratching out an existence for you and two offspring? What kind of life would that have been for them? How would you have cared for them? It would have been a death sentence for you all."

Adia pulled from Acaraho's embrace to answer. "I do not know, I do not know."

Urilla Wuti looked into Adia's eyes. "If you cannot figure it out now, older and wiser as you are, how could you expect your younger self to have figured it out?"

Adia found Nimida in the quarters she shared with Tar, busy with her toolmaking.

"May I speak with you?" she asked.

Nimida looked up and silently motioned her to come in.

"I have to go to the Far High Hills for a while. I wanted you to know."

"Nootau will return with you?"

"Yes. As well as Urilla Wuti."

"I see." Nimida hesitated. "How long will you be gone?"

"I'm not sure. I hope not long."

Nimida put down her rock-cutting tools, brushed off her hands, and stood up. "I have talked to Tar about moving to another community. Maybe even returning to the Great Pines." She felt a rush of gratitude for how supportive her mate had been, holding her and listening to her without judging her feelings. Not trying to tell her how to deal with the situation, just allowing her to work through her emotions. And they were many.

"If that is what you want."

"I do not know what I want—other than to stop feeling how I do now."

Adia took a step toward her daughter, who put her hand up and stepped back.

Nimida continued, "I talked to Nootau, and I want you to know it helped. You know he and I are close. I already thought of him as a brother. Imagine my surprise. He and I spoke about how you kept the truth a secret for good reasons."

Then she continued, "I do not want to make this any harder than it is. For any of us. I thought it might be better if we left."

"For what it is worth," and Adia's voice cracked, "I hope you do not leave. You are part of me. You have a family here, and you always will have. Don't let my actions take that away from you."

"At first, I wanted to punish you; I did. But as I said, I have gotten to know you over the years. I know your heart is good, and I agree that I would be punishing myself, which makes no sense. So I am trying very hard to understand."

"Going back to the Great Pines would help you heal?"

"No. Leaving would not work—and besides, that is the last place I want to go."

Silence.

"Deep in my heart," Nimida said," I know leaving is not the answer. I would just be taking my pain with me, and nothing would be resolved. I would lose all the good things that are here, and there are many. I know that."

"Then do here what must be done to take care of yourself. Take your time; you are loved at the High Rocks, and welcomed. Do not let what I did rob you of the belonging you have found here."

"What is really sad is that I am jealous of the twins. That they will have the life I never did. How petty is that, to be jealous of innocent offspring." Nimida was trying not to cry.

"I can understand. That life should have been yours too, growing up with your brother here, with us. I am so sorry I could not find a way to make that work."

"I did not have a terrible life; I do not want you to think that. I know I have told you how difficult my father was. My mother shielded me from it until she died. I guess I am grieving a fantasy life where everything was perfect."

Adia's voice shook. "If you did leave, know I would miss you every day and that you are always welcome back any time." She turned and left without another word.

Nadiwani was waiting for Adia in the Healer's Quarters, busying herself with packing things for the trip.

"You talked to Nimida?" she asked as Adia came in.

Adia sat down. "Yes. I told her I was leaving for a while. She said she has thought about leaving Kthama."

"Oh. I am so sorry. We have all lived with this hanging over our heads for so long, wondering if she should be told or not. I wish I could help you." Nadiwani sat down next to Adia.

"You help me by being my friend," Adia replied, taking Nadiwani's hand in hers and leaning her head on her friend's shoulder.

After a moment of silence, Nadiwani said, "May I ask you something?"

"Of course. Anything." Adia sat up straighter.

"You and I both always believed we would never be paired or have offspring. But now, here you are. You and Acaraho are so much in love, and you now have three new offspring. The sacred laws forbade us from being paired and having offspring partly for fear it would interfere with our dedication to our calling. Do you feel it has?"

"Not interfered. But it is a lot to manage. It was not so much with Oh'Dar and Nootau because I had so many other issues to contend with that they were mostly just a joy to me. But, I admit, I am tired. It is becoming more and more difficult to balance my role as Healer with that of mate and mother."

"That is why I am here to help you. I knew it was not allowed," said Nadiwani, "so I never let myself think about it. I never imagined being with a male or allowing myself to feel physical attraction to one. But I do now. And I cannot stop thinking about Awan. I want more of him. More of his time, his thoughts, his views, his touch."

Adia smiled. "Being paired and having a family is a great blessing. Do not think otherwise for a moment. Having a mate, taking comfort in his strength. Knowing you are not walking this life alone. Watching your offspring grow and learn, become strong and independent. But it also has its down moments, as you know. You try to make the best choices you can. You pray that where you fail, they will have the strength to overcome your short-comings and, at some stage, find it in their hearts to forgive you. No one can do it perfectly."

"I think you have come close," Nadiwani said.

Adia sighed. "It is gracious and generous of you to say that. I suppose if anyone has lived a charmed life, I *have* come close. I have been given many bless-ings and granted much grace. But no one escapes heartache, loss, or moments of despair. You celebrate the good and pray for strength to get through the bad. Lean on those who love you, then support them when it is their turn, and they need someone. I have been doubly blessed even though my heart aches for Nimida."

Nadiwani shook her head, "It is a tribute to your character that with everything you have been put through, what Khon'Tor did, the High Council, Hakani, you have lived a blessed life.

"I have had Ithua on my mind lately. All those years of loving Chief Ogima—and him loving her. And she let it slip through her fingers. I realize I must not make her mistake."

"She has aged since his passing," Adia said. "Honovi fears she will not be with us long."

"Why do you think she never accepted his love?"

"You would have to ask her to know the reason. Perhaps fear of change or maybe thinking there would always be more time. And then, one day, there is not any time, and it is too late. There are many possible reasons. We must pray for her that she will find peace one way or the other. And you are right, Nadiwani. Are you making the same mistake?"

At Kht'shWea, Pan and Haan met with the Sassen Guardians.

"I want to stay with my mate," Lellaach said. "We will be safe; I am not concerned about your brother's son, Guardian. Especially if you are here."

Votas, paired to Zok, agreed with Lellaach. "I would also like to stay."

The third, Eyota, said she would like to go with Adia to the Far High Hills. "I feel a call to go with her. I am not sure why."

The remaining two female Sassen Guardians, Nin and Lyra, said that they preferred to stay at Kht'shWea.

"Then, Eyota," said Haan, "please prepare to leave by tomorrow morning. You will need to be at Kthama by first light."

Harak'Sar, Khon'Tor, and High Protector Dreth had been alerted that Acaraho was bringing a group, including one of the Sassen Guardians and her offspring, to stay at the Far High Hills for a while.

The news of the visitors garnered a great deal of interest. Not only was there the possibility of seeing the Healer and An'Kru again, but also of being in the presence of one of the white Sassen Guardians.

As the group arrived, the People did their best not to stare, but it was almost impossible.

Nootau embraced his mate Iella, happy to see her again. He held her for a long time, reveling in the comfort that she was safe in his arms again.

Khon'Tor asked Acaraho if he was staying a while. "No, only to get my family settled. But there is much I have to tell you both after this commotion settles down," he said.

Urilla Wuti was surprised to see Apricoria in the

gathering. She frowned, not understanding why the young healer was there.

Seeing Urilla Wuti's expression, Harak'Sar explained. "Apricoria came here to speak with you."

"How did she know I was coming ba—" Then Urilla Wuti remembered that Apricoria could sometimes see events before they happened. "Of course," and she raised her hand in acknowledgment.

The First Guard had taken charge of getting the guests settled and led them away. All eyes followed Eyota and her offspring as they left with the others.

Finally having some privacy, Acaraho told Harak'Sar and Khon'Tor about the arrival of Moart'Tor.

"A Mothoc? At Kayerm?" Harak'Sar remarked.

"Pan arrived shortly after," Acaraho explained. "She suggested that Adia and our offspring should come here for a while as she is not confident that the Mothoc's motives for coming are benign."

"To say the least. I would not be, either. He must be from the rebel camp, as you said. And Pan told us they are committed to annihilating the Sassen and us," Harak'Sar said. "Your mate, your offspring, and their fellow travelers are all welcome as long as necessary."

"It will also do Adia good to be here with Nootau. She draws strength from him," Acaraho said.

"That is easy to understand," said Khon'Tor. "He has a pure heart. You did a great job raising him."

"As far as the Sassen Guardian and her offspring are concerned," Harak'Sar said, "there is no way they will not draw a crowd. But it will be up to her how much she wishes to interact."

"There is something else I need to let you know," Acaraho said, and he told them of the possibility that another Waschini might be joining his people at the High Rocks.

The cool fall weather made traveling easy for Oh'Dar and Ned. It was no longer hot enough to be burdensome, and the weather was, in fact, quite enjoyable. They traveled by day and rested at night after making an evening fire for comfort and to take the chill off of the cool autumn air.

Oh'Dar had kept from asking Ned how he was feeling; though he was curious about it, he did not want to pester his friend. So he was relieved when Ned brought it up one evening while they were sitting out under the twinkling canopy of stars.

"This is a much more relaxed trip than the last time," Ned joked. He picked the meat off the piece of rabbit he was eating. "You gave thanks to the rabbit after you killed it."

"Yes. Its life was sacrificed to nourish ours. It is our way. You will learn."

"Please tell me more; I am anxious to know."

"Living with the Brothers, that is what they are called, requires basic skills. Far more involved than those of the general Waschini world. That is what white people are called. Waschini."

"Does it mean anything?"

Oh'Dar chuckled. "Yes. White Wasters."

"Oh. So that is how they see us?"

"It is not undeserved. For the most part, when white people come into an area, they squander the resources and hunt a species to extinction, not leaving enough alive to allow for future generations to be born and thrive. They pollute the waters, exhaust the land by not rotating crops, destroy the beaver dams, causing floods and denying water flow to areas downstream that it had previously nourished. Not all of them are like this, but the mindset is growing, and there seems no apparent end to it."

"I know our people are threatening the— The Brothers."

"Yes. The very ones they should be learning from."

"I am willing to learn," Ned said earnestly.

"I believe you." Oh'Dar finished his portion and wiped his hands on the grass next to him before continuing.

"So, there are similarities to the white culture. Each healthy male contributes to the community and provides for his own family. The elderly and infirm are not expected to; the community comes together to take care of them. Females step in to help older females whose families are gone. They also help nursing mothers with their added burden. Beyond that, there is always work to do. In the winter, there is more socialization because of the cooler temperatures. Planting and harvesting are done by then.

"Every person has a role and contributes some-how. Though every male hunts, some have a partic-ular affinity for it. Others excel at toolmaking, preserving hides—there are many critical tasks. Past a certain age, children are introduced to chores and start building skills so they can later become contributing members of the village."

"So, in addition to providing for myself, my place will be helping Ben?" Ned asked.

"No doubt, yes, but you must be open to other possibilities. I was raised with them, but you and my grandparents are the true emissaries for our kind."

"Again, I am in awe of how brave you were, Grayson," Ned said. "To set off all alone to find us."

"I had the love of my family behind me, surrounding me. Even though I knew I would have hurt them by leaving, I knew their love for me would never falter. And I had the guidance of the Great Spirit. I was not alone."

"Well, I am grateful to have you to help me." There was a moment of silence. "Grayson, tell me about the Great Spirit. What do your people believe?"

"The Great Spirit is the focal point of our lives. Beyond family and loved ones, beyond duty to the community, it is the foundation of all we believe and do. We listen to hear his voice. Though I say *his* because it is easier. I do not think the Great Spirit is male or female, but rather embodies both the active male and receptive female aspects."

"I don't think I have ever heard the voice of the Great Spirit."

"It is in the quietness of our own soul that we hear his voice. For me, it is not in words—though some have experienced it that way—but it is there in the longings and yearnings that call to you in your heart of hearts."

"Like my wanting to come with you?"

"Could well be. There is an unsettled place in each of us that lingers, unsatisfied, quietly unrelenting until we surrender to our path. It does not mean that the path is always smooth, but there is a peace that comes from finally following what is calling to us. Whether to do, to be, or to understand. But always, to yield."

Ned let out a sigh. "I will be happy when I have made a place for myself."

"You must be patient. I understand you want to take this in one big step, but that will only overwhelm you. You must trust me that your preparation will unfold in a series of small steps. Striving to be other than where you are at the time will only slow your progress."

"I don't want to fail."

"You can't fail. No matter what happens, whether this is meant for you or not, in the end, you will have peace, which is something you do not have now. And peace is the product of being in line with the will of the One-Who-Is-Three. Now, before we go into that, let's get some rest."

"One last thing. Will I get to meet your wife and daughter?"

"If you pass the test, yes, eventually," Oh'Dar said.

Urilla Wuti could see Apricoria was anxious to speak with her.

"My Adik'Tar, Lesharo'Mok, sent me here to see you after I told him about my growing gift and what I had seen."

"Your visions?"

"Yes. I continue to get them, though I cannot summon them at will. At first, they were the small things, as I told you at the High Council meeting, but the last few unnerved me so much that I was unable to settle down. Not even our Healer, Veturia, could help me. Both she and Lesharo'Mok agreed I should come to the Far High Hills."

"You came here to tell me of the things you have seen?"

"No. Not only that. They both feel I should

apprentice with you here. Veturia feels I need the guidance only you can give me."

"I see," said Urilla Wuti. "Tell me what you are seeing."

"It is about the future. The Waschini. We know they have terrible weapons, but what they have now is only the beginning. They have much ingenuity and that, combined with their drive to conquer, leads them to present a great threat to Etera. Greater than anything you or I could imagine.

"The tools they create will make it nearly impossible for any of them to hear the voice of the Great Spirit. There is something about these inventions that are intoxicating. They are a constant distraction and will entice them to constantly keep something before their eyes, ears, or in their minds. They become alienated from the forest. From nature. They move at alarming speeds, and their lives are lived in a rush. They become primarily indoor dwellers in artificial structures they build for themselves, often crowded together in large settlements.

"And so they drift further and further away from living in harmony with everything else. Their disregard for nature and for the creatures they share our world with becomes criminal. If the path they are on is not averted, I have seen all of Etera destroyed at their hand."

Urilla Wuti was spellbound.

"There is more, though not related. Just another example, but I do not know if it is true. I saw the

Guardian Pan. And she was at the High Rocks. And there was another Mothoc, newly arrived, who looked a bit like her."

Urilla Wuti's eyebrows rose. "What you saw is true. The Guardian has returned to Kthama, and another Mothoc, as you described. Similar but without the Guardian's full silver coat."

"If that vision is true, does that mean the other one is true? Will come true?"

"I believe it is the future that lies ahead, as of now. But one that hopefully can be avoided. Now, as for you coming here—"

"I know you already have your niece, but—"

"It will work out, do not worry," Urilla Wuti reassured her. "You are welcome here. Please let me know if you see anything else. I believe your gift is true and that it will greatly serve our people and all of Etera."

Urilla Wuti sought the will of the Great Spirit before speaking with the parties involved. Once she had what she thought was the best next step, she sought out Adia.

"I am glad to see you have some time to yourself," she said, joining Adia in the eating commons. "Where are your offspring?"

"Iella and Nootau are watching them. Both are so good with them, and I appreciate the help so much."

"That is something I want to speak with you about."

Adia took another bite of dried meat and chewed while waiting for Urilla Wuti to continue.

"You are exhausted. Everyone sees it. Too much is being asked of you. You cannot fulfill all the demands on yourself. You are wearing down, and it cannot go on."

"I know. I fear I am failing. At being a doting mother, a loving life-walker to Acaraho. Being the Healer to the People of Kthama."

"Not to mention serving as Third Rank."

"Yes. But I do not know what to do."

"You do not?" Urilla Wuti asked.

"What I want to do, I do not feel I can."

"And what is that?"

"Step down as Healer. It is the only optional role I have. But I would feel I am letting my people down. And it is such as part of me I am not sure I even can."

"An exhausted Healer is not giving her best. And you are right, it is the only role you can step away from, but you do not have to do so entirely. So, I have a suggestion.

"Let Iella and Nootau come back with you and live at Kthama. Iella can continue her apprenticeship under you. Apricoria has asked to move here and apprentice with me. Your uncle feels it would do her good, and so do I. That frees up Iella to go to Kthama. And that would put both her and your son there with you. And with An'Kru and the twins."

Adia closed her eyes briefly. "I can see no drawback to your solution. Are Iella and Nootau amiable to this?"

"I spoke with them first. Yes, they are excited about the possibility. Of course, Iella does not relish leaving her home, but she heartily welcomes the opportunity to learn from you. I think it is a good idea and we should perhaps consider rotating all the apprentices. That way, they could learn from each of us and would gain and pass down a larger wealth of knowledge. Once Iella takes over as Healer, you can still consult with me as needed, but without the daily responsibility."

"That would be," Adia sighed, "wonderful. A great relief, really. Nadiwani is not a Healer, nor does she want to be. And I know she and Iella would work well together. Thank you, Urilla Wuti. Thank you." And Adia leaned over and hugged her old friend.

"There is more to Apricoria apprenticing under me. It has to do with her gift."

"That she believes she sees events before they happen?"

"Yes, and apparently some that are happening from afar."

Urilla Wuti told Adia about them.

"It fits with everything Pan has said about the threat of the Waschini," mused Adia.

"They are carrying us all toward the destruction of Etera. I pray we can divert their path and create a different future."

Adia left Urilla Wuti and took An'Kru down to a pool of the warmest shallowest waters around Amara to let the little fish nibble his toes. It made him squeal with delight, and as usual, creatures from everywhere gathered around or circled overhead. Before long, she felt and heard footfalls behind her. She turned to see Eyota approaching with her daughter Tansy.

The ground seemed to shake as Eyota plunked down next to Adia. "Sorry," she laughed. "That was not very graceful."

Adia laughed with her. "No, but at least you landed squarely."

Eyota looked at An'Kru's feet where the little minnows, which had scattered when her shadow fell over the water, were re-gathering.

"He seems to like that!" she said, arranging her daughter on her lap.

"He likes everything, and my others were also easy to raise, so that is saying a lot. He attracts a following wherever he goes." Adia motioned around them.

"They sense the presence of the Aezaitera in him. I can feel it myself. He is imbued with the creative life force, more so than anything I have experienced. Even Pan, I have to say."

Adia's eyes widened at that.

"Pan told us something, and I will convey what

she said if it will not offend you that she did not tell you herself?"

"Please, go ahead."

"Pan explained that when we were created through the tremendous release of the Aezaiteran life force when Kht'shWea was opened, our transformation took place at the smallest pieces of our being. This means that we have been re-created down to tiny invisible parts of ourselves. We are pure Sassen. New creations. Not only that, but we have no impurities in our blood and can interbreed as we wish. And so can our offling."

"That is fascinating!" Adia said.

"Yes. And she included An'Kru in this. He was transformed within your water cradle at the same time we were." Adia remembered the moment and had since realized this for herself.

"He is a perfect Akassa and able to mate with whom he chooses. But she also said he is that and something more. We do not know what she meant. But it intrigues me as I am sure it now intrigues you too."

Adia pulled An'Kru's feet from the water, dried them off, and set him on her lap. He looked up at her with his startling steel-grey eyes, and she kissed him and held him close.

"I fear for him," Adia said.

"I know. All mothers fear for their offling. Here, want to trade?" Eyota asked.

Adia smiled, and they exchanged offspring. She knew Eyota would be gentle with An'Kru.

"Oh, how sturdy Tansy is! And so soft!" Adia exclaimed. "Her covering is like bunny fur, so light. She is precious." The same steel-grey eyes looked up at Adia, though much larger and more deeply inset than An'Kru's.

"And An'Kru is so small yet so powerful. Oh, Adia, I can feel the power coming off of him. No wonder Pan says he cannot stay at the High Rocks too long. The rebels will certainly know the Promised One has come when his powers are strong enough to feed back into the vortex."

Adia looked over as Eyota continued.

"As Pan said, he will become so powerful it will be obvious to the Mothoc downstream that the flow of the Aezaitera into Etera is being augmented, pulled into our realm with a more intense force. But now that I experience it for myself, I can imagine that his energy might even extend through the magnetic field like waves! Either way, they will figure out it is coming from the Promised One. Yes, he must be taught how to manage his power, and only Pan can do that."

"What will become of them?" Adia wondered, looking off into the distance. "Your offspring, the others. They are Guardians, and they will outlive us all. Oh, that's not quite true; you and your family will outlive us all. But what of An'Kru; what is his Guardian lifespan?"

Eyota indicated she was ready to switch back, and Adia handed Tansy over with a bit of an oomph.

The Sassen chuckled. "I know; she is much heavier than An'Kru." She put Tansy up to her shoulder and patted her back. Then she reached out and clasped Adia's smaller hand in hers and gave it the gentlest of squeezes. "An'Kru will not be alone; he will have all of us. Try not to worry, Healer; none of us knows what the future holds. Pray for the best and trust the Great Spirit and the Order of Functions."

With An'Kru resting in his sling on her hip, Adia went to claim Aponi and Nelairi from Nootau and Iella.

Nootau spoke up immediately. "Mother, did Urilla Wuti talk to you?"

"Yes, she did, and I am very happy about it."

"So are we," said Iella. "I am anxious to learn from you and for Nootau to have time to spend with his family."

"That is gracious of you," Adia said. "I know you will miss your family."

"I will. But we are so close, really. I can visit any time I wish." Then she added, "As long as you can spare me, of course."

"Here, let us carry them back for you," Nootau

offered, and he and Iella each picked up one of the twins from their cozy nest.

"You are so kind," Adia said. "Just like your father." She glanced away for a fleeting moment, remembering that Khon'Tor was also Nootau's father.

"Thank you, Mamma. That is the highest compliment anyone could pay me. Acaraho taught me everything I need to know about being a male and a provider."

"I could not be more proud of you," Adia smiled. "Come, and on the way, I will tell you what has happened at the High Rocks. It will explain why we and the white Guardian and her offspring are here."

CHAPTER 8

With their plans agreed upon, Pan and Haan approached Kayerm. When he saw them approach, Moart'Tor dropped the tree trunks he had been collecting. *Thunk.* The birds scattered, and he squinted, trying to make out what type of creature was with the Guardian. He opened his mouth to speak but then closed it again.

Without any ceremony, the Guardian said, "This is Haan. He is the Adik'Tar of the Sassen."

Moart'Tor ran his eyes up and down the newcomer. Though it was much smaller than him, there were so many similarities. The heavy body coat, the color of many of his own kind. The face was also similar, though more chiseled, the nose not as wide or flat as those of the Mothoc. It had deep brown eyes, small ears set high on the side of the head, and a broad chest above a solid core. He was waiting for it to speak but then realized he should introduce himself.

"I am Moart'Tor, son of Dak'Tor, son of Moc'Tor and E'ranale. Are you Sassen?"

"I am Sassen. My name is Haan, and I am the Leader of my people."

Moart'Tor knew he was staring but could not help it. The Sassen was a smaller version of himself, and he could see the influence of the Brothers in him, in the facial features and size, if nowhere else.

"You no longer live here?"

"No. We left some time ago. I have come to meet you at the Guardian's request. I imagine you have never met one of our kind before."

"No. Only the Elders in our village have. Those who lived here," and he motioned behind him at Kayerm, "before they were banished by Straf'Tor."

"Kayerm served us well. Have you come to live here? Are there others coming?" Haan asked.

"It is just I. Alone."

The Guardian had been eyeing him closely; in his peripheral vision, he could see her steady gaze on him.

"I came to seek asylum among my own kind. I came to find the Mothoc who remained here."

"Asylum? From what?" the Sassen asked.

"From where I was raised. What I believe you refer to as the rebel camp. I cannot live there among them any longer."

He knew the Guardian was waiting for more.

"The Leader there, he burns with hatred for the Akassa and the Sassen. He seeks to destroy them. I have lived under his tyranny all my life. I have never agreed with him, and I can no longer bear to listen to it. I wish only to live my life in peace, but there is no peace there."

"Tell me about your community. It has been a long time since I visited," the Guardian said.

"It is small. Much smaller than I understand it was when you came. We barely scratch out an existence on the land because most of the community are older, and there are not enough strong males to provide for everyone. The few females who could bear offling no longer wish to mate. They fear their offling will be deformed. It is a dying community, and I seek life and vitality. I thought I would find it here."

"Tell me of my brother."

"He is a strong influence. He paired with a female named Iria shortly after he arrived. They have several grown offling."

"If there are so few remaining, how is it your Leader still intends to annihilate the Sassen and the Akassa?" the Guardian asked next.

"He realizes it is not possible with the small numbers he has, but that does not quell the fire in his heart. If anything, it makes him angrier. He is not one to bear feeling powerless. I cannot support him or his beliefs, and I no longer want to be part of it, though it has no chance of coming to pass. But this hatred is disrupting their lives and robbing them of joy and happiness. Guardian, they said you spoke of someone. The Promised One. Could you tell me about him? I need some hope for the future."

Moart'Tor saw the Guardian tilt her head. *I have gone too far. I should not yet have asked about the Promised One.*

"The Promised One will usher in the Wrak-Ashwea. The Age of Light. It will be a renewal of hope for all Etera. Does my brother not ever speak of this?"

"No, Guardian, there is almost no talk about it. The Leader forbids it, though there are a few of us who would gather together in hidden areas to discuss it. But there is no more known about it than you told the Elders long ago. Your brother has had nothing more to add. But even that little bit gave us hope when we have so little otherwise. Hope drove me to come here, to try to find our people at Kayerm."

The Guardian looked at the Sassen. "Let me confer with Adik'Tar Haan. I will return later. As I requested, do not leave the area. Is there anything you need that I can bring you when we come back?"

"I can make what I need, thank you. This area appears rich with resources."

Moart'Tor watched the two walk away. The only place he could think they would be going to was Kthama.

Haan had called his advisers together. Haaka his mate, High Protector Qirrik, and Artadel, the Healer. Lellaach and Thord, Leaders of the Sarnonn Guardians, were also there.

"He is not being honest," Pan said. "He did not come here seeking sanctuary but, no doubt, seeking information about the Sassen, the Akassa, and those of my kind, the Mothoc, whom the rebels believe still live here among you."

"Do you believe their numbers are so few?" Haan asked.

"That, I cannot tell. He could be telling the truth. With no others to breed with, they might well have stopped mating altogether. That would certainly add some tension to an already challenging situation," Pan said. "The fact that he is actively trying to block my ability to read him only adds to my suspicion."

"Has he come here to harm us?" Haaka asked, thinking of Kalli.

"There is only one of him. If harming us was the intent, there would be others with him. We must, of course, be on the lookout should others arrive. But no, he is not here to harm us. It is clear he expected to find you and your people still living at Kayerm with my own—his own. He asked about the Promised One. Once he has learned what he has come for, he will no doubt go home. I am sure they want to know if the An'Kru has been born."

"How do we keep him from learning that the Mothoc are gone? If they know that we and the Akassa are no longer under their protection—" Qirrik looked troubled.

"I know," Haan agreed. "If they have any numbers at all, they could certainly kill many of the Akassa. Of course, they would have to get through us first. But we cannot keep him there forever. In time, he will venture out and perhaps learn the truth."

"No, we cannot force him to stay here," Pan agreed. "We cannot confine him. He says he came here looking for others, to join another community, so that is what we will give him."

The others looked at Pan, waiting for her to explain.

"Haan, speak with your people. Find a number of them who would be willing to return to Kayerm and live with Moart'Tor."

"Live at Kayerm? For how long?" Haaka asked as respectfully as she could manage.

"I do not know how long, but we must change his thinking. Right now, he sees you only negatively. We must help him see that his Leader is wrong. He must get to know you to understand that you are not an abomination. The best way to defeat an enemy is to turn him into a friend," Pan explained.

"What about Thord, Lellaach, and the others?" Haan asked.

"For now, we will keep their existence a secret."

Pan addressed the Sassen. They were all entranced by her presence, those who had been at the High Council meeting when she appeared, just as much as those who had not.

After she finished explaining what had happened, she said, "Consider this carefully. He is not here to harm any of us. He is here to learn about you, the Akassa, and anything possible about the Promised One, most likely to take the information back to the rebels who would attack both the Sassen and the Akassa. So you must not mention anything about Kht'shWea, Kthama, or anything about your way of life here. He must not know that the Mothoc or the Akassa no longer live among you. If any of you who have no offling feel led to return to Kayerm to be part of a community living with him, let your Leader or High Protector know. I will take you there myself, no matter how many of you there are. You may enjoy the return to your first home, as you have fond memories there, I am sure."

By the next morning, a decent-sized group had gathered, Haan among them. They had some of their personal belongings as well as practical items like tools. A spirit of anticipation, even adventure, permeated the group. Once they were quietened down and ready, Pan raised her hand.

With no lapse in time, they were standing just below the ridge before Kayerm.

The Sassen released gasps of astonishment. "Guardian!" one of them gasped.

"All is well, fear not. I have gained many abilities through my centuries of living."

"Is this how you brought Notar's community to us?" someone asked.

"Yes. The concentration of the Aezaitera in your blood allows me to relocate you."

Haan nodded. "And in this way, there are no tracks to lead him to the High Rocks. Can you do this with the Akassa?"

"Yes. But I have not dared to test it with the Brothers or the Waschini. All living creatures have the Aezaitera within them, but I do not know if they have a high enough concentration to survive it."

Pan gave them a few moments to collect themselves and then led them to Kayerm.

Moart'Tor was inside cleaning up the area he had selected for his living quarters while he was there. He heard voices and stepped outside to see the Guardian, the Sassen Leader, and a group of other Sassen approaching

For the briefest instant, he felt a flash of fear.

Ridiculous. But the Guardian? Pan, he would not want to test, even though his father had said she had no supernatural powers.

"I have brought you some friends," Pan said. "These Sassen are returning here to live with you."

Moart'Tor frowned. "For how long?"

"We will see. They will introduce themselves to you over time. For now, know that they come in peace and brotherhood. They are looking forward to getting to know you, Moart'Tor," Pan said.

This was not going in the direction Moart'Tor needed it to go. Where was Kthama? Where were the Mothoc? He wanted to see the Akassa, how big they were, and if they were as puny and helpless as his father had described.

The Guardian stepped back, and the crowd started to gather around him. He listened as each one told him his or her name, then filed past him to find a living space. They seemed to know exactly where they were going, and there was a sense of homecoming about it.

"How long ago were you here last?" he asked Haan.

"In comparison to our life spans, it was only yesterday. For many, it is a bittersweet homecoming. Ah, but it is good to speak the ancient language again."

Moart'Tor thought he was going to burst from wanting to ask where they were living now, but he knew. It had to be Kthama. Somehow they were all living at Kthama with the Akassa. It occurred to him to try to follow their tracks, but he could not see how he would have the opportunity. The Guardian would know he had broken his promise to stay here. Then what? Would he be detained? Or would he be allowed to return home, though with no real information for his father? He was discouraged, but it had only been a few days. Somehow, he must win their trust.

"How have you been spending your time?" the Leader, Haan, asked him.

"Exploring the immediate area. The river not far from here is rich with resources. They are so plentiful, I could reach into the shallows and catch the fish by hand if I did not mind getting my arm wet."

"Yes," the Leader chuckled. "We have a common aversion."

"Instead, I made a spear and dined well last night."

"You will find there is more than enough provision. Since the time of the great division, we lived here for centuries in peace and harmony."

Finally.

"The great division was the time when our community split, some following Moc'Tor and some following his brother Straf'Tor?" Moart'Tor asked.

"Yes. They were in disagreement about how much of the Brothers' blood to incorporate. The varying concentrations caused the differentiation between the Akassa and us."

"The Akassa are more like the Others?" Moart'Tor asked Haan. If he was going to learn what he came here to find out, he needed to keep the Sassen Leader talking.

"Yes. But we worship the same Great Spirit. We honor the same sacred laws. Consider the birds of the air. Some have larger wing spans, some smaller. Some ride the air currents, their wings outstretched, gliding gracefully, effortlessly. Some flap their wings continuously from one destination to the next. Some are brightly colored, and others blend in with their habitat. Yet they are all birds, created by the loving hand of the Great Spirit."

Moart'Tor felt his anger rise. *Except the Great Spirit did not create you. Or the Akassa.* They did not belong here on Etera. None of them should ever have been born.

The Guardian had been standing there listening. "My hope is you will find a sense of community with those who have volunteered to bring their lives here to help you."

"I— I thought—"

"You came here expecting to find the rest of us, others of your kind. If that is all you are interested in—"

"No," Moart'Tor stammered. "I welcome the chance to learn about the Sassen. And the Akassa."

"Very well. I am only a thought away if you need me," Pan said. Then she turned to the Leader, Haan, her face averted. He could not see her expression and did not know what, if anything, passed between them.

Moart'Tor watched the Guardian climb the ridge and disappear from view down the far side. He turned his attention back to the Leader. Most of the others had gone inside to get settled, though a few had come back out and were talking among themselves.

"Where are the offling? Have there been no new Sassen born lately?"

"You are unknown to us. We have no belief that you have come to do us harm, but you can understand our hesitancy to expose them to a stranger," Haan said.

"Of course. But I promise you, I have not come to harm you. Any of you."

Haan replied, "I believe you. And the Guardian does too."

Moart'Tor believed the Leader when he said that.

"Where does the Guardian go when she leaves?" he asked, trying another approach.

"We do not know."

Moart'Tor screwed up his face, "Really?"

"Truly. She comes and goes. We do not know when she will appear. But she comes at times of need. She is thousands of years older than any of us," Haan continued.

"Her father was Moc'Tor. My grandfather," Moart'Tor explained. "We know so little about her or any of the Guardians. What can you tell me about them?"

"Not much. Little is known other than that they are practically immortal. That they have tremendous healing power and that they are far more closely connected to the Aezaiteran stream than we are. Pan is said to be the last of the Mothoc Guardians. But we have found that much of what we believed to be true is not, so we try to keep an open mind about what we *think* we know."

Moart'Tor thought carefully before he said his next words. "I know you are testing me. I do not blame you, but I came here looking for a new home. I will accept any test you give me. I have nowhere else to go. It is my prayer that you will accept me and incorporate me into your communities. I am not here to harm anyone, so please, give me a chance."

"We are. Do you not realize that?"

"Yes. You are right. I am impatient."

"If this is your path, trust that it will open before you as it is meant to be. Trust the Order of Functions."

"What is the Order of Functions?" Is it something new? Or is it knowledge known only to the Elders but was somehow lost? Or intentionally withheld?"

"Ah, that is a great question, one I will let Pan answer when she returns. For now, I would like to walk through Kayerm again. There are many memories here, many pleasant ones, some painful, but that is life, is it not?"

The Leader walked away and entered Kayerm, leaving Moart'Tor standing alone. Within a moment, several of the Sassen came over to speak with him.

"Welcome! You have a beautiful coat. So striking!" one of the females said to him. Moart'Tor looked at her. She was smaller than the Sassen male standing next to her. Her coat was almost black, with no variations even in her undercoat. Very becoming. No one in his community had exactly this coloring. The closest was Dak'Tor's mate, Iria. This female's eyes were brown but darker than any he had seen. Almost as black as her coat. He almost forgot for a moment that she was a Sassen.

"I am Eitel. This is my brother Naahb. If you need help finding the best red berry patches, we can show you. They are still producing fruit and will be for maybe another month."

Moart'Tor did not plan on being there in a month, but he nodded agreeably and smiled. The female smiled back at him. She really was attractive. For the most part, just a smaller version, really, of their own females.

He needed to befriend one of them, maybe her? Perhaps then he could coax out some real information. He had never been with a female and found his imagination taking over. He had been raised knowing he had a great mission to accomplish, and his father had told him a family would distract him from his cause. He had been promised a female when he returned, though. It would be a great reward, and he anxiously looked forward to it. Not everyone was allowed to mate any longer. The privilege had to be earned, even for the son of the Leader. His loins ached when he thought of it.

He caught himself, realizing he had lapsed into distracted silence. "I am sorry, I was remembering something back home."

"What is it like, the rebel camp where you live? We have no other name for it."

"Zuenerth. We call it Zuenerth. It means refuge. I am told it did not have a name for a long time until my father named it."

"Dak'Tor, the Guardian's brother," the male said.

"Yes. His naming it helped us make peace with living there. Until then, there had been great unrest. The first Leader, Laborn, was difficult. He did not seem to want anyone there to find happiness. It is said it was because his mate was killed in a rock slide in the first place they found after leaving here. But my fath— The Leader, Kaisak, changed that for the better. Between his and my father's efforts, they have carved out a peaceful living."

"Yet the Guardian said you no longer wanted to live among them," the brother said, still eyeing him.

"True. Their ingrained hatred of your kind and of the Akassa. I want no part of it." Moart'Tor realized he had just contradicted himself. He had told the Guardian that their community was a place of unrest and unhappiness but had now told this one that they had carved out a peaceful living. Deception was harder than he had realized it would be. He worried how much of their seventh sense was left to pick it up. He also wondered how much stronger the Guardian's abilities were. Was it possible they knew he was lying and were somehow leading him into a trap by appearing to befriend him?

"You will find that everyone here understands that. After all, it was a difference in belief that caused the great division," the female said. "Our beliefs are at the core of who we are. We must first discover them for ourselves, then honor them. Only then can we be true to ourselves and the Great Spirit. You will find kindred spirits here," and she reached up and gently brushed his forearm.

He instinctively pulled it away, then saw the hurt in her eyes. "I am sorry. You just startled me," he did his best to apologize. He was surprised at his reaction. Her touch had sent a shock wave through him. He had expected to be repulsed by them, but he was not. And he was anything but repulsed by this one. He started to consider their size difference, wondering—

Stop it, he admonished himself. How could he think such a thing? He would lie with an abomination? "I need to replenish my water supply." He somewhat abruptly walked off.

Haan had been observing the exchange the whole time and was anxious to tell Pan about it.

CHAPTER 9

Oh'Dar and Ned were not far from the Brothers' village. Oh'Dar had changed into his traditional clothing and rolled up the Waschini items to be washed later.

"You look like one of them, Grayson. Except for your eyes," Ned said. "I never will, not with this mass of hair."

It was true. Grace and Ned had the same coloring, curly hair the color of winter wheat, and green eyes. There was no way Ned would ever blend in with them.

"Your clothes look comfortable."

"They are," replied Oh'Dar. "Much more than the Waschini ones. No more pinching boots and tight arm holes. It is always a relief to take them off."

"I was only at the village once, but I imagine we are nearly there?" Ned asked.

"Yes. We will make it by first light tomorrow

morning. I suggest you rest as much as you can tonight because busy days are ahead."

Oh'Dar lay in his blankets and thought about tomorrow. He was sure that Is'Taqa's scouts would let their Chief know that he and Ned were almost there. He longed to see his family again but knew that was still days away. They had to send word to Chief Kotori for someone to come and bring them to his village. That would take a few days, so Ned would stay with Oh'Dar until then.

The next morning, they pulled up in sight of the village. Oh'Dar paused Storm and turned to Ned. "Are you ready?"

"Let's go!"

Pajackok rode out to meet them, turning a snorting Atori around in circles in front of them. Then he went on ahead, and they followed him.

Before long, several people had gathered to watch. Oh'Dar pulled up and dismounted. He motioned for Ned to come with him and walked over to Chief Is'Taqa.

Ned once again met the Chief, and with Oh'Dar to translate, thanked him for allowing his visit. Oh'Dar explained that some of the Brothers would take care of the horses and introduced Ned to Snana, who was another of the Chief's daughters. She took him to a small shelter where he would be staying. Ned looked around; it was small but enough for him. There was a sleeping blanket already waiting, as well as gourds of water. He thanked her, and she told him he was welcome to mingle among the rest of their people though no one but she and her brother Noshoba would understand him.

Ned heard Oh'Dar talking to the Chief in the villagers' language. It made him uncomfortable not to understand it. Not that he was concerned about what they were saying, but because he had never been in a situation where he couldn't understand. He knew this was just one of many unfamiliar circumstances to come, and steeled himself. Despite Grayson's wisdom that either way, he could not fail, he felt if he was not able to learn how to live among them, he would be failing. He could not imagine returning to an ordinary life in Wilde Edge, or anywhere else for that matter.

His reverie was interrupted by Snana cautiously opening the flap of his shelter and calling his name. "Here, I brought you some clothing," she said. She set a bundle down inside the opening along with a woven basket. "You can put your Waschini clothes in this."

Ned walked over and examined the bundle. There was a small white bulb on top. "What is this?" he asked, lifting it to his nose and sniffing.

"To wash with. You peel off a layer and rub it between your hands in the water. Oh'Dar is waiting for you. Bring your new clothes and the basket."

Ned did as she said, and Oh'Dar led him to a small pond and started to remove his clothes. "Come on," he said. "You don't want to put your fresh clothes on without cleaning up first."

Ned watched as Oh'Dar stripped all the way down and dove into the pond, the splash creating circles of ripples. "Is it cold?" he asked.

"Absolutely!" and Oh'Dar laughed, shaking the water from his hair.

Ned soon joined him, exclaiming at how cold the water was.

"It gets warmer when the summer sun beats down on it," Oh'Dar said. After they had paddled around a bit, they washed. Snana was right; when Ned peeled off a layer of the white bulb and rubbed it between his hands with water, it made a nice lather. Finished, they got out and walked back up on the bank.

Oh'Dar lay down on the grass, and Ned followed suit. Then Oh'Dar grabbed some leaves close by and threw a bundle at Ned.

"You might want to cover up," he said as Ned heard giggling coming from the bushes.

"The young girls will be curious about any new man. Especially a Waschini, I imagine."

Ned quickly placed the leaves over his manhood.

"Could have given me a few more," he complained, trying to position them sufficiently.

Oh'Dar laughed. "The Brothers are much more relaxed about some things than the Waschini are."

After a few moments, somewhat dried off, Oh'Dar stood up, clutching his bunch of leaves, and said something in the direction of the bushes. The giggling started up again, and then Ned could hear whoever it was leaving.

"It is clear now; we can get dressed."

Ned pulled on the legging first, then put the hide tunic over his head. Grayson was right; they were far more comfortable. He wiggled around, testing them. The shoe coverings, moccasins as he would have called them, were also comfortable. He wondered how they fared over rough ground—if they would protect his feet from being cut. But they seemed tough enough. He had noticed the soles of Grayson's feet when he had taken off his boots and socks the past few nights. They were thicker and much tougher than his. Either from the footwear or perhaps from going barefoot. It was just one of the few changes that awaited him. He had not thought of how this adventure might affect his body. Considering it now, no doubt he would end up stronger, more agile, healthier even.

"That soap worked well," Ned said, somewhat surprised at how clean he felt.

"You will find there are medicinals everywhere if you know where to look and how to prepare and use them. The Great Spirit has provided for all our needs," Oh'Dar said, hopping a bit as he pulled on his second moccasin. "Let's get something to eat. I am starved!"

Ned had thought that meant something else, but before too long, they were deep in the forest with bows and arrows.

"You know how to shoot?"

"With a bow? Not as well as with a rifle."

"Well then, breakfast is on me," Oh'Dar pulled the bow up to shoulder height, pulled his arm back, leveling it and sighting the arrow. Ned knew that he would have to hold the bow and arrow like this for some time, waiting for breakfast to wander by. He marveled at the upper body strength it took to stay in position. Oh'Dar was tall with long arms, the perfect archer's body.

Ned's job was to stay equally quiet. After what seemed like forever, he heard the arrow leave the string with a zzziing and then a dull thud. Oh'Dar waited, then went over to claim his kill. He knelt down and gave thanks to the groundhog for its sacrifice before picking it up by the tail, after which they walked back to the village.

Sometime later, they were seated around a fire with the groundhog on a spit.

"I could have gotten it with a rifle," Ned said.

"Yes, and also scared away any other wildlife in the area for the next two days. You will learn to use the bow and arrow. If you can sight a rifle, you can learn to hunt this way."

A younger boy came over, one of the Chief's children whom Ned remembered as being called Noshoba.

"That looks good," Noshoba said, pointing at the slowly roasting meat.

"There is enough for you too," Oh'Dar smiled.

Noshoba asked if he could go with them next time. Oh'Dar said if his mother approved, and the boy sat down next to them and waited for the meal to be done.

Within a moment, his sister, Snana, came over. "Noshoba, what are you doing?" she asked in Whitespeak.

"Waiting for breakfast!" he said heartily. Snana shook her head. "Do not let him fool you. He has already eaten. I swear he is always hungry." Then to her brother, she said, "Go. You are old enough to know better than to invite yourself to another's fire."

Noshoba got up and left reluctantly, longingly looking back at the meat, which had started to smell oh so wonderful.

"Wouldn't there be enough for him too?"

"Yes, but his sister is trying to remind him of his manners. He is no longer a child. Don't worry, he won't go hungry."

The smell of the meat made Ned realize just how hungry he was. When it was time, he ate ravenously and enjoyed the feeling of satisfaction afterward.

"Most of the days have a pattern, a routine," Oh'Dar told him. "It starts with a morning fire, which is not always for warmth but does provide comfort, especially in the dark. Fire is an amazing creation. It is beautiful to watch, it smells good, and its flames dance - just as our souls should in gratitude for the remarkable provision of the Great Spirit."

"What will we spend today doing?" Ned asked, savoring the last remnants of his food.

"Living," Oh'Dar answered, smiling.

Ned was relieved to realize that some of this he already knew. He knew how to build a fire, and he knew how to hunt, though not that well with a bow and arrow. He knew how to skin and gut an animal and properly dispose of the leavings. He did not realize, though, how much of it could be used. Very little was discarded; almost every part had a purpose. The fur was used to make blankets and warm-weather clothing. The hides were turned into rawhide or used for clothing, buckets, the soles of their moccasins, drums, and other things. Very little was wasted.

"What did you throw into the fire?"

"Some pieces of the wuchat, the groundhog, in gratitude as a sacrifice," Oh'Dar answered.

Oh'Dar knew that Ned had a great deal to learn. So while they were waiting for the escort from Chief

Kotori's village to arrive, he suggested Snana might show Ned some of the more dangerous plants in the area. She agreed, and she and Ned went off into the forest together.

Oh'Dar turned back to see Pajackok glaring at him before going after the two. Oh'Dar had forgotten that Pajackok had a distrust of the Waschini, and Ned being a male of about Snana's age, did not help.

He could hear loud words being exchanged, followed by Snana stomping out of the forest with Pajackok storming along right behind her. A moment later, Ned followed out sheepishly.

He headed over to Oh'Dar, "That fierce-looking fellow took exception to your suggestion. I take it that is his girlfriend?"

"Wife. Life-walker. A mistake on my part. I had forgotten Pajackok's disdain for our kind. But she is one of the few here who can speak English with you."

Oh'Dar had hoped to have some more time to talk to Chief Is'Taqa but instead took Ned out himself to start his training. Late, he would hunt down Pajackok and apologize.

It had been a full day, and Ned was grateful to slip into his shelter and lie down on the blanket. He pulled the nearby hide up over him, though he was not sure he needed it. He closed his eyes and waited for sleep to come.

But it wouldn't.

He rolled over, trying to quell whatever was bothering him. Then he realized what it was. He felt closed in. The shelter was small, big enough for one person, but it was too close quarters for him. He got up and padded out into the night.

Oh'Dar was still sitting at the fire next to the Chief. Ned waited at a distance, not wanting to interrupt what looked like a serious conversation. Finally, Oh'Dar got up.

"I can't sleep. It is too tight in there."

"Would you prefer to sleep out here next to the fire? I would be glad to join you. My wife and daughter are not here. I can sleep in our family shelter, but I would be just as happy out here."

In the distance, coyotes yipped and howled. Though Ned was used to it, for some reason, it made the hair on his arms stand up.

"Are we safe out here?"

Oh'Dar replied, "You will never be any safer than you are right here. I can promise you that."

Ned didn't understand the answer. He wanted to believe, but felt he would be safer if he had his loaded rifle tucked up next to him.

Oh'Dar lay down next to Ned, thinking over what he and Chief Is'Taqa had just talked about. The Chief had told him how, while Oh'Dar was gone, the constable had returned with Snide Tucker and a posse of questionable men. Oh'Dar felt sick thinking of what could have happened. But after hearing how the Sassen watchers had surrounded the village center and terrified the men with their earth-shattering stomach-rumbling screams, he doubted they would be back.

Despite everyone's advice that Constable Riggs drop his vendetta against Grayson Morgan after what they had experienced at the Brothers' village, he could not. In fact, it had inflamed his curiosity even more. Ben Jenkins had been an established and successful horse breeder. He knew a great deal about matching up characteristics to produce a specific outcome. And the constable's mind started to wander. What was going on up there? Was Grayson Morgan involved in some devilish experiment? Were they breeding monsters up there? Monsters who were somehow under Grayson Morgan's control? Morgan had no loyalty or regard for keeping his own race pure; that was obvious. What else was he capable of?

Sheriff Boone at Millgrove slammed his fist down on his desk. "Dammit, Samuel. I am telling you to drop it."

"I won't drop it. You and your men searched that village well over two decades ago. That Morgan child was not there. You have sworn to me on that more than once. It means he was somewhere else, so where? Who was taking care of him?"

"For gracious sake, any of them could have seen us coming and figured out why. One of the women could have taken him into the woods until we left. That isn't hard to figure out. I don't know why you can't let this go."

"That quickly? And for an indefinite period of time? Not knowing if you and your men would have been there for days? I don't believe it. No, there is something else going on up there. Something unnatural."

"Up until now, Samuel, you have enjoyed a solid reputation. I know it stung that the prosecutor lost that case. But if you continue with this, you are going to be the laughingstock of the territory. And you won't be constable for long if that happens."

The Sheriff pushed his chair away from his desk. "You were trespassing by going up there."

"I was on official business."

"Poppycock, and you know it. You were on personal business, a personal vendetta against Grayson Stone Morgan the Third, though for the life of me, I can't imagine why."

Riggs leaned over the desk, nearly in Sheriff Boone's face. "Now you listen to me. I am not crazy, and I know I am right. Someone told me about a man two territories over who shot a creature. Something he had never seen before and said he hoped never to see again. It was tall, unbelievably tall, probably eleven foot, he said. More like a man than anything else, but all covered in hair."

"Oh, hell, he was probably drunk, and it was probably a bear, only the story of a tall hairy man got him some free drinks. Did you talk to this man? Hear this story straight from him?"

"No, he has traveled on, and no one knows where he is."

Sheriff Boone stood up, forcing Riggs to back away from the desk.

"I am telling you this for the last time. Drop it. If you continue, I won't cover for you, and I won't help you. We may be related, but that doesn't mean I'm going to ruin my reputation to save yours. You're a grown man; you ought to know better than to believe in monsters. As for Grayson Morgan, he did exactly what he testified to, and the Judge agreed. He risked his own life to help his grandparents enjoy the rest of their lives in a way that, though unconventional, is certainly theirs to choose. Now, please, you have your sister over in Appleton. I suggest you go and stay with her and her family for a while and get some perspective."

Constable Riggs picked his hat up off a nearby

chair and glared at his cousin. Then he roughly pulled off his badge from his shirt pocket and stared at it for a moment as it rested in his open palm.

"Don't do it, Samuel. I'm talking to you as a friend now. If you resign your position, you won't get it back. You know that. The Governor is not a forgiving man, and he has vested on you a great deal of standing. Don't throw away a position most men would give their right arm to have."

Riggs clenched his jaw but hesitated. Then he slowly pinned the badge back on his shirt and left, closing the door behind him considerably harder than was necessary.

CHAPTER 10

I t was time for Acaraho to return to Kthama. He held Adia lovingly and kissed the top of her head, then raised her chin with his finger so he could gaze into her eyes. "It will be alright, Saraste'. Neither of us knows how long you must stay here, but it is the safest place for you all. Try to enjoy your time with Urilla Wuti, Nootau, and Iella. I am so happy they will be coming to live with us at Kthama."

"I am too. But I cannot help wondering if Nimida will still be there by the time we return."

Mapiya was helping the other females in the food preparation area when Nimida found her and asked to speak to her.

"I am sorry to interrupt. Do you have a moment to spare?"

"Of course." She could see that Nimida looked sad, so she stopped what she was doing and guided her to an empty table.

"I want to thank you for being so kind to me when I first came here. You befriended me and let me stay with you. You are so dear to me; I do not tell you enough."

"And you are like a daughter to me," Mapiya hastened to reassure her. "You know I have only sons, and you enrich my life so much. I'm looking forward to your first offspring, sharing that with you."

Then Mapiya reached out and placed her hand over Nimida's. "What is troubling you?"

"Oh. It is something I do not want to go into. I just wanted to see you."

"You look worried. Remember that there are many here in addition to me who love you and who you could talk to. I know you and Nootau became close almost right from the start. And Adia. I have often heard her tell people that you are like an adopted daughter to her, just as you are to me."

Nimida became very quiet. Her heart was breaking. She loved Mapiya. And she loved Nootau too. What was she doing? She had just told Adia she knew leaving wasn't the answer, and yet here she was, almost ready to tell Mapiya that she and Tar *were* leaving. Finally, she could admit to herself that she loved Adia too. But could she completely forgive her?

Of all the places she could have ended up,

Nimida was at the High Rocks. With her birth family, with her birth brother, at the invitation of her birth mother. And now, if she could open her heart to accept them, she had three new siblings to love and make part of her life. Did it matter if no one knew the truth? That she shared Adia's bloodline. What did it really matter? Were families made up of bloodlines or of heartlines? Then she thought of Mapiya. What if Mapiya returned to the Great Spirit and Nimida was not there? Could she leave and never know what became of her? Not be with her in her final moments?

"Please tell me what is going on? It feels as if you are saying goodbye," Mapiya said, her seventh sense picking up what Nimida was struggling with but not revealing.

Nimida got up and then leaned over and hugged Mapiya for a long time. Mapiya leaned into her embrace. "I am sorry if I upset you. No, I do not want to leave Kthama. I do not want to leave those I have grown to love and who love me. And, especially, I would never want to leave you. You are right; I will work through my troubles here."

The females held each other for some time. The others in the eating commons watched the display quietly, touched by the depth of the love between the two.

If Eyota had thought she would not know what to do with herself at the Far High Hills other than caring for Tansy, she was mistaken. She drew attention everywhere she went and spent many hours with the people there. She was a mystery to them and a living sign of the still undiscovered secrets of their world. The delicate Akassa offling were as enamored with Tansy as the adults were. But through it all, she maintained her humility and patience, answering their questions the best she could. They asked her what her life had been like before she was transformed and what it was like now. She told them that she had always been healthy, but it was nothing like the vigor she felt now. They asked to touch her silver coat, and she graciously obliged. The females asked to hold her daughter, and as long as it was not tiring Tansy, she let them. As Adia had, they always commented on how soft Tansy's coat was. They examined her little toes and fingers and were delighted when she smiled at them, which was frequently.

"She is a good-natured soul," said Eyota. "She seems happy and content. Of course, everything will become more complicated once she starts crawling."

The other mothers laughed and nodded. Motherhood was motherhood, whether your offling was a Sassen Guardian, one of the Brothers, or one of the People. It was one of the common threads that bound them all together.

"What does she think of An'Kru?" a female asked.

"I do not know. She has only met him a few times. She is too young to play, and of course, she will always be too strong to play with any Akassa offling of her age." She went on to tell them how each of the other Guardians had become seeded at about the same time and that there were three males and three females. If they found that peculiar, no one said anything, and Eyota did not tell them what Pan had said about the Sassen Guardians being able to mate with any of the others without concern for bloodlines.

One day, while Eyota was surrounded by a similar crowd, Adia came to join them. She had the twins with her in a double sling that she had designed with Tehya's help. She sat down and propped them up so the crowd could see them too.

The others fussed over them, and the offlings' little heads wobbled about as, with open mouths and unfocused stares, they looked at the strangers.

When the crowd thinned, Eyota said to Adia. "I am glad you came by. I enjoy your company."

"And I enjoy yours!" Adia smiled.

Eyota felt a kinship with the High Rocks Healer that she could not explain. In fact, it was the main reason she had come to the Far High Hills. She had felt called to go with Adia.

"May I ask you a personal question?"

"Of course," Adia answered.

"Are you often cold?"

Adia laughed. "Very seldom. But then I just put another layer on. I am sure it works in reverse for you."

"I love the beauty of the spring and summer, but the summers, in particular, are terrible. Too hot, too humid. How refreshing it would be to live somewhere cooler most of the time. It would be much easier if we did not mind getting wet. I imagine the Great River is cool and refreshing."

"I hear it is. My son Oh'Dar loves to swim. As do many of the Brothers."

"Do all the Waschini swim?"

"I do not know," Adia chuckled. "If he joins us, we can ask the new Waschini."

"We Sassen lived at Kayerm all those years and now look at what is going on. We never know what is around the corner, do we?"

"No. But as you said before, we have to trust that it is for our good. Even if we cannot see it at the time."

"When will the new Waschini arrive?" Eyota asked, putting Tansy up to nurse.

"He has to pass a test first. A trial. To see if he can adjust to such a different life. My son fears that his friend is too young to make this significant a life choice. I believe Oh'Dar will make it as hard on him as possible but only wanting the best for him. Ned. His name is Ned Webb."

"Nedwebb," Eyota said. Then faster, "Nebwebb."

Then the two looked at each other and laughed as they said it together quickly at the same time.

"Well, when you say it together like that, it sounds comical." Eyota said it again three times in a row even faster, and they laughed again.

By arrangement, a messenger was on the way to Chief Kotori to let him know that the Waschini man had arrived at the Chief Is'Taqa's village. When the Sassen appeared, they knew to have Pakwa follow them back to where the young man was waiting. Though Oh'Dar was anxious to get back to the High Rocks, he felt he needed to go with Ned.

When Pakwa arrived, he was welcomed, and along with his pony, was given quarters, food, and a chance to rest. Oh'Dar had not met the brave before, so introduced both himself and Ned. Ned stood patiently, not understanding a word they said but carefully listening to the cadence and intonation. Oh'Dar showed Pakwa the bow, quiver and arrows he was giving Ned. Pakwa hefted the bow and turned it side to side, checking the balance and examining the feathered arrows. He frowned, nodded, and then grinned, handing it back to Oh'Dar, saying, "Che'sa'halla." Oh'Dar smiled at the compliment, looked at Ned, and nodded.

Ned was pleased, not knowing exactly the

meaning but knowing it was positive. He had just learned his first word.

Chief Kotori had met with his people and explained why the Waschini was being brought there, what his training would consist of, and who would be delivering it. He explained that this white man had much to learn about living in the way they did. They were not to make it harder on him than necessary, but he had to prove himself if he was to be accepted into the People's culture.

All of them knew of the Waschini's growing persecution of their people, but the Chief helped them understand the vision of the Guardian of Etera, Pan, and how they must all come together, Sassen, People, and the Brothers, to help turn the Waschini from their destructive path.

"It is said they are not teachable," said Sakinay, one of the braves assigned to teach the Waschini how to hunt.

"All men, regardless of skin color, are teachable if to be so is the only way to achieve that which is out of their reach."

"So you think they are the same as us, other than their appearance?" Sakinay had lowered his voice.

"Every creature that walks, or swims, or flies through the air was created by the hand of the Great Spirit. Every living thing seeks that which is pleasurable and avoids that which is not. The Waschini can be no different. It is their methods for achieving their desires that are misguided. It is the hope of our newly formed brotherhood that we can help them back onto the path of peace and harmony."

"It is difficult to teach someone who would kill his own teacher," Sakinay said before walking away.

His father, listening from a few feet away, came over to Chief Kotori. "I apologize for my son. He means no disrespect."

"I have watched Sakinay grow to manhood. I know his heart is good, and I take no offense from his words. It is better that a man say them straight out than let them fester and ferment in a dark corner of his heart. He is our best hunter; he will teach the Waschini more quickly than anyone else."

"He will not fail you. But I will speak with him and ask that he not make it harder on the white man than need be."

Oh'Dar knew that Ned would be left out of the conversation on the way to Chief Kotori's village, but there was not much he could do about it. He would occasionally point to something along the way and give Ned the Brothers' word for it. Trees, rocks, creek, moss, birds— It was a start.

Oh'Dar found Pakwa to be a friendly chap. Whatever Khon'Tor or someone had said had been effective.

Soon, Pakwa also started teaching Ned words. He took it further, though, and started teaching Ned verbs for sitting, stumbling, talking, riding. By the second night, Oh'Dar could see that Pakwa and Ned were going to get along fine. He surmised that Ned would feel comfortable about the situation by the time it came for him to be left alone at Chief Kotori's village.

It was late morning on the following day when Pakwa said they were almost there. Ned took a moment to try to straighten out his clothes and wet down his hair, which was sticking up all over the place.

Oh'Dar chuckled. "You look a fright."

"Thank you. I was starting to feel nervous; now I feel much better," Ned laughed good-naturedly, rubbing his hand over the stubble on his chin.

Pakwa rode on ahead, and within a few minutes, returned and motioned them ahead. When they broke through the underbrush, Ned saw a circle of the villagers waiting to greet him. He quickly scanned one face to the next. Only one seemed to have a sour look on his face, a rather tall, regal fellow standing to the right of who could only be the Chief.

They dismounted, and Pakwa introduced them

while Oh'Dar translated for Ned. First was Chief Kotori, then the Second Chief, and then the grim-looking fellow on the right who was named Sakinay. The next was a female, their Medicine Woman. Ned's heart sunk a little at hearing that the sour-faced one would be his first teacher. He would teach him the basics of their hunting practices. Ned decided that this made sense. It was a tangible skill that probably required less talking than other skills. And eating was a primary need.

After the introductions were made, one of the women showed him to his living space. Ned was grateful it was larger than the one he had been given at the Chief Is'Taqa's village. He didn't need claustrophobia on top of his other nerves.

He dropped his belongings inside the shelter, and when he came out, Oh'Dar was speaking with the Chief and another female. Ned waited and joined them only when Oh'Dar beckoned.

The female was becoming. She had very long dark black hair that shone in the sunlight. Her cheekbones highlighted very pretty brown eyes. He could tell she was young, though no longer a child by any means. He looked away when she caught him staring at her.

There seemed to be some sort of discussion going on, and Ned assumed it had to do with him. He guessed that this woman would have some part in his training, and she didn't seem too happy about it.

Just then, the sour-faced one, named Sakinay,

came over to join the circle. He looked at Ned, frowned, then wrinkled his nose in Ned's direction.

Ned immediately became self-conscious and sniffed at his tunic. They had been traveling on horseback and not that long, so Ned couldn't see how he could be offensive but asked anyway, "Chief, Grayson, is there a stream nearby where I can clean up after we take care of the horses?"

Oh'Dar translated, and the Chief raised his hand, indicating they could leave. With the horses cared for, Ned went back to his shelter to find something else to put on when he was clean, and as he came out, an older woman was standing there holding a pile of clothes. She held it out to him and said something. He took the bundle and thanked her, hoping she understood what he meant.

This time as they bathed, there were no children peeking at them from the bushes. Ned enjoyed getting clean and though the water was cool, would have stayed longer, but Oh'Dar encouraged him to hurry.

"I will stay a day or two, and then I need to get home. I want to make sure you're relatively comfortable before I leave." Oh'Dar stood up, brushed the excess water off himself with his hand, and flicked the droplets onto the bank.

Ned pulled on the leggings and the tunic. They were a bit large.

"The woman who made them said she would alter them once she could see how they fit. We will find her when we get back, then leave them outside your shelter when you go to bed, and she will have them back by morning."

"They are going to a lot of trouble to make me feel welcome." Ned was now pulling on the last of his new outfit, the moccasins. "I'm surprised they want to help a Waschini after what my people—our people—are doing to them."

"This is more important than you realize. It is important that you succeed for reasons beyond your own personal ones," Oh'Dar said.

Ned was learning not to push for more than Oh'Dar was willing to share. He trusted that in time it would all make sense.

That evening, the entire village was gathered around an enormous fire. The flames shot up into the night and released glowing embers, which drifted up higher and higher before blinking out of sight. In the background, the village children laughed and played, their voices adding joy to the mood.

The Chief spoke in long, vibrant sentences, obviously telling a story. His deep voice was mesmerizing. Many of the villagers nodded and smiled and made approving or excited comments as he spoke.

The story was not lost on Ned, as Oh'Dar was sitting next to him and quietly translated.

The closeness of the village members was palpable. Ned longed to be part of it, to know without Oh'Dar's interpretation what story was being told, to feel he belonged there with them. But no matter how well he learned the Brothers' language, he knew he could never be one of them, and it made him sad.

Oh'Dar lived with this feeling all his life. No wonder he set out to find his blood family. But even after finding the Morgans, where did he feel he belonged, if anywhere?

Chief Is'Taqa's story had them all spellbound and then came to a climactic ending with everyone oohing and ahhing and broad smiles everywhere. Next, it was the Second Chief's turn to tell a story, and Ned enjoyed it as much as the other. He hoped that they would be told again someday when he could understand what they were saying.

Eventually, the fire was dying down, and many of the villagers had left. The children were long put to bed by their mothers. The woman who had brought him the clothes came up and stood over Ned, saying something and gesturing back to his shelter.

"She says you have to go to bed now or take your clothes off and sit here naked if you prefer," Oh'Dar chuckled. "She says she does not want to be up all night sewing for you."

Ned smiled and stood up and faced her. She reached out and pulled the tunic out and let it go, then she ran her hands up and down over his leggings. Ned's eyes widened, "What the—" he exclaimed.

"She is just checking for fit," Oh'Dar laughed.

"Is *that* what she is checking for?" Ned asked.

"I imagine," Oh'Dar smiled. "Unless the other women have asked her to check for something else." Then Oh'Dar quickly added, "I am just teasing you. You can relax. In the women's eyes, we Waschini men are generally no match for theirs."

Finally, she was done and walked away, though she was still chattering back at him as she left and pointing again to his shelter.

"I had better turn in. Please thank the Chief for his hospitality," and Ned smiled at the Chief.

Grace was sitting on the floor playing with the puppy she had gotten from the Baxters. She had named him Pippy. The puppy tugged at her skirts, and she admonished him and gave him a little hide ball Newell had made. He forgot about her skirts and chased it across the wooden floor. Newell was due home at any moment, and dinner was already cooking in the hearth. She loved making their house cozy and welcoming for him, and she loved working in their garden, seeing the new shoots of the fruits and vegetables poke up through the soil. Since Tucker had disappeared, they had enjoyed a quiet day-to-day existence. Newell's business was picking up, and they had no financial troubles. Grace only worked a few days in the office with him now as Newell preferred her to be at home, and she didn't mind; there was lots to do.

Even though he had been gone only a short time, Grace missed her brother terribly. She imagined that had contributed to getting a puppy from Alicia. It was a tie to her brother since he was Buster's puppy. And he was company for her during the day. One day, hopefully not too soon, she would also have children to occupy her. At times she thought she wanted a houseful of children—seven was the number that came to mind. When she had shared her thoughts with Newell, he had looked surprised but said it would be just wonderful if that was how it turned out, as long as it was not too hard on her and did not wear her down.

In the backyard was a little pen with three goats in it. The farmer Oh'Dar had spoken with about the goats had asked her to go ahead and take them since they were paid for, and Grace was glad to do it. She loved the goats' milk and the sweet butter it made. She had gained a little weight since she and Newell had gotten married, and he said it made her all the more delightful. Newell promised her he would replace them when Oh'Dar finally took the goats. He had gotten used to having the rich butter himself!

Later, at dinner time, Grace was clearing the

table and thinking about her brother. "I miss him," she said.

Newell knew without asking that she was speaking of Ned. "I know you do, honey. But you know Grayson is taking good care of him."

He stood up to help her clear the table. "This is what Ned needs. It is the only way he is going to settle this for himself. You don't know, he might be back, but I know you want him to find peace, whether it is here with us or there with Grayson."

"Alicia seems to have moved on quickly. The Thompson's oldest is courting her now."

"Well, that tells you something right there, doesn't it? Ned hasn't even been gone a month," Newell said, setting the last bowl in the sink.

He brushed what was left on his plate into the puppy's bowl, and Pippy scampered over and immediately licked it up.

Grace gave him a look.

"I know; I shouldn't give him cornbread."

"Dogs don't digest corn well, I am told."

"I've never seen one chewing on a cornstalk, that's for sure," Newell quipped.

"I'll bet Ned would enjoy some cornbread right about now," Grace sighed. "But, if Ben and Miss Vivian could adjust to such a life, I believe my brother can too."

CHAPTER 11

Eitel had left Moart'Tor alone since their first conversation when she had reached out to touch him, and he had pulled away. Though she tried not to take it personally, it had made her feel rejected. After that, she left it to others to befriend him, though she did watch him when he was unaware.

In the end, Eitel decided that her people were not that different from the Mothoc. They had a similar build, though both Pan and Moart'Tor were much taller and heftier than the Sassen. And their coats were heavier. The undercoat seemed to be fuller, making the top coat extend further. She wondered if all the Mothoc were the same color but did not know if it would be too personal to ask. From his torso down, Moart'Tor was a very dark brown, almost black, in stark contrast to the white coloring on his upper body. Sometimes that looked almost translucent when the sun hit it just right.

Eitel could see the Brothers' influence in the Sassen's more defined features. Though nowhere as delicate as the Brothers', their noses fitted in between the Mothoc's flatter, wider ones, and the Brothers' more pointed ones. As for herself, she had inherited her solid black coloring from her mother. Sometimes she wished it was not so different from everyone else's, but her brother told her she made too much of that and that most males would find it becoming.

She and Naahb were very close, barely a year apart. They had been each other's constant companions growing up, and Naahb preferred her company to that even of his friends. He always looked out for her, which prompted him to speak as she was spearfishing down by the Great River.

"Missed that one," he said as he came up behind her.

"Only because your looming shadow scared it off!" she retorted.

"Excuses make for a meager meal," he teased her again.

"Grab a spear and help me then," she said. Naahb did as she asked and walked a few feet downstream.

"I saw you watching that one," he said.

"You mean the stranger? Moart'Tor?" she asked as she plunged the shaft in quickly, pulling it out with a huge longfish impaled on the end. "Ah ha! It was your shadow after all!" She held it up and waved it about so he could not miss it.

"Yes. And if I noticed it, so did others," Naahb chided her.

"I am sure I am not the only one studying him. He is—unprecedented."

"That he is. But we know nothing of him. There is no reason to believe anything he tells us about who he is or why he is here."

"And there is no reason not to believe it either," she said.

"I am just saying be cautious. I do not want you to get hurt."

"You say that as if you think I am particularly interested in him." Eitel frowned.

"It is hard not to think it. I have never seen you watch anyone so."

"He certainly would have no interest in me. We are not even the same—people."

"We are not all that different. It is mostly the size."

"You saw him pull away when I tried to touch him. He is not interested in me."

"He would be a fool not to be. Just promise me you will be wise about your actions. I am certainly not encouraging you."

Eitel turned her attention back to the waters. She was starting to feel sorry for Moart'Tor and thought perhaps she should give him another chance.

After a moment of stillness, she had another fish on her spear.

"Seeing as you have two fish and I have no fish, I could use an invitation to dinner," her brother teased.

"You had better catch up. Two fish are not going to feed you and me and mother and father!"

Though he felt guilty about it, cloaked within a nearby grove of hickory, Moart'Tor had been sitting watching them. There was some variation in the language, probably formed over the thousands of years that separated his people and theirs. But his ear had adjusted, and he could make out what they were saying.

When Eitel pointed out how he had pulled away from her, he felt a pang of regret. She was indeed comely. Her black coloring was in sharp contrast to Moart'Tor's own upper body coloring, and he found it enticing. And her brother was right; they were not all that different. They were about as different as the Brothers were said to be from the Akassa.

He did wonder if he would ever get to see the Akassa. He had not been there long enough to have a right to be impatient, but he was.

He spent his days foraging and gathering for himself. He nodded and greeted the Sassen as they came by. Sometimes he talked with them briefly, just passing friendly remarks. He watched them as often as he could without being obvious about it. In the back of his mind, it was bothering him just how alike they were to the Mothoc. They worshiped the Great Spirit, and they gave thanks for their blessings. They gathered around the night fires just as they did back home. Moart'Tor was having a hard time seeing what made them so different from his own kind.

A branch snapped, and he turned to see Pan standing behind him. He realized she could see him even though he was cloaked. Moart'Tor stood up, though remaining cloaked, unsure if Eitel and her brother could see Pan.

"You are watching Eitel and her brother."

"Only curiosity," he answered.

"You are unpaired. Why is that?"

Moart'Tor looked over at Eitel again, then turned back to answer the Guardian. "Our numbers are few. A female must be earned."

"And how is that done?"

"Bravery. Valor. A male must prove himself worthy."

"Perhaps by completing a task? A—quest even?" Pan asked.

Moart'Tor felt shame rising in him. He could not meet Pan's eyes and looked away. He tried changing the subject. "Do you have a family?"

"I did. A long time ago."

"You came to Zuenerth once. You never returned. Did you know your brother, my father, was there?"

"Not when he first left Kthama. But eventually, I did. I could feel he was well and not suffering. That was all I wanted to know. What do you know of the formation of your group, Moart'Tor?"

"That we were expelled from Kthama by your father, Moc'Tor. That we then came here to Kayerm until his brother Straf'Tor took it over and banished us once more. From then on, we wandered until we eventually came to settle where we are now."

"And do you know why your founders were expelled from Kthama?"

"Because they did not support your father's vision for our people's future. That he did not protect the sovereign nature of the Mothoc. He allowed our blood to be diluted with that of the Others. He betrayed the trust of those we were created to protect," Moart'Tor explained.

"Your original Leader was Norcab. He and my father never got along. Norcab would challenge my father at every opportunity. In the end, they came to blows. Norcab lost the fight but, in the end, tried to kill my mother, who was still carrying your father, Dak'Tor, within her. It was that moment when my father killed Norcab."

Moart'Tor fell silent. He had every reason to believe the Guardian. But he did not want to.

The Guardian picked up a rock and held out her hand. She asked him to do the same. Then she pricked her finger, and a drop of blood formed at the tip. She handed the stone to him, and he followed her lead. A similar rich red drop formed on his finger.

"This," Pan said, indicating the blood. "This is the life of Etera. Without our blood, everything on her will perish. Our people were dying. Faced with extinction, my father made a choice that only a great Leader could bear to make. A choice that he paid for in ways, unbearably painful ways, that no one will truly ever understand. Your Leader seeks to annihilate the Sassen and the Akassa. I will tell you this and make no mistake that what I say is true. If he were to succeed, that would be the abomination."

Just then, the drop on the Guardian's finger pooled and dripped to the ground. It landed on a small shriveled brown plant. Moart'Tor watched as the plant trembled, and then, miraculously, it grew, changing from brown to light green and then dark green, doubling in size right before his eyes.

"How can that be? What happened?"

"Our blood contains the life force of Etera. The Aezaitera flows through our veins. Mine more so than any other of the Mothoc. In the many thousands of years I have lived, the concentration of the Aezaitera in my blood has doubled, tripled even. But regardless of that, this, this blood of ours, and that of the Sassen and of the Akassa, is precious. Without our blood, even in the diluted form that flows in the Sassen and the Akassa, Etera will die."

When she finished speaking, Pan turned and walked away. After a few steps, she shimmered out of view. Moart'Tor stared into the empty space where she had just been, then back down at the plant, which had continued to grow and was now pushing out a delicate pink blossom.

Moart'Tor suddenly felt lost. Completely, utterly lost. What he had believed to be true, was it, or was it not? Were these people not an abomination? An affront to the Great Spirit? Was their existence not what was causing all the troubles his people faced? Had Moc'Tor, his very own grandfather, not betrayed the Great Spirit by creating the Akassa and the Sassen? What was true? What was not? How was he to know? What had seemed so clear a few days ago now seemed murky and obscure.

As he was standing there, he heard footsteps approaching. He turned to see Eitel and her brother coming up the little rise to where he was standing in the grove.

"We have been blessed today," Eitel said, holding up a large collection of longfish. "Would you care to join us at our fire tonight? You would be welcome."

Moart'Tor was shocked that they could see him. He had not uncloaked. Had the Guardian uncloaked him herself? Did she have that power? Or, in his confusion, had he dropped his guard?

Moart'Tor frowned at Eitel; it was as if he could not think for a moment. Then he looked at the fish she held up. Her brother held an equal number. Finally, he stammered, "Yes. Thank you. Yes. I would."

Eitel looked at him briefly, then at her brother. When Moart'Tor said nothing more, she said, "We will expect you then." And they turned and walked off.

Ｏ

"That was peculiar," Naahb said as they walked away.

"No doubt. Who was he talking to? Himself? It seemed like he was finishing a conversation when we came over the little hill and saw him."

"Who knows," Naahb said. "And who knows how long he had been there. I did not see him when I joined you, and I walked right past there. As to who he was talking to, perhaps he talks to the *Shissu*."

An ancient word, seldom spoken.

"Those already returned to the Great Spirit?" Her eyes widened. "Do you think that is possible?"

"I do not know. As I said earlier, we know nothing about him. Come on, let us show mother and father our catch and then prepare it."

Ｏ

The fish were nearly done by the time Moart'Tor arrived. Eitel smiled up at him as he approached, and she scooted over quite a bit, making room for him between herself and her father. Her father greeted him, welcoming him to their evening meal, and motioned for him to sit.

"It smells wonderful," Moart'Tor said, sniffing the air loudly. His nostrils flared, taking in more of the delicious scent.

"My mother taught me how to season it just right," said Eitel.

Moart'Tor looked at her mother. She had dark coloring similar to her daughter's, though not as uniformly black as Eitel's. It was late enough and dark enough that the fire cast a warm glow over them all. He felt a flood of comfort come over him. He had not felt that in a long time.

Eitel's father handed out the fish, making sure that Moart'Tor received the largest portion.

"You do not have to do that. Do not go without because of me," he said.

"You are our guest. It is fitting that you should be well provided for, as the Great Spirit provides for us as well," the father said.

Moart'Tor had not had anything prepared by anyone but himself for a long time. He tried to eat it slowly but could not help himself and gobbled it down. He licked his fingers and said, "That was delicious. Excellent. I do not think I have ever tasted it so well prepared."

"That is kind of you to say," Eitel answered.

As they were finishing up, Haan and a female Sassen came over to visit. A very young offling was walking with them.

"This is my mate, Haaka, and my daughter Kalli,"

Haan said. "They have come on a brief visit to Kayerm."

Moart'Tor stared at the offling standing at Haaka's side, reaching up to hold her mother's hand. He could not pull his gaze away.

"She is part Akassa," Haan explained. Moart'Tor then realized how intently he had been staring at the offling.

"How is that possible? I thought they were small. Like the Others."

"Not as small as the Others, but you are correct; it is a miracle she was born. Her mother almost died giving birth to her."

Moart'Tor frowned at Haaka, not understanding.

"It is a long story. One for another time," Haan said.

"What is going on here? Sassen breeding with Akassa? Are there no restrictions? No limits to—" Moart'Tor suddenly caught himself and stopped talking.

"Thank you for dinner. I must leave now," he said, rising abruptly and quickly heading off.

"What just happened?" Haaka asked.

Haan turned to her. "The shell concealing the truth of his true beliefs is breaking open."

"You should tell Pan," Haaka said.

"She knows. Trust me, she knows."

Moart'Tor moved quickly to his living quarters. He pulled the hide curtain closed as tightly as possible, not that anyone would disturb him, but it was still comforting. It was a large room, and it should have been comfortable. But right now, there was no place on Etera where Moart'Tor could find comfort.

For a fleeting moment, he had felt comfort while sitting with Eitel and her family. And then the Leader had appeared, with that—thing. So the Sassen had continued Moc'Tor's depravity, this time breeding with the Akassa? Where would it end? He caught himself—had he not just thought of mating Eitel?

I should go home. Moart'Tor was getting nowhere except more and more confused. He pictured the disappointment on his father's face if he returned with no news of the Promised One and with no information about the Akassa or the Mothoc. And where were the Mothoc? Where were the Akassa? At Kthama, he assumed. But after his reaction to that mixed offling, he doubted he would be able to find out anything more than he already had. Whatever trust he had earned, his uncontrolled reaction at Eitel's family fire had just destroyed it.

CHAPTER 12

It had been three days, and Oh'Dar was preparing to leave. With Pakwa's help, Ned had made a little progress, learning some of the basic words of the Brothers' language. Still, he hated to see Oh'Dar go.

"When will you return?" Ned asked.

"In three months. I will be back in three months. It will be winter by then. However, if you decide earlier that you do not want to continue, they will bring you back to Chief Is'Taqa's village and let me know."

"I will be fine; Sour Face seems nice enough. And I think he likes me." They both laughed, knowing that Sakinay was not the cheeriest fellow, and if he did like Ned, he certainly would not show it. He seemed to have a permanent scowl and barked at Ned more than he spoke.

"I brought my bow for you to use so you would

not waste away immediately, but I was told not to leave it. Apparently, your first task will be to make one of your own. Try not to starve before you learn how."

"Give me some credit. I am told I am smarter than I look. And give my regards to your grandparents, please," Ned added.

Oh'Dar gave him a hug. "I will. See you before you know it."

"You won't recognize me when you return!" Ned called out after him.

"Oh, I bet I will!" Oh'Dar laughed, "There's not much you can do to hide that curly yellow mop on top of your head, white man!" he called out.

Ned laughed again, but as soon as Oh'Dar was out of sight, he felt a huge sadness. Lonesomeness. He realized he was now lonesome. He and Oh'Dar had become friends, and he already missed his friend.

Ned heard his name called and saw that Sakinay was looking for him. Whatever the brave was saying, the gist of it was to get to work. Sakinay led him into the forest and started pointing out trees, different trees, some taller than others, some with leaves, some without. Ned was not sure what Sakinay was trying to teach him, so he waited and hoped it would make sense.

Sakinay started looking at various trees. Ned saw him pass up the softer woods, the pine, cedars, and spruce trees. He pulled at various ash and walnut branches, finally settling on a birch. He used his hatchet to cut two long pieces, then stripped the bark from both.

He came back to Ned and handed him one of the long branches. Ned realized that Sakinay was going to teach him how to make a bow by making one alongside him. Ned had never in all his years made a bow.

Ned watched and copied exactly what Sakinay did. It took them all day, from preparing the bow itself to stringing the sinew for the string, to selecting the wood for the arrows, notching the ends, and setting the arrowhead and feathers appropriately. By the end of the day, Ned was proud of his bow and felt that surely he had passed that test.

That evening at the fire, once everyone was settled down, Sakinay stood up to address the village. He spoke for some time, pointing to Ned off and on. Then he stepped away and came back with Ned's bow.

Sakinay continued talking. The Chief looked at Ned and then back at Sakinay, who had continued talking. When Sakinay was finished, he held Ned's bow up for everyone to see it clearly. And said, *"Che'sa'halla."* Ned knew this word. He had heard Pakwa use it in complimenting Oh'Dar's bow. It meant good, accomplishment, success! Ned felt a blush of pride at having passed this first test. Then, to his horror, Sakinay tossed his bow into the fire.

Ned caught himself before calling out. He looked

around, confused. He looked down at his bow with the flames slowly licking around its edges. What had he done wrong? Why had Sakinay destroyed it? He had worked so hard all day, and what was he to hunt with now? No one seemed disturbed except him. He wanted to go to his shelter and collect himself, but he felt it would bring shame if he did so. Instead, he watched Sakinay talk some more, not understanding and hardly listening.

Finally, others left to go to their shelters, and Ned felt it was alright for him also to leave. He refused to look at Sakinay, fearing that he would be unable to hide his anger.

The next morning, Ned found Sakinay waiting for him. Sakinay signaled for him to follow back into the woods, and before long, they were at the same place as the day before.

Sakinay handed Ned a knife and motioned to the birch tree. He said something and then said it again. He held up his own bow and motioned back to the birch tree.

Ned finally understood that today he would make another bow, only this time on his own, not with Sakinay to show him each step. This seemed unfair. Ned had only seen him do it once. Surely this was not how they taught their children, expecting them to learn by watching only one time?

Ned did his best to remember every step that Sakinay had shown him. His teacher watched him, making a few corrections along the way, pointing here or there where a notch needed to be deeper or an edge smoothed. Finally, by the end of the day, Ned was where he had been the day before. He had another bow and a set of five arrows. Despite his anger, he had not let Sakinay beat him.

That night at the fire, Ned was doubly relieved that the day had ended well. He watched Sakinay stand and address those gathered there. He saw Chief Kotori nod at him as Sakinay spoke, and he heard the word *che'sa'halla* again. And watched again in horror as, once more, Sakinay threw the bow and, this time, all the arrows into the fire.

Ned looked around, incredulous. No one seemed shocked. They all looked as if this was perfectly normal behavior. But how could it be? He had worked just as hard on the second bow. He had done what Sakinay asked. It was just as good as Sakinay's bow. Both had been. And for a second time, Sakinay had thrown his work into the fire.

This time Ned could not help himself; he got up and left to go to his own shelter. He lay on his blanket and tried to understand what was going on, but he could not. For the first time since he had arrived, he wished he could go home to Wilde Edge and forget about this. Whatever Sakinay was up to, it seemed he had no intention of letting Ned succeed.

The next morning, it was the same routine. Sakinay was waiting for him. For the third time, Ned spent the entire day making a bow and arrows. This time when it was done, he was sure it was perfect.

There was no way Sakinay would throw this one into the fire. He was satisfied that this time he had succeeded; there was no question that he had passed the test.

This time, when he returned, Ned made sure to tuck his bow and arrows away in his shelter, and he went to the evening fire, confident that tomorrow would bring a new lesson and he would move on to another skill.

The evening fire was almost finished, and Ned was relieved. Sakinay had not gotten up to speak to the village people again. He had sat quietly while others talked and laughed, and the children played in the background. But just when it seemed it was time for others to start leaving, Sakinay stood up. This time he spoke for a while and then pointed at Ned. Ned, not knowing what else to do, stood up. Sakinay pointed back to Ned's shelter and gestured as if he was asking Ned to go and get his bow and arrows and bring them back to the fire. Ned stared at him, and Sakinay motioned a second time. Ned looked at Chief Kotori, who nodded as if saying, yes, do as Sakinay asks.

Reluctantly, Ned went to his shelter and came back out with his bow in one hand and his arrows in the other. He stood next to Sakinay, who smiled at him and reached out to take the bow and arrows. Ned stepped backward, putting them behind his back and shaking his head.

"No," he said.

Sakinay scowled and took a step toward him, talking and pointing to the bow and arrows Ned was holding behind his back and putting his hand out as if demanding them.

Ned stepped back once more and said again, this time strong and with a frown on his face, "No. No. They are mine. You cannot have them just to throw them into the fire."

Sakinay looked at the Chief and then lunged at Ned, knocking him to the ground. Ned got up and pushed the taller man away just as he almost had his hands on Ned's bow. This time, Ned shouted, "No!" He took a firm step toward Sakinay and firmly said it again. "No. I said no!"

Suddenly, Sakinay started to chuckle and then looked at the others around the fire. Ned looked at them too and saw them all smiling at him, even the Chief. Then Sakinay stepped forward and put his hand on Ned's shoulder. "Che'sa'halla," he said. "Che'sa'halla."

Ned was confused. What was happening? He had just attacked Sakinay and was receiving admiration for it? What was this about? Then it dawned on him. The test was not about making the bow and arrows. Well, at least not all of it. He had passed that test the first day. The other part of the test was standing up to someone who was treating him unfairly. It was about being a man and protecting what was rightfully his. No man had the right to destroy another man's property. When Ned figured it out, all his anger disappeared. He looked at Sakinay and smiled. "Che'sa'halla."

Then Sakinay went over to where Ned's bow and arrows lay and bent down, picked them up, and handed them to him. "Che'sa'halla," he said once again and then sat back down by the fire.

While Ned was still standing there, the older woman who had sewn his clothes brought over a newly made quiver for his arrows. She handed it to him, and he thanked her for the generous gift. She chattered something at him before smiling and walking back to join her family.

Ned put his arrows in the quiver and slung it over his shoulder. Then he raised his hand as if to say goodnight and went back to his shelter. It had been a long day, but at least tonight, he would go to sleep with his bow and arrows at his side. Finally.

Sakinay left him alone the next day, so Ned was free to do whatever he wished. He decided he would go down to the river and catch some fish. The weather had turned warm again, as it often did at the beginning of fall.

He followed the bank around, trying to avoid stepping in the crinkly fallen leaves and keeping his eyes on the shallows. Up ahead was a small crop of rocks and a place he knew that Myrica liked to linger. Perhaps he would meet up with her. But as he got closer, he heard water splashing. He reached a boulder, and looking around it, saw Myrica bathing. She was facing away from him and her long black hair cascaded down her back. The tips were wet from touching the water. Her reflection highlighted the curve of her waist leading down to the swell of her hips, just showing above the water. In a hurry to leave, he lost his footing, and a twig snapped. He saw her head turn to see who was there. She called out and sank down into the water. Ned crept off as quietly as he could; the vision of her beauty seared into his memory.

Myrica finished bathing and returned to the village. Her friend Awantia was waiting for her. "You took long enough; did you enjoy yourself?"

"Yes, but I caught the white man watching me."

"Oh!" Awantia said. "Were you scared?"

"Of course not."

"What do you think of him? I almost gasped out loud the second night that he let Sakinay throw his bow and arrows into the fire. I think we were all relieved when he finally stood up for himself."

"He is either very brave or very stupid, leaving his people to come here," Myrica said.

"Do you know that the Waschini who lives at the High Rocks, the one who brought him here, is life-walker to the Chief's daughter there?"

"I know you. What are you getting at? That I should bond with the white man? Because he watched me bathing, as any man would watch any woman given the chance? Seriously?"

"And why not? He will not always be helpless. He has already passed the first and second tests. And you say there is no other man for you here, anyway."

"That part is true, but I can do better than a crazy man. And a white one at that."

"Well, why else was he brought here? He wants to learn our ways, and he clearly is enamored with you."

"So, because I have no mate and neither does he, and he managed to make a bow and arrow and stand up to Sakinay before he died of starvation, you think he was brought here to be my life-walker? Now I think you are the one who is crazy," Myrica said, and they both laughed.

"Well, until you take a life-walker, no one will give me a second look. So please hurry up," Awantia remarked.

"Why do you say that?" Myrica frowned at her friend.

"You know why. I am tall, lanky, and plain compared to you. As long as you are available, I will always be overlooked."

"You are a skilled tool-maker. You have a happy spirit and beautiful smiling eyes, and you are the better cook. Any man would be blessed to have you tend his fire. Beauty fades; it is the least important of all things in a life-walker."

"Tell that to all the males who cannot keep their eyes off you," Awantia replied.

The next day, Sakinay took Ned to Myrica. He blushed when he thought of her bathing in the river and hoped she did not realize it was he who had seen her.

She had a pile of stones around her with a small bunch of dry grasses to the side. She beckoned to Ned to sit down and picked up a stone, which he recognized as flint. Then she gathered the dry grasses in front of her and struck the flint against a stone containing pyrite, making a spark that ignited the little mass of fine dried grass. Ned nodded, understanding what she was doing. Next, she showed him how to create a deadfall. Ned's father had taught him how to do this long ago, but he was enjoying her company, so he did not let on. He felt a little guilty, but he was lonely, and after the hard time Sakinay had given him, sitting across from Myrica, so beautiful and so gracefully demonstrating her skills, was pure pleasure.

That afternoon, Ned went out hunting. He shot a nice plump grouse, took it back, and offered it to Myrica. She looked at the bird and then at him but smiled and took it. Not knowing what else to do, Ned turned and left.

Awantia came over to her friend. "He brought you a gift, I see."

"He is thanking me for showing him how to start a fire using pyrite stone and flint. That is all."

"He has good manners," Awantia said.

"If he really had good manners, he would not have hidden behind the rock watching me bathe, now would he?"

"So he has a way to go. No one is perfect. What are you going to do with that grouse?"

Myrica sighed. "I suppose I will prepare it and offer to share it with him over tonight's meal."

"That would be showing good manners, too," Awantia teased her friend.

"I will do that, but you must join us. So it does not look—personal."

"Has he learned any of our language?" Awantia asked. "Otherwise, it will be an awkward meal."

"Hmmm. He knows some simple words. But you are right. He needs a teacher. Why do you not try to teach him?"

"Me?" Awantia asked. "It was not me he watched naked in the river."

"Exactly. He will not get the wrong idea if you offer to teach him. He has no manly interest in you!"

Awantia laughed good-naturedly. "Alright. I will do that. But only so he will know the proper words when he asks you to be his life-walker."

Myrica swung the grouse to swat at her friend, who dodged out of the way and laughed some more.

Awantia spent the afternoon thinking about how best to teach the Waschini their language. He was learning the names of things and the words for some actions, but he was not stringing them together in any usable form. She decided that if he learned some phrases, perhaps it would help him along.

She found Ned finishing off some arrows and motioned to him to come with her. He got up obediently and followed her over to where Myrica was roasting the pheasant and had a stew cooking.

Awantia bent down and stirred the stew, looking up at Ned as she spoke a word. He looked at her. She repeated herself, exaggerating the stirring motion. He repeated her words. She said the phrase again, and he repeated it once more. Close enough.

Then she turned the spit but noticed he was no longer watching her. He was looking at Myrica.

"How am I supposed to teach him when he is not even paying attention to me," she lamented.

Myrica scowled and answered, "Why did you bring him here? Now he is staring at me. It is rude. Take him somewhere else. Please."

Awantia got Ned's attention and took him down to the river instead. She bent down and splashed water on her arms and rubbed them back and forth.

"Washing," she said. He repeated it. She pointed to her arm and said the word for arm. Then she repeated the motion and said, "I wash my arm." Next, she pointed to her leg and said the word for leg. Then she washed her leg as she had her arm and said, "I wash my leg." It seemed to be working. She spent the rest of the day teaching him simple phrases like that, teaching him the sentence structure they used and some more of the names and phrases that Pakwa had started with. Eventually, Awantia realized it was most likely time to eat and took him back to Myrica's fire.

"How did it go?" Myrica asked.

"Hard to tell, but I think he is learning. How interesting it is that as children we learn to speak so easily, yet when we are grown, it is difficult to learn another's language."

Awantia leaned over and tasted Myrica's stew. "Delicious." Then she said, "This takes a great deal of time. Who else could we get to teach him?"

"Maybe some of the older children? They seem curious about him."

"Should we worry about them being with him?"

"I would worry more about him," Myrica said. "They must be told he is not for them to entertain themselves with."

Awantia laughed. It was true. The children could easily take him out into the woods and abandon him or teach him nonsensical things. Not out of spite or cruelty, but just as childhood antics.

Myrica took her idea to Chief Kotori, who identified several of the older children to be assigned to help teach Ned Webb their language.

With the children teaching him, Ned made great progress. They seemed to have infinite patience. And after their parents had admonished them not to trick the white man, making them realize they had been given a great responsibility, they all took to the task in earnest.

One of the oldest proposed that they teach him just as a child would learn. So they started with the basic functions of life. Eating, sleeping, bathing, walking. He had to do these things daily anyway, so one of them was with him at all times, describing to Ned whatever he was engaged in. By the end of a week, he had learned quite a few new phrases and was starting to string words together into sentences of his own. From that point, life in Chief Kotori's village became a lot less lonely.

Ned learned the village ways and routines. He often hunted by himself. He made sure to offer Myrica and Awantia some of his bounty, which they gratefully accepted. He wondered why they had no males providing for them, then eventually figured out they were not married. Later, he would learn that life-walkers were often found when the tribes got together at community events. Still, it seemed a haphazard way to find a spouse.

What he did not know was that Sakinay did not like Ned frequenting either Myrica's fire or Awantia's. It was one thing for a white man to be learning their ways, but another for him to be attracted to their women.

In the time Ned spent with the children, one younger boy stood out. His name was Kele. He was quiet, smaller than the other boys his age, and often hung at the back. He seldom spoke, and Ned noticed the older children looked out for him. After a while, Ned decided that Kele was impaired in some way, and from that point on, made sure that Kele was always included and close to him. One day, he got up the courage to ask Awantia about the boy. She explained it had taken a long time for him to be born. Far too long. They had not been sure he would live, but he did. Only, as a result, he turned out the way he was. Slower than the others and not as physically or intellectually adept.

Ned did not know if he was succeeding or not, other than, as Oh'Dar' had teased him, he had not yet starved to death. The other males now acknowledged him and treated him with respect, but there was so much he did not yet know. And the truth was, he missed his mother and father. And his sister. He also missed Buster. He missed the morning chatter over breakfast, the sounds of his mother and sister at the cookstove while he and his father sat at the table.

Of course, Grace was married to Storis now, but there were still many family get-togethers. In short, he missed everything he had taken for granted, and he started to wonder if Grayson had been right. What if it was too much to give up?

Ned had kept a calendar of sorts since the day he arrived. He made a mark on a tree branch he kept in his shelter for each day he was there. He found himself counting the days until Oh'Dar would return.

CHAPTER 13

Moart'Tor's reaction to Kalli had not gone unnoticed. "He looked at her like she was—" Haaka said, "I do not know. Like she was—wrong. A mistake, somehow."

"An abomination?" Haan said. It was a cruel word, but it fit exactly.

"Yes. But she is not, is she?" Haaka looked at Haan, her eyes searching for reassurance.

"She is not. Of course not. He only enhances your fears for her, that she will live and die alone because she is different."

"I hope his reaction did not register with her. But she is old enough, and I fear it did," Haaka said. Then she added, "Haan, I want to have an offling. Somehow, by an Akassa."

Haan had expected this day would come. He knew Haaka worried about his daughter as if she were her own. Kalli was different. Not that different, but not enough like the Akassa or the Sassen for either to find her attractive. He was fairly certain no Akassa would. He was uncertain if any of the Sassen would either, but doubted it.

"I am not suggesting that I mate with one of the Akassa. But there has to be a way for me to be seeded by one. The Ancients figured it out when it came to the Brothers. Surely we can too."

"We will speak with Adik'Tar Acaraho and the Akassa Overseer about it. If this is what you really want, perhaps they can advise us."

"I cannot let her live alone like this. Isolated. You and I will not live forever. Yes, hopefully, eventually we will have offling of our own, but Kalli will still be the different one."

"Even though they would not be related by blood, there is no guarantee that the new offling will be a mate for her. It could be a female, or it could turn out that they have no such interest in each other."

"I know that. But at least she would not be the only one of her kind. She would have an ally who looks like her."

At Urilla Wuti's request, Harak'Sar assembled his Circle of Counsel. His mate Habil, High Protector Dreth, First Guard Gek, Khon'Tor as chief advisor, and Iella—who would have been the next Healer at the Far High Hills. Urilla Wuti had also asked that Adia and Harak'Sar's son, Brondin'Sar, be invited, so he had included them.

"I am considering postponing the High Council meeting," Urilla Wuti said. "There is no guarantee that the situation with Moart'Tor will be resolved by then as we do not know what is going on at Kayerm. And to bring all the Akassa together at Kthama with the rebel Mothoc still in the area seems unwise. That much activity might well draw his attention."

"He might not know where Kthama is," Harak'Sar said. "And Acaraho says he does not have supernatural abilities like a Guardian. The Sassen Adik'Tar, Haan, told Acaraho that they could control him, stop him if need be."

"I do not think there is anything to be afraid of. There is no way Pan would allow any harm to come to any of us," Adia added.

"And yet she sent you here, Healer," said Habil.

"I do not think that decision was made from fear on her part," Adia said. "She sent me here so An'Kru would not be discovered. The Guardian does not want it known that he has been born. And as for the Sassen going against the Mothoc, Pan said the last thing she wants is an altercation and bloodshed."

"There is no reason for them to believe that the Promised One would be an Akassa, either," Urilla Wuti said. "Quite the contrary."

The others looked at each other. "You are right.

They most likely assume that it would be one of their kind." Habil exclaimed.

"How interesting. We are the least powerful of any of the three, Mothoc, Sassen, and Akassa. That the Promised One is an Akassa would be a surprise to them."

"Or, more likely, a shock," Adia added. "An insult, even.

"The Guardian does not believe Moart'Tor is being honest about his reasons for coming. She believes he is here to gather information for his father, the Leader of the rebel camp. They no doubt believe that the Mothoc still live among us as they did thousands of years ago. If the rebels were to find out that they have left our communities, it might make us appear vulnerable to an attack."

"It would not just be a question of appearance. And there is no might about it, I am afraid," Khon'Tor added. "Those of us who have seen Pan can attest to the Mothocs' far superior size and strength."

"Had the specter of Straf'Tor not appeared, we could have all been destroyed when the Sassen came to take Kthama. Imagine what an army of Mothoc could do," Khon'Tor added.

Khon'Tor's mention of Straf'Tor's appearance got them all thinking. They had seen wondrous things, amazing things. The opening of Kthama Minor, the transformation of the twelve Sassen into the White

Guardians, the birth of An'Kru, and now many of their Healers were developing unheard-of abilities.

"Adia is right," said Urilla Wuti. "The hand of the Great Spirit is upon us and our path forward, and Pan would not allow any of us to be harmed. But that does not provide assurance that Moart'Tor might break his word and stray from Kayerm and see the large number visiting Kthama. It would not take him long to realize there are no Mothoc protecting the People or the Sassen any longer. No, there are too many variables to try to control. We must postpone it. The High Council meeting will not take place as scheduled. Please send word."

Adia left the meeting to collect An'Kru and the twins. She had left them under Apricoria's care in the Healer's Quarters.

The twins were sleeping peacefully in their nest, and An'Kru was interacting with a small rabbit that had insisted on following them inside the Far High Hills. The rabbit was eating some greens out of An'Kru's little hand. When he noticed her, he glanced up at Adia, pointed at the rabbit, and giggled.

"I thought Oh'Dar and Nootau were happy offspring," Adia said, "but this one—" She crouched down next to her son, and the little rabbit hopped away. An'Kru reached out his hand, and it came back and resumed eating.

"So now we have a pet rabbit?" Adia chuckled, looking at Apricoria. "I am afraid to think of what he will attract next! And we must keep it away from Kweeuu. He is elderly and seldom leaves Tehya's side but still—"

"Yes. The wolf. I have seen him in the distance with Tehya."

"He was a gift from my mate to our Waschini son, Oh'Dar. Then, after a tragic series of events, the wolf ended up coming to the Far High Hills with Tehya. It will be sad when the day comes that he is no longer with us."

"It will be some time yet," Apricoria said. "Has the wolf met An'Kru?"

"No, he has not, now that you mention it," Adia said, smoothing a piece of silver hair from An'Kru's forehead. "I am sure it is just a matter of time. All animals seem drawn to my son."

"Iella can talk to the animals. Maybe she or An'Kru can somehow tell Kweeuu not to eat the rabbit," Apricoria said casually. She held out a nice fat shoot, and it slowly disappeared into the rabbit's little mouth.

"I know you do not know when you will be returning to the High Rocks, but I will miss An'Kru and the twins when you leave." Apricoria leaned forward and scooped An'Kru up in her arms. He grabbed her nose, and she pretended to chew on the little fingers of his other hand, making quiet animal noises.

"Can you see when it might happen?" Adia asked.

Apricoria closed her eyes for a moment. "No, I am sorry, Healer, I cannot control what is shown to me and what is not."

For a brief moment, Adia thought about asking about An'Kru's future. But she did not. She would have to learn on her own how to deal with her concerns. She knew she could not keep seeking reassurance from others. It was part of her path, trusting the Great Spirit at deeper and deeper levels.

It was a long time since E'ranale had called her to the Corridor and Adia saw this as more evidence that she needed to trust the Order of Functions on her own.

Apricoria helped Adia take An'Kru and the twins back to Adia's quarters.

After they had all nursed, they settled down quickly. Adia had learned that the twins needed to be close to each other; when they were separated, they tended to fuss until reunited. She had learned from other mothers who had also had twins that this was often the case. Her heart ached even more for Nootau and Nimida—that they had been forcibly separated for so long. But where Nootau and Nimida had been, Nelairi and Aponi would not be.

"Are you my second chance?" she asked out loud,

leaning over the twins in their nest, "to redeem myself?"

"What was that?" Apricoria asked.

Adia had forgotten she was still there. "Oh, nothing, I was just musing out loud."

Urilla Wuti announced herself, and Apricoria left the two Healers alone.

"I know you are anxious to return home."

"I miss Acaraho," admitted Adia. "And I am unaccustomed to not knowing what is going on."

"They are all sleeping," said Urilla Wuti.

"Apricoria entertained them all while we were meeting. She is a good soul."

"Yes, she is. And she has been given a tremendous gift."

"As the others have. Imagine being able to influence the weather and the elements. Or to make plants grow and flourish. I wonder what other abilities are yet uncovered."

"And to what end," Urilla Wuti mused.

Adia sighed and rested her head in her hands. "I want to go home."

Urilla Wuti walked over and put her arms around Adia's shoulders. "I know, my friend. I know you do."

Acaraho received word that the High Council meeting would not take place as planned. He had wondered about that himself, with Moart'Tor's appearance, and sent word back with Harak'Sar's messenger that Moart'Tor was still at Kayerm. Despite the Mothoc's presence, routine continued at the High Rocks and Kht'shWea. With his mate gone, Acaraho spent even more time among the People or visiting with the Sassen. The yellow moon appeared, proclaiming harvest time, and during the daytime, the fields were filled with both the older offspring and the adults. After this, with the colder months, activities would move inside, the opposite of how the Sassen lived. They cherished the times of cooler temperatures. And so it made for a balanced rhythm, the Akassa spending more time outside in the warmer weather and the Sassen spending more time outside when it was colder.

As far as Acaraho knew, the Waschini who had threatened to take Honovi, Acise, and the other Brothers of mixed blood had not returned. The soul-shattering howls of the Sassen had driven them away. Fear was a powerful tool; through the warning of the Rah-hora, it had kept the Sassen from the Akassa for thousands of years. He hoped it would do the same for the Waschini. But for how long? Acaraho feared that the secluded, peaceful way of life the People had known since they were formed by the hand of the Great Spirit was at risk.

Samuel Riggs traveled through the neighboring territories looking for the man who had reported shooting a very tall hairy creature several years back. He occasionally came across someone else who had heard the story but no one who could tell him where to find the man himself. Some said he was a drifter who had died; others said he had moved far up north. Most of the time, Riggs could see them snickering at him even as they answered his questions, but nothing discouraged him. He knew there was no way any of his kind had made the noises that scared away him and Snide Tucker's hired guns. And he was going to get to the bottom of it if that took the rest of his life.

He didn't know what had become of Tucker or the other men after they all separated. None of them had waited for the money he had promised—in fact, they could not seem to get away from him and each other fast enough. He had seen how frightened they were. And he could tell from this that they would never speak of the experience again. Tucker had taken off with the rented horse, which ticked Riggs off, but in the end, it canceled out the money he didn't have to pay. Riggs wished he could forget it and get back to living a normal life, but he was changed forever, and there was no going back, so he tried to figure out how to go forward.

He traveled from town to town, usually checking at the local inns and drinking establishments, asking if anyone had any 'peculiar' experiences in the woods. But if they had, no one was talking. So he tried a different tactic, putting up posters offering a reward for any information about tall human-like hairy creatures living in the woods. When that failed, he wondered whether whatever these things were lived only in one specific area. Which only convinced him further that they were perhaps abominations of nature created by Grayson Stone Morgan.

Riggs needed another tactic. A way to get as many men as possible up into that land to look for whatever these things were. In one way, it was good that Tucker's men had kept their mouths shut. If they hadn't, no doubt Riggs would not have been able to find anyone willing to go up there. Well, at least not the sane ones. Most people had lives to live, families to care for, and if the whatever-it-was wasn't bothering them, they had no cause to bother it. Still, all he needed was a few, and in his own jurisdiction, citizens were bound to assist him when requested.

Having learned his lesson with the posters, he did not try that in Millgrove. Instead, he went from house to house, calling on able-bodied men who needed to make some extra money. Riggs explained that he needed hunters to go deep into the forest to look for a bear. Not just any bear, but a peculiar bear, deformed. Some might say, the largest bear anyone could imagine. He said that he would give a handsome reward to anyone who could find the deformed bear, kill it, and bring back its hide. It was the only way he could think to describe what they were looking for that might make sense to them if they did come across whatever had made those sounds.

They had questions. He had answers.

In the end, he had commissioned about twenty men. But just as their conversation was coming to a close, he always added, "Now, of course. It might not be a bear. I am not saying it isn't a bear, but it might not be. So, if you run into something different, something not a bear and not a human, I will pay triple."

Most of the men just grinned at him and shook his hand. If anyone believed there might be something other than a bear up there, they never let on. As for why Riggs had a personal vendetta against a particularly large bear that lived 'up there', most didn't care either. They had all grown up hunting bears. And if some fool was willing to separate his money from his pocket because of a particularly large or unusual bear, who were they to argue?

With the harvest in, Franklin Jones and his sons had some time on their hands, so Jones decided they would head up into the Morgan Territory and look for the Bear, as it had started to be known.

"I'm not scared," his youngest boy boasted.

"Of course not. It's just a bear. They are as dangerous as you already know, so there's no need to let your imagination run away with you. We don't even know if it exists. Could have been Riggs's imagination. Or perhaps he had too much to drink one night, and fear got ahold of him, being out there all by himself. But we have some time, so let's go. If nothing else, we'll spend some time together, the three of us."

"Mama doesn't want us to go," his oldest said.

"I know. Womenfolk! But there is nothing to worry about, I promise you. Sometimes a man has to do what a man has to do, even if the women don't like it. You'll find that out soon enough once you settle down yourself. We leave in the morning."

Jones and his sons set out with supplies enough to stay for nearly a week. They set up camp a bit outside the local village there. They had brought dried meat and canteens for water and planned on hunting for anything else they needed. Both Jones boys were crack shots, and their father had no concerns for their safety. The only threat was the deformed bear—if it even existed.

Nimraugh whispered to his fellow Sassen watcher, Inrah. "Three Waschini, and they have the fire sticks Adik'Tar Notar warned us about."

"We will watch them and make sure they do not go close to the village. Perhaps they will leave peacefully in a day or so."

"Why are they here?" Nimraugh said. "Wherever

their home is, it seems they are far away from it. I do not like this."

Nimraugh and Inrah kept a close watch on the Waschini, never letting them out of their sight. If Franklin Jones and his sons had known who was watching them, they would have been frightened indeed.

One morning, the youngest boy was out on his own. He spotted a doe and quickly felled her. Nimraugh and Inrah were watching from the ridge above. The boy field-dressed the animal and took the meat back to camp.

The watchers had earlier seen the doe with her fawns, which still had their spots, meaning they were late born, perhaps still nursing.

"The fawns are too young to be without their mother. Without her protection, they will easily be killed by coyotes." Inrah had always been a kind-hearted soul.

"What can we do?" Nimraugh asked.

"I must take them home. Artadel there will know how to care for them."

"What of the white men?"

"You stay and watch them, and when I come back, we will deal with them. The stories are right; they have no care for Etera's creatures. At least these do not. Anyone could see that the doe had fawns with her, and anyone who cared would not have left them to be attacked or starve to death. I do not like these Waschini."

Inrah quietly approached the two little fawns. At the moment, they were not in peril, but that would not last long. He sent calming vibrations out to them, then he gently picked up the first one and then the other and cradled them protectively against his chest. They nestled up against him as if knowing they were being protected.

"Wait here; I will return as soon as I get them safely home."

Franklin Jones and his sons had finished eating and were about to settle down for the night. They had set their sleeping rolls around the fire and banked it so it would burn a while longer and then safely die down.

The stars overhead were spectacular; the night was so clear that it seemed they lit up the sky. In the distance, coyotes howled. An owl hooted from high overhead. And then suddenly, everything became very quiet. Very, very quiet.

Plunk.

"What the—" one of the sons called out, sitting up and raising his arm over his head. "Did you just throw a rock at me," he accused his brother.

"Wasn't me. What are you talking about?"

Just then, another stone came whizzing by, just missing the other boy's head.

Then another. One landed right in the center of

the fire, spewing burning embers about and making golden sparks fly up.

Jones jumped to his feet. "Whoever is out there, you'd better leave us alone. We want no trouble. Show yourself or go away!'

Another round of rocks flew by, each one missing them but close enough to unnerve all three.

"That's it," Jones shouted. "You're asking for a lesson." He looked down for his rifle. It was missing.

"Did either of you take my rifle?" he asked.

The boys reached for theirs.

"Mine is gone."

"Mine, too."

"They're all gone. Whoever is out there must have taken them."

For a few moments, the rocks stopped flying. The man and his sons stood with their backs to the fire, searching the dark to see who was out there.

"Those guns are ours, not yours. You got no right to steal them. We haven't done anything wrong. Now give us back our guns and be on your way."

Suddenly, a long dark object flew toward Franklin Jones and landed a safe distance from his feet. It was his rifle. Or at least had been. Only it was curled up like a pretzel. Twisted back on itself.

He glanced at his sons, who peered over at the twisted piece of metal lying in the middle of their camp.

"Pa," said the oldest.

"Stand your ground. Nobody moves. If whatever

is out there wanted us dead, we would be by now. As soon as day breaks, we're out of here."

"Maybe we should go home now," the youngest said.

"Hold on, son, we need the daylight. Only a few more hours before we break camp and head home."

"Pa's right. Whatever twisted that rifle could certainly have killed us if it wanted to. Or hit us on the heads with one of those stones. Look, some of them are pretty big. I would say whatever it is just wants us gone."

"Listen to your brother. Stay calm and wait it out."

"I never want to come back here!" the younger boy lamented.

"Me neither. And we have to warn everyone else not to."

"No, sons, that's the last thing we're going to do. No one would believe us."

"They will when they see that!" and he pointed to the twisted rifle.

"Alright, maybe; we'll talk about that later. For now, let's just be as quiet as possible. I think once they see we are not fighting back, they will stop harassing us."

Franklin Jones took his own advice and slowly eased himself into a sitting position, never taking his eyes off the dark woods in front of him. He then motioned for his sons to do the same. Soon they were sitting quietly, listening to the eerily-quiet woods.

The morning sun broke through the canopy of leaves and woke the oldest son first. He sat up with a start, looked around, and saw that they had all eventually fallen asleep. The fire was out. He crawled over to his father and shook him. "Pa, wake up. Wake up. Let's go home."

Jones rubbed his eyes. "Wake your brother and be grateful we are alive. Then pack up, and let's head out."

After looking around, the younger boy exclaimed, "Papa, the rifle is gone. The one that was all bent up."

"Well, there went our proof. Listen to me. No one talks about this. Not a word about what happened here. We will go back and act as if nothing happened."

"But what if others come out here, trying to find the bear?" asked the elder boy.

"Bear? No bear throws rocks. And no bear twists a rifle up like a piece of warm bread. I suspect Riggs knows whatever is out here isn't a bear, and he is putting ignorant folks like us at risk, hoping someone will kill whatever it is for him."

"So we aren't going to warn others?" the younger child asked.

"Warn them of what? None of us was hurt. Was either of you hurt?"

Both shrugged. "No. But scared nearly to death, yes!"

"Well, that was the point then, wasn't it. We aren't coming back, and we aren't telling anyone about it. If others come, they will no doubt get the same treatment we did, and they will also keep quiet about it. We aren't going to have people thinking we lost our minds or made this all up for attention. You boys have lives to live. You won't find any women willing to settle down and raise a family with madmen. We can talk about it on the way home, but once we get there, we never mention it again. Even between yourselves, understand?"

"Not even tell Ma?" the youngest asked.

"Not if you ever want to be able to go hunting with me ever again. She'll put a stop to that right there."

"But you're the man; what can she do to stop us?"

"Son, there are things about marriage and women you don't yet understand, so you have to trust me on this one. I should have known something was up. Since when does the constable have to pay anyone to carry out his orders? Now, come on. Let's get a move on."

Jones and his sons did just as he had said. Neither of them pointed out that their father's comments contradicted what he had said about men having to do what they had to do regardless of what the women thought. And they never told anyone about what had happened. As their father had told them, the sons did their best to never talk about it together, though they did occasionally slip up. But thanks to their father's wisdom, they both did grow up to find good wives and raise their own families, and they took the story of what had happened to their graves.

CHAPTER 14

Moart'Tor was avoiding Haan. In fact, ever since the incident with Haaka and Kalli, he was avoiding all the Sassen. He rose before first light and came back after dark. He hunted and ate by himself.

Haan's Watchers kept track of him, and the Mothoc kept his word; he did not stray from the boundaries set for him. But it disturbed Haan that Moart'Tor was no longer interacting with the community.

Haan found Moart'Tor gutting a stag he had just taken down. "You came here looking for a new home, a new place to belong, yet you now avoid us all."

"I am confused. I thought I knew what I wanted when I came here. Now I am no longer sure."

"You are thinking of returning home? To Zuenerth, to the rebel camp?"

"I am," he answered, not looking up from his task.

"And what of your Leader's commitment to destroying us, both Sassen and Akassa. To wipe us from the face of Etera? You would return to live among such hatred, which you said you came here to escape?"

"What do you want from me, Adik'Tar? I told you, I am confused."

"You did not seem confused. In fact, you seemed as if you were settling in here, making a place for yourself. Until you saw my daughter."

At that, Moart'Tor looked up to face Haan. "I cannot make peace with what she is."

"What she is, is a living being just as the rest of us are. She was created by the Great Spirit, as were we all."

"You were not created by the Great Spirit. The Akassa were not created by the Great Spirit. It was Moc'Tor's doing that you exist. A mistake. He made an unforgivable mistake. And he betrayed the Brothers' trust in doing so. As for her—"

"Her name is Kalli," Haan said sharply. "She is the product of the love I shared with an Akassa female. It is no fault of her own that she is here or that she is different. But your words now reveal the truth. You agree with your Leader, after all. We are an abomination, both Sassen and Akassa. You have just said yourself that we were created by mistake, without the blessing of the Great Spirit."

Haan remained silent; he could feel the anguish boiling within Moart'Tor. Finally, the truth was coming out, and only when the truth came out could they move forward.

"What will happen when you go back?"

"I have not decided to go back. But if I do, my father will be displeased."

"Don't you mean your Leader?" Haan frowned. When Moart'Tor didn't answer, he continued, "So your father would not be pleased to see his only son return?" Something wasn't adding up.

"I am not his only son, just his firstborn."

"But it was to you that this mission fell. To come here and learn what you could about us, then to take the information back so your Leader could better prepare for the time when you would return here and annihilate us all."

"Yes," Moart'Tor held his head in shame. "I lied. I lied about it all. And there are not just a few of us. There are hundreds. My father has prepared an army, an army ready and able to destroy you all when he gives the order."

"You said your father was Dak'Tor, the Guardian's brother."

"He is. I was raised by two males. Dak'Tor is my seed father, while Kaisak is Zuenerth's Leader and my adopted father."

The details did not matter to Haan, only that Moart'Tor was finally being honest. "And you think the Great Spirit would allow this? For all of us to be annihilated?"

Moart'Tor stood up, towering over Haan. "I could kill you right now, and nothing would stop me."

"That is not true." A voice spoke out of nowhere, and Pan shimmered into sight. "Were you to raise a hand against Haan or anyone here, I would strike you down before you could brush against a single hair of his coat."

"You have such power?" Moart'Tor said.

"I do."

"Then prove it. Strike me dead now. I have nowhere to go. I belong nowhere. My soul is in anguish, and I have no future to live for." He hung his head in despair.

"It is true that you are suffering; I can feel it. But it is not true that there is nowhere you belong or that you have no future to live for. You do belong. We all belong to each other and to the Great Spirit."

"But where are the others of my kind? Of your kind? I came seeking them, too. Is all that is left of us those who live at Zuenerth?"

"No. I assure you that is not true. Your settlement is not the only community of Mothoc. I will not explain any more now, but you must trust me that it is true."

"You may be the only one I do trust," he answered. "You knew I was lying all along."

"Of course."

"Why did you not seek out my father, your

brother, at Zuenerth? You knew that is where he was, or you would have had more questions."

"My brother has his own path to walk, as does each of us. I thought of it many times, and each time, I chose not to. But I will see him again when the time is right."

"You would truly kill me to protect the Sassen and the Akassa?" Moart'Tor asked.

"Until the true deliverer rises and takes his place, I am the Hand of the Great Spirit on Etera. And yes, I would."

"But my father said Mothoc would never rise against Mothoc. They would stand by and let the Akassa be destroyed before they would rise against another of their own kind."

"Your father was wrong. It is not about Mothoc against Mothoc," Pan continued, "or Mothoc against Akassa. It is about right against wrong."

"Who is right and who is wrong? You believe you are right as passionately as my father does!"

"I would only harm you to protect another from your unfounded aggression, yet your father would slay innocents merely because they are different from his own kind. Your father would destroy the Akassa and the Sassen because of an idea, not because of any wrongdoing on their part. No. It is your father who is wrong."

"I no longer know what to believe," Moart'Tor said, and Pan could feel that his despair was genuine.

"I advise you to make no decisions until your soul

is clear about this, Moart'Tor," Pan said. "I am only a breath away. If you need me, or if I am needed to intervene, I will return. Until then, search your soul and find the truth. Find what you believe and know to be true."

With that, Pan disappeared.

Moart'Tor turned to Haan. "Please forgive me, Adik'Tar; I had no right to threaten you."

"Rest, Moart'Tor. If you decide to rejoin the community, you will be welcomed back."

Moart'Tor knew what Haan meant. He was still living with the Sassen at Kayerm, but he had been keeping to himself and avoiding everyone else. Within a few nights, he once more joined them at the evening fire. Sitting a few seats down from him were Eitel and her brother. He listened absentmindedly to the conversation; someone was telling a story about life previously at Kayerm. Life was being lived around him, and in every way that mattered, it was no different than life back at Zuenerth.

Eitel got up to turn in, and as she passed him, she laid a hand lightly on his shoulder. This time Moart'Tor did not pull away. For the brief moment she rested it there, he took comfort from the gentle contact. He wanted to thank her, but in an instant, she was on her way. He looked over at her brother Naahb, who had been watching the whole thing.

Moart'Tor got up to leave, and Naahb stood up at the same time. "A word with you?"

Moart'Tor stopped.

"You would destroy us all; is that the truth? Is that why you came here? To learn about us only to later use it as a weapon?"

Moart'Tor let out a long breath. "It is true. I came here under false pretenses."

"You would use our hospitality and kindness against us."

"Yes."

"You never intended to be one of us, to accept the comfort and inclusion we freely offered you."

"Everything you say is true." There was no denying it. In fact, there was bitter relief in having the truth be told.

"And what is it you want now? Do you know? Have you decided?"

"I will not be staying."

"I see," Naahb said.

"But I will not be returning to Zuenerth. I did come here to betray you. I did come here thinking you were all abominations deserving to be destroyed. But I no longer believe that. At least about the Sassen."

"And yet you will not stay with us. Where will you go?"

"I do not know. There may be no place for me on Etera. I cannot go home, yet there is nowhere else."

Eitel had almost made it to the entrance when

she turned to see them talking together. She made her way back just in time to hear the last piece of the conversation.

"Why would you not stay with us? We came to Kayerm to help you."

"But you do not live here. You live elsewhere and only came here because of me."

"That is true. Yet we are willing to remain here with you and create a new community for you so you would have somewhere to belong. And a people to belong with."

Moart'Tor was overcome with feelings of sadness, regret, remorse, and once again, shame. A few short months ago, he would have relished seeing them all destroyed. And yet now they were still saying he was welcome.

Haan soon joined the conversation. "Have you come to a decision about your future?"

"I have. But I will do nothing until I speak with Pan, as I promised."

"I see," Haan said. "Whatever your decision is, I pray you find the peace and happiness you seek, and may your soul walk in harmony with all of Etera's creatures for the rest of your days."

Ned made another notch on his stick that tracked the days since he had come to Chief Kotori's village. It was nearing time for Oh'Dar's return. He felt he had accomplished what he had been brought there to do. He had mastered enough of the Brothers' language to be able to follow most conversations unless the speaker was excited and speaking very quickly. While he was not the best hunter, he could provide for himself—and a family if it came to that. He had earned the respect of the braves, and the children no longer mocked him behind his back. Instead, they teased him openly about his curly yellow hair, and he knew they meant it for inclusion, not exclusion.

Whoever it was who had set up this test had been wise to do so. He had succeeded at all of it, except the most important part. There was only one thing he had not learned how to do, one he had been so sure would not be a problem. And that was how to forget about his family back home.

It wasn't that he wouldn't miss the Waschini way of life. Yes, he would miss the soft bed sheets and the welcome glow of the gas lamps in the dark of night. The gaiety of a barn dance, seeing the pretty girls fixed up and flouncing around in their party dresses amid the music, clapping, and laughter. There were equivalents here for all those joys and comforts. But there were some things that could not be reproduced. The comfort of hearing his parents' voices already planning the day in the kitchen downstairs when he was just waking up. His sister's laughter. His father's comforting hand on his shoulder now and then when he needed it most. The way his mother looked at him, with so much love in her eyes, he could feel it warming his heart. The pieces of his life that mattered the most he had taken for granted, and he could not let them slip through his hands like the sand next to a passing stream.

And so he counted the days to Oh'Dar's return.

Others in the village witnessed the change in him. He had come to them a stranger and had become a friend. They had learned about his ways too. The ridiculous amount of splashing he made when he first entered the cool water, and while he was bathing, the groans of pleasure that he seemed to have no ability to keep to himself. How he would confuse words and end up saying something so comical that no one could keep from laughing. It had taken a while for him to realize what he had done and that they were not laughing at him unkindly, but it endeared him to them, along with his other quirks and idiosyncrasies. And most of all, Ned's friendship with and care for Kele had bought him a special place in the villagers' hearts.

Myrica had grown fond of him. He was generous to a fault and would go without or give up far more than his share to others. He was a quick learner, and he was willing to be taught. Even Sakinay, who had set out never to give him quarter, had learned to respect him.

Everyone knew the time was approaching when Oh'Dar would return, but no one knew if Ned would go and live with the Akassa or not. It was only he who didn't understand the scope of what lay before him. Ned didn't even know they existed, and no one had said anything to him about them.

"I do not think he is staying," Awantia said to Myrica one morning.

"Why do you say that? Did he tell you?"

"No. But he seems sad all of a sudden. And as the day draws closer for Oh'Dar's return, he seems to be getting quieter and quieter."

"He has done all that was asked of him and more. He has passed the test. He should be pleased with himself," Myrica said.

"I think he knows that, but his heart is sad. I think that now that the time is here for him to leave behind his Waschini way of life forever, he is having second thoughts."

"It is to be expected. He was not leaving to run away from what he knew, but to answer his soul's calling."

"If that is true, then he will not easily set aside the pull to move forward, either."

"I do not envy him," Myrica said.

"Neither do I. And too bad for you," Awantia added, unable to keep a smile from turning up the corners of her mouth ever so slightly. "Now you will die an old woman with no man in her bed and no children to keep her company, only an empty fire."

Myrica aimed and threw the hide she had been working on. Throwing things at her friend seemed to have become a habit.

Awantia dodged and quipped, "Oh, but there is Sakinay. I hear he fancies you!"

"That sour soul? Please, I would rather bond with the Waschini!" And they laughed some more.

After the laughter subsided, Awantia became aware of her own sadness. She would hate to see Ned Webb leave; they had spent a great deal of time together. She looked over at his shelter off in the distance and imagined it being empty, and the sting of tears surprised her.

Oh'Dar arrived as he had said he would, and the entire village turned out to welcome him. He brought greetings from Chief Is'Taqa and Honovi to Chief Kotori and his life-walker. He told them that both were looking forward to seeing him again at the next High Council meeting, whenever that would be. The Chief thanked him and asked Oh'Dar to send similar greetings to Chief Is'Taqa.

Finally, Chief Kotori motioned for the crowd to part so Ned could step forward to greet Oh'Dar. "Your friend has done well. He has proven himself a man. He can go with honor where he chooses."

Then the Chief left Oh'Dar and Ned to themselves.

Oh'Dar stepped back to look at him. "You look well. Robust!"

"Yes, I have gotten a workout living here the past few months."

Oh'Dar did not ask the question that was on both their minds, as he wanted the topic to surface naturally. Ned invited Oh'Dar to his shelter to show him the tools he had made during his stay. Oh'Dar hefted the bow and tested its balance. "This is fine work. Anyone would be proud of this." Then Ned told the story of how Sakinay had thrown the first two he had made into the evening fire in front of everyone. Oh'Dar laughed, though he probably shouldn't have, as he immediately understood the lesson Sakinay had been trying to teach Ned.

"Did you finally tell him to stop?"

"At the third bow, yes!"

"Things are not always as they appear. What seems to be the obvious lesson is not always the only lesson."

"So I have learned," Ned agreed. Then Ned showed him the flints and the hatchets, the spears and other items he'd made. He had even learned from some of the women how to weave baskets. When he was done showing off his handiwork, Ned said, "I could live like this. If I wanted to."

The mood turned solemn.

"If you wanted to—"

"Oh'Dar, I'm sorry," Ned said.

Oh'Dar raised his hand. "You do not need to apologize; this is why you came here, to find your true path. I told you on the journey here that there is no failure either way, whether you decide to continue with me or return to Wilde Edge."

"I want to continue with you. But I feel I have to go back."

"Only you can decide which is right for you. Whenever you are ready, we can return to Chief Is'Taqa's camp, and you can be on your way home from there, but first, you must pack up your belongings and say your goodbyes here."

Oh'Dar knew from experience that, either way, it would be hard. No doubt Ned had made friends here, and leaving those you care about is never easy.

That night Ned looked at the faces lit by the firelight. He knew them all now, their names, who they were bonded with, the names of their children. He knew which had a great sense of humor and which had a quick wit. He had even come to like Sakinay for his ways. He would miss them. He would miss them all. But most of all, Kele lay heaviest on his heart.

Everyone knew that Ned was leaving and would be returning to the Waschini world. One by one, they came up to say their goodbyes and wish him well. Some of the children brought him presents, a special stone, a small carved figure. One had carved him a little wolf out of wood. He carefully put each in one of his bags. He could see Myrica standing in the back. He wondered if she would come to say goodbye. He had grown to respect her. Coupled with her physical beauty, she was not one he would forget. And then there was Awantia. Taller and more plain, she didn't have Myrica's physical beauty, but he had come to care for her patient ways and her quick wit. He would miss them both very much.

It was time to leave. Ned waved to them all. His heart was saddened further when Kele came to say goodbye. He knew he would often think about the young boy and pray that he was alright.

"This time, you did not need Pakwa to show you the way here?" he wondered.

"No. Don't worry, I can get us safely back."

"How are your wife and daughter?"

"They're good. The earlier troubles are gone. They have adjusted to life—" and Oh'Dar stopped himself, realizing he had almost said something about Kthama. "I'm sorry you won't be able to see Ben and my grandmother. But I'll give them your regards."

"Will you ever tell me, Grayson? Even though I'm going back to Wilde Edge? Will you ever tell me about the mystery here?"

"Perhaps. I don't know. It is possible, but not probable—if that makes sense."

"It does," Ned said.

By the time they arrived in the center of Chief Is'Taqa's village, there was a crowd gathered. At the forefront were the Chief and his life-walker, Honovi, who had returned from her visit to the High Rocks.

As they approached, Ned called out a greeting in the language of the Brothers.

"Welcome back," Chief Is'Taqa said.

"Thank you. I have learned a great deal. They treated me very well." Ned was relieved to be able to converse directly with the Chief and Honovi and understand them in turn. What a difference it made, not being dependent on a translator and missing everything but the very basics of what was being said.

The question everyone wanted answered was whether Ned was going to return to the Waschini world or move forward as he had intended to do when he came there. But it would be impolite to ask, so they all waited patiently to find out.

Meantime, the Watchers carried word back to Acaraho that Oh'Dar and the other Waschini were back.

Ben and Miss Vivian were so excited to hear the news, and of course, Acise was happy and relieved. The question on their minds was the same—would Ned be joining them or returning to Wilde Edge?

The next morning, Ned told the others that he was indeed returning to Wilde Edge. Honovi tried to hide her disappointment. She had wanted Ned to stay, not only because she believed so strongly that this was his calling, but also for Oh'Dar and his grandparents' sakes—and for I'Layah's.

Oh'Dar prepared the horses for the return trip, and they said their goodbyes.

With his parents' permission, Ned gave Noshoba the bow and arrows he had made.

The young boy took them, and gratitude filled his eyes. "I will keep them for you. Perhaps you will change your mind."

"Thank you," Ned answered. The rest of his tools he left for Honovi and the Chief to decide what to do with them.

Oh'Dar had sent word to the High Rocks that he was taking Ned back to Wilde Edge. He regretted that Ben and Miss Vivian wouldn't get to see Ned before he left, and he knew they would be disappointed that he was returning home. There was no way to get word to the Webbs that they were on their way back, but Oh'Dar knew how happy they would be to see Ned come home.

❁

Mrs. Webb was kneading the day's bread when she heard a knock on the door. She wiped the flour off her hands and opened it. "Ned! Oh, you're back. You're home! What a surprise. And you're here too, Grayson. Ned, your father's out back; you must go and find him. And we must go and tell Grace as soon as you are settled in. How long are you staying?" She was afraid to know.

"I'm home for good," Ned said.

"Oh, I'm glad! You can tell us about it at supper. You must both go and get cleaned up and then tell Grace you are home, if you're not too tired. Have them come back with you for supper."

"Where is Buster?" Ned asked, but just as he said that, Buster appeared as if out of nowhere and jumped straight into Ned's arms.

"Oh, I have missed you so. Where were you, huh?"

"Probably upstairs on your bed. He has hardly left it since you went away."

Matthew Webb came in just then and exclaimed, "Ned, you're home!" He gave Ned a strong hug and then looked him over. "You forgot how to cut your hair?" he teased his son before giving Oh'Dar a warm welcome.

❂

Before long, Grace also had a knock at her front door. "Ned! Grayson!" she exclaimed, and a similar scene unfolded.

"Marriage must agree with you; you've put on weight!"

"Marriage does agree with me," she laughed.

"That is wonderful. I am sure Newell is just as content."

"He is."

Then the puppy padded in from around the corner, a sock in his mouth.

"And who is this?"

"I got him after you left." Introductions were made, followed by a furious string of Pippy puppy kisses.

"Mama wants you to come for supper."

"Of course! We'll be over as soon as Newell's home from work. I can't wait to hear about your adventure."

"Yes, Mama said there was no sense going into it until we were all together."

Matthew Webb said the blessing, making special mention of Ned's being home safe and sound. After the dishes were passed around and several bites down, Ned started telling them about his time at Chief Kotori's village. He was an excellent storyteller, and they laughed and gasped with him through it all and were saddened at the end when he told them how hard it was to leave. For some reason, he did not tell them about Kele, whose sad face kept haunting him. But he did tell them about Myrica and Awantia.

"They liked you?" Nora asked.

"Yes, and I liked them too. I liked all of them."

Nora dropped it and did not press him further. If anything had grown between him and any of the women there, it apparently hadn't been strong enough to keep him.

"I mean, I didn't want that to be the reason I stayed. Besides, I would not have lived there with them anyway. Had it worked out, I mean." Ned pushed his mashed potatoes around on his plate.

They grew quiet.

"I'll be leaving tomorrow," Oh'Dar said, "if Storm is up to it. This is a time of great challenge for my people, and as much as I would like to stay, I must return home."

Home. The term was not lost on any of them. Nora found herself wondering if Grayson had finally now made peace with where he belonged. Perhaps having his grandparents there had settled it for him.

"Alicia Baxter is dating the oldest Thompson boy," Grace said.

"Good; I am happy if they are. I never truly saw myself with her," Ned said.

"It sounds like you learned a lot there, son," his father said. "I hope you got your questions answered about where your future lies."

"He's back for good now," Nora Webb pointed out. "I take that to mean he did."

More silence. Grace shot a worried glance at Newell but said nothing.

Once supper was finished, Grace and Newell said their goodbyes, and Oh'Dar excused himself and went to the room he always stayed in. Ned retired soon after, also exhausted.

The cushiony bed and smooth linens were as wonderful as Ned had remembered. The soft moonlight coming into his bedroom window fell on Buster, who was curled up next to him, his little legs kicking in some dream, no doubt chasing squirrels and rabbits through a magical forest.

Ned was home. This was what he wanted.

Wasn't it?

CHAPTER 15

Constable Riggs was becoming impatient with the lack of results from anyone he had talked into finding whatever monstrosities Grayson Morgan was creating up there. None of the parties who had gone out came back with any reports of encounters, and it was eating away at him. He'd been neglecting his official duties as constable, and he was well overdue in checking in with the Governor, who he was now on his way to see.

Governor Wright looked at Riggs. "I was wondering when you would show up. You should have checked in a month ago."

Riggs was apologetic, knowing his good standing with the governor was at risk. "I apologize, sir. The Morgan trial took up more time than I expected." He glanced around the richly appointed office, looking for a place to sit, but as the Governor remained standing, he did too.

"I hope I can trust you to regain your focus," the Governor continued. "The situation with the locals is at the forefront of our concerns. Land to the west has been set aside to which to relocate the villages. It is not as rich in resources as the lands they are currently inhabiting, but that is the point. I'm going to put you in charge of overseeing the mission to move them all out of your territory."

The Governor walked over to his large walnut desk and rolled out a map. Riggs followed him as he pointed to a marker, "There is a newly established outpost here; I am sending you there to talk to the outpost commander. He will know of any local villages. I don't care where you start; just start."

Riggs noticed that, if what Grayson Morgan said was true, this new outpost had to be in what was now private land. Word had apparently not reached the Governor that the area was no longer owned by the government, but he kept his mouth shut, not wanting to miss this opportunity while being able to hide behind the Governor's authority.

"I don't have military standing," Riggs pointed out.

"They will answer to you." The Governor handed him a piece of paper sealed with an official wax seal. "This will explain everything. They are to start moving them out, one village at a time. Once you deliver the order, return here."

"May I ask what the orders say?"

"They command the outpost regiment to collect as many villagers as they can back at the outpost. Then when they have several hundred together, they will move them to the designated location out West. There's a map included, showing them where they will eventually end up."

Without a word, Constable Riggs took the official papers, along with a rough hand-made copy of the map showing him where to find the outpost.

Weeks later, Constable Riggs arrived at the northern outpost. He handed the Governor's sealed orders to the outpost commander and watched as the man quickly read them, folded them back up, and put them in his jacket pocket.

"This is going to take a long time."

The constable said nothing, and the commander relented. "We have no way to feed their horses. The closest village is about thirty days south of here, as a man walks. That will be a long walk back for them. They will have to hunt along the way, just as will my men. Even at the best time of year, it would be difficult. Now, with the cold weather set in—does the Governor realize there could be severe casualties among the weak and elderly?"

"If he does, he didn't mention it." Riggs didn't give the commander's concern a second thought.

Whether the locals survived the trip or not meant nothing to him. As far as he was concerned, the world would be better off without all of them.

Chief Kotori saw several of his braves running toward him. "There is a large group of Waschini riders coming in our direction. I have never seen them dressed as they are," one of them said.

"They carry their weapons," said another.

"We will see what they want," the Chief answered. "Send the women and children to their shelters."

The militia rode into the center of the village, their horses' hooves cutting through the snow that covered the ground. One of them dismounted and walked over to where Chief Kotori and Second Chief Tawa were sitting calmly, waiting for them.

The man in front looked around at the mostly-empty village. He turned to the Chief and said, "We are here by order of the Governor. You and your people must come with us. You can no longer live here."

The Chief knew nothing of what the Waschini was saying, though he knew by the tone that it was not for their welfare. Behind him, the rest of the Waschini remained mounted on their horses, their fire sticks raised and aimed in his village's direction.

The Waschini pointed around the empty village

and talked some more. The Chief knew that if he answered, the Waschini would not understand him, nor would it make any difference. Whatever they were here to do, they would succeed.

"What do they want?" Sakinay asked the Chief.

"We have heard the stories," Second Chief Tawa answered. "They want the land we live on. We knew this day would come. They are here to take us from our homes,"

"Is it not better to die with honor? To fight them?" Sakinay asked.

Chief Kotori answered, "Perhaps. But in the end, it is the women and children who would pay the greatest price. If we go with them, we will still be alive to take care of our families wherever they are taking us."

Second Chief Tawa agreed, just as the Waschini barked out more orders.

Chief Kotori stood, followed by his Second Chief and Sakinay. He called to the villagers, telling everyone to come out. Then he addressed his people.

"The Waschini are here to take us from our homes. We will not fight them. We will trust the Great Spirit who watches over us to keep us safe on the journey ahead."

Seeing that the rest of the villagers were coming out of their shelters, the outpost commander stopped talking. He motioned for his men to wait and see what happened. He could see them slowly gathering up their belongings. Realizing that they were complying peacefully, he told his men to lower their rifles.

It took some time for the people to gather their things. They did not know how long the trip would be, so they packed all they could carry. The women quelled the children's fears as best they could, keeping them busy with tasks. The men gathered their bows and arrows, watching the Waschini carefully to see if they would be allowed to take them. One of the Waschini said something to the one who seemed to be in charge. However, whatever he said must have meant that they would be allowed to take their weapons as no one stopped them.

Myrica and Awantia exchanged worried glances but said little, just going about collecting their supplies and belongings.

When there was a free moment, the Medicine Woman, Tiponi, said under her breath to Awantia, "Take a large handful of maize seed and keep it handy. Try to stay near the end of the group, but with other women, so you will not be noticed."

"The seed is for planting. Why do you want me to carry some with me? It will not nourish us along the way; we need the dried meat."

"It is for another purpose. Trust me," Tiponi whispered back.

The militiamen took turns on watch. Much to the commander's relief, so far, the locals had not given any trouble. He would let the men take their bows and arrows, so the soldiers would not be burdened with hunting for everyone. But he would collect the primitive weapons and disperse them when it was time to hunt. He was counting on the men not doing anything stupid as long as the women and children were still alive as collateral.

The next morning, Chief Kotori and his people took a last look at what had been their home. He was relieved that the Waschini had not harmed anyone so far or burned their shelters. As he watched the solemn faces of the men, women, and children who trusted him, he was filled with regret that he had not accepted Khon'Tor's offer to put Watchers around his village. Had he done so, at least someone would know what had happened to them.

At last, they set out. It was slow traveling, as the Brothers were not permitted to take their ponies and so had to travel on foot. At least the white men untethered and scattered the ponies, so they would have a chance at surviving.

The garrison escorted the Brothers, some in the front and a few taking up the rear. As much as they could, the villagers carried the younger children and supported the elderly so they could keep up. So far on the journey, the Waschini had not been cruel, but there was no guarantee that the treatment would not change.

Kele's mother was having trouble calming down her son. He buried his face in her skirts as they walked together, her arm around him. She was worried the Waschini would notice he was different. She would do her best to keep him and his behavior hidden from them as long as possible.

The Waschini did not seem to care if the women spoke to each other and the children, though they did not allow the men to say much. Myrica and Awantia stayed close to each other. Every now and then, Awantia would do as Tiponi had instructed her and reach into the pouch on her hip and drop out a few kernels, looking around first to make sure no one was noticing.

"What are you doing?" Myrica whispered to her. "If you think you're leaving a trail for someone to follow, you know the birds and animals will eat it up before anyone could ever find it?"

"I am not leaving a trail. I am leaving a memory," Awantia said.

"Who is going to remember you dropping the seed?"

"The creatures of the forest. They are seeing us being taken away. They will remember."

"And who are they going to tell? Have you lost your senses?"

"They will tell the one who speaks to them. The People's Healer, Iella. The animals will tell her we have been taken away, and her people will come looking for us. They found us before; they will find us again."

The longer they traveled, the harder it became. The militia let the men have their bows long enough to hunt but felt compelled to watch them from a distance. It was that, or the soldiers had to hunt for everyone, which would leave fewer to guard the group. Having the soldiers nearby made hunting much harder, and they were not allowed enough time, so all had less food than they needed. The soldiers did not seem to care that their charges were dramatically losing weight.

Hopefully, they would not have that much further to go. Wherever they were being taken, they would still have to build shelters and prepare for the worst of the cold months.

The Brothers witnessed how the Waschini hunted with no gratitude or humility. It sickened them to see how little they valued any but their own lives.

Kele had unfortunately come to the attention of one of the soldiers. "There is something wrong with that one. He is holding everyone else up," he complained to the commander.

"I don't think he is holding anyone up. It is taking a long time because they're on foot. We have to give them time to hunt, gather, and rest. Ignore him. He is of no importance."

"What if he is sick? Maybe that is why he is slow, something infectious maybe," the soldier said.

"He is not sick; he doesn't have anything you can catch. That's enough; say no more of it. And that's an order."

Since it was now apparent that the soldiers did not like Kele slowing them all up, the men started taking turns carrying him on their shoulders.

Eventually, Awantia told Tiponi that she was nearly out of maize seed. Tiponi said that they should instead start speaking to the forest animals and birds as they passed.

At first, nothing was said about it, but then it started to irritate the same soldier who didn't like Kele, and he angrily reprimanded Awantia. From then on, she was careful only to speak when he was further away from her.

Even though the High Council would not reconvene as had originally been planned, Khon'Tor decided to visit Chief Kotori, hoping to keep him involved in the newly formed brotherhood. He promised Tehya he would return as soon as he could and tenderly kissed her goodbye.

Khon'Tor was lost in thought as he traveled from the Far High Hills to Chief Kotori's village. He thought of how the Great Spirit had led him to find U'Kail, whom they had later named Ahanu, and how Larara now had peace that her daughter's son had been returned to her. And how they would not have connected with Chief Kotori's village otherwise. He put one foot in front of the other and made good time.

It was a quiet winter afternoon with a biting breeze blowing across the landscape. He approached the river where Pakwa was often to be found fishing, but not seeing the brave, Khon'Tor continued on to the village. As he approached, he noticed the silence. No offspring's laughter broke the quiet. No sounds of normal village chatter. As he drew closer, a stray pony crossed his path and traveled on. A sick feeling gathered in his stomach.

The village was empty. The shelters were still standing, but there was no one around. The place was clear of any footprints in the snow other than those of animals. Khon'Tor walked about, checking inside to see if anyone was left. To his relief, he found no bodies or evidence of bloodshed, just not a single person.

He felt the fires and found no trace of warmth even at the bottom of the ash beds. As far as stored provisions and small tools were concerned, few were left. Chief Kotori and his people had left their village. But why?

Then, in an area where the winds had not allowed snow to accumulate, he noticed faint impressions in the frozen ground. The tell-tale prints of the Waschini, as their horses' tracks were clearly distinguishable from those of the Brothers. The Waschini 'shod' their horses, as Oh'Dar had called it, putting metal plates on the bottom of their hooves, whereas the Brothers did no such thing.

Chief Kotori and his people had not left their village. They had been taken from it.

Khon'Tor could not tell how long they had been gone. Unable to find a trail good enough to follow, he hastened back to the Far High Hills.

Harak'Sar immediately called together the Overseer and his Circle of Counsel. "We must find them, but how?" High Protector Dreth lamented. "The frozen ground will have left no record."

Iella spoke, "The forest knows. The forest knows where they went and where they are now."

The High Protector frowned. Urilla Wuti reminded them of Iella's gift and how she could communicate with the forest creatures. "Iella will be able to lead us to them."

"But to what end?" the High Protector said. "We cannot show ourselves. What good is it going to be to find them?"

"Dreth is right," Harak'Sar said. "The only people who can help rescue them from the Waschini are the Waschini."

"I'll go," Khon'Tor said.

Oh'Dar had returned from Wilde Edge a few days previously, and he, Acaraho, and Awan listened with growing concern as Khon'Tor told them what he'd discovered. "Chief Kotori and his people are gone. The village is empty. What little tracks there were suggested Waschini riders," Khon'Tor explained.

Oh'Dar paled. *Oh no.* It had escalated.

"Iella says the forest creatures will tell her where the Brothers are, but we cannot free them without showing ourselves." Khon'Tor continued.

"We should consult Ben and my grandmother," Oh'Dar suggested. "They know more about the Waschini world than I do."

"Where is your Waschini friend?" Khon'Tor asked.

"He returned to his world."

"He failed the test?" Khon'Tor asked.

"He passed the test but realized he was not ready to give up the life he knew," Oh'Dar explained.

"Then it achieved its purpose," Khon'Tor remarked.

In their living quarters, Ben and Miss Vivian listened carefully. Ben's bad leg was propped up on one of the chairs.

"So it has come to this," he said, thinking out loud. "I did not think it would. Hard to believe that anyone can be so cruel as to take people from their homes. It has to be the military, no doubt under orders from the Governor. There's no doubt that they are being relocated so the government can take over the land they were inhabiting. And it also follows that their new home will not be as hospitable or rich in resources, or the Governor would want that too. We had heard rumors it was coming. I didn't think I would live to see the day."

"But the land is owned by the Morgan Trust," Oh'Dar said. He was pacing back and forth, unable to control his agitation.

"Even though the deed has been recorded, it doesn't mean the maps have been updated," Ben pointed out. "It's true they were living on private land, but the commanders of the military that took them did not know that."

"The military is—?" asked Awan.

"An organized group of males under the command of another, all with weapons."

Ben thought a moment. "The only way anyone can help them is for Grayson to find them and prove that they were on private land as guests of the Morgan Trust. It would be best if you had others with you, though."

Oh'Dar sighed and stopped pacing. "You mean like Newell Storis?"

"Yes, especially Storis, with some proof of the recorded paperwork showing the land ownership."

"Do I have time to go all the way to Wilde Edge and back?" Oh'Dar asked.

"It can't be helped. There is no other way that I can see if you want to free them," Ben said.

"The Brothers would be traveling on foot," Khon'Tor mused. "And that is to our advantage. If you remember, Pan told us the Healers' abilities would be augmented. Iella from the Far High Hills has developed the ability to communicate with Etera's creatures. She was sure she could find them and said she could send someone to lead you to them," Khon'Tor explained. "Most likely a hawk or an eagle."

Oh'Dar glanced over at Ben and Miss Vivian, who were looking at each other with wide eyes. His mother had told him about Iella's abilities, as well as the developing abilities of the other Healers, but he could only imagine what Ben and his grandmother were thinking. For a moment, he deeply regretted that Ned had changed his mind. He was missing out on incredible wonders, and he would have been a great help right now, but Oh'Dar also missed him as a friend.

"Yes, I have to do this," Oh'Dar said. "I am the only one who can. I will go to Wilde Edge and talk to Newell Storis. I will do my best to convince him to come back with me. Please look after Acise and I'Layah. It seems I am gone even more now than I was before."

"Iella will know when you have returned, and you will recognize the guide she sends when it appears," Khon'Tor said. "But it is not enough.

Finding them is not enough. When Oh'Dar finds them, assuming the Waschini military releases Chief Kotori and his people to him, what is he to do with them? Surely they will be weary. We do not know if any are ill. What of their elderly?"

"You are right," Acaraho said. "It is not enough to free them from the Waschini abductors; they must be provided for on the way back to the village. And we don't know what shape they will be in by then."

"Oh'Dar cannot provide for all of them by himself," Awan pointed out. "We must send our people to help them. Once the Waschini are out of sight, they can show themselves."

Acaraho thought for a moment. "Oh'Dar will be on horseback, and Haan's people travel faster. They are stronger, and they can cloak themselves. I know they would help get the Brothers back to their village. Come, we will speak with Haan and ask for his people's help."

The two Leaders and their Circles of Counsel met. When Acaraho finished speaking, Haan said, "The time has come for us to step into the place of the Ancients as the Brothers' protectors. The Rah-hora was satisfied at the opening of Kthama Minor. We are no longer bound to the shadows, leaving their care to your people. Whatever is needed, we are ready."

So, once again, Oh'Dar bade his family goodbye and set out for Wilde Edge. He'd had only a few months respite following the ordeal of the trial, then delivering Ned to Chief Kotori, fetching him, and now once more traveling back to Wilde Edge. He was growing weary, the burdens wearing him down both physically and psychologically.

He had a great deal of time to think on the return trip but could come up with no other solution if this failed.

CHAPTER 16

As surprised as they were to see Oh'Dar back so soon, the Webbs, Newell, and Grace were equally horrified to hear that one of the local tribes had been abducted and taken from their home.

When Oh'Dar mentioned that it was Chief Kotori's village, Ned's face fell. "What? The military took them?"

"From what Ben said, it had to be the military."

Mr. Webb said, "It's wrong, It's just wrong. They were there first."

"Unfortunately," said Newell, "not everyone cares. At least not those in power. So what is our plan? Though I can think of one too."

Oh'Dar reached down to pet Buster who was making circles around his legs, "We have to find them and show whoever is in charge that the locals were living on private land. Morgan Trust land."

"You're right. That is the only way to stop them," Newell said.

"What if they don't believe us?" Oh'Dar asked the attorney.

"Oh, I think they will. You don't realize who you are, Grayson. Your grandfather was a very powerful man. His legend lives on, as does the loyalty of many he helped get into power. But with power comes the resentment of others, which is why the constable wanted so much to find you guilty of the murders of Ben and your grandmother. It is a shameful side of our natures, I'm afraid."

"So you will go with me?" Oh'Dar asked Storis.

Before he could answer, Ned spoke up. "I'm going too."

His parents' heads snapped in his direction.

"You said you were home to stay," Mrs. Webb said.

"Yes, but I have to help. These people are my friends; I know them all, every one of them. I can't stand by and let them be treated like this. And the more of us, the better."

Storis looked at Grace, "I need to go with Grayson, and I want you to move back in with your parents."

"I will be fine on my own," Grace said.

"I'll feel better if you're here with your family."

"Your husband is right, and I agree." Mr. Webb looked across at Grace. "We will look after you for however long it takes."

"I hate to leave you, Grace, but I know you will be safe with your parents. And if I don't do this, it will haunt me for the rest of my life."

"I understand," she said. "I will be fine, I promise."

"There is a big problem here," Mr. Webb said. "How are you going to find them?"

They all looked at Oh'Dar.

"We have means that I can't explain. But trust me, we will find them."

Everyone said their goodbyes, and the men were soon on their way. Each had much on his mind, which made for little conversation. Finally, one night at the fire, Ned asked the question that had been bothering him since they decided to go after Chief Kotori's village.

"Grayson, what are we going to do with the Brothers once we find them? Always assuming the military accepts proof that they were guests on private land and lets you take custody of them?"

Oh'Dar knew Haan's people would help feed the Brothers and get them back home, though he had no idea how he was going to explain that. "We will take them back to their village. I just pray they are all in good health and have not been mistreated. We have the advantage they have had to travel on foot, so they could not have gotten that far away."

What he didn't add was that being on foot would have caused more suffering, and it would also take longer to get them home.

Iella brushed off the snow and sat on a fallen tree trunk. Urilla Wuti, Nootau, and Khon'Tor were with her.

After a silent moment or two, she announced, "I see them!" The eagle she had connected with dipped his wings and swooped lower, and she could see the long line of weary travelers. They had their wraps wound tightly about them and were methodically putting one foot in front of the other across the frozen ground. Most of the younger offspring were being carried. Many adults walked bent over, their heads covered with blankets.

"There are many Waschini on horses. A frightening number."

Khon'Tor and Urilla Wuti looked at each other, their glances expressing their concerns about the plan. Yet it was the only way.

The eagle swooped even lower, and many of the women turned their faces upward. A few pointed and called to others so they might notice the eagle too. "They see me," Iella said, and everyone knew she was speaking as if she were the eagle. "They look tired and worn down, but they see me, and despite everything, they are smiling up at me. They somehow know I have come to help them."

"That is good," Urilla Wuti said. "That will give them the hope they need to hold up a bit longer. I cannot imagine how hard this is on them in every way."

The eagle swooped around again, making another loop, and this time some of the Waschini took notice and also looked skyward. Iella told the eagle to fly higher, out of any danger from the weapons. The bird rose high above the treetops.

"I see where they are. They must have been traveling for some time; they are far from their village," Iella said. Her eyes moved under her closed lids as if she were looking at the scene itself.

Finally, she opened her eyes. "They left a trail for me to find."

"I looked for a trail," Khon'Tor said. "There was none; the ground was too frozen."

"They left a different trail. They are smart, and they remembered I could talk to the forest creatures. The women were leaving maize seed for them and then later talked to them along the way. They did that on purpose—I know they did—so the squirrels and birds would remember their kindness and tell me where they passed. That is how I found them so quickly."

"Their faith in the Great Spirit is strong," Urilla Wuti said.

"When you think it has been long enough for

Oh'Dar to have gotten back, let me know, and I will send the eagle to Chief Is'Taqa's village."

Honovi was surprised to see Ned Webb returning. He had decided to return to his Waschini world, yet here he was with Oh'Dar. And there, too, was the attorney named Storis.

Storis and Ned stood listening while Oh'Dar spoke to Chief Is'Taqa and Honovi. Ned could catch only bits and pieces of it as they spoke quickly. He recognized the word for eagle and walking, but that was about all. He did see Honovi glance over at the rifle in Ned's hand.

When Oh'Dar, the Chief, and Honovi were done speaking, Oh'Dar explained to Ned and Storis, "We will stay here tonight and rest up. Tomorrow morning we will leave at first light. Honovi asks that you keep your rifles out of sight, unloaded, and in a safe place, please. The children here will be curious to examine them."

"Of course," Storis answered. Ned nodded and clutched his rifle tighter, realizing he should not have carried it so openly.

When the horses were tended to, the three men ate a hearty meal and then tried to get a good night's rest.

Oh'Dar was up earlier than the others. Pajackok helped ready the horses. "You trust that one?" Pajackok asked.

Oh'Dar knew Pajackok meant Ned. "I do," he said, tightening the cinch.

"How will you explain how you are going to find the villagers?"

Oh'Dar shook his head, "That is a problem. No doubt they will wonder how I know where to go. And if they do notice the guides, it will be difficult to explain. I can only avoid the question so long."

"You walk a difficult path," Pajackok said. "But you walk it with honor."

Oh'Dar put his hand on Pajackok's upper arm, and Pajackok returned the gesture.

Noshoba came over to tell Oh'Dar that the other two Waschini were awake and that his mother had food ready to eat. They went back to Honovi's fire, where Storis and Ned were already eating.

Snana and Honovi had packed supplies for them as best they could, but the men would have to hunt along the way. Despite it being later in the year, the land they would be passing through would have some vegetation, even under the snow, to sustain the horses.

Oh'Dar searched the skies for a sign of the screech of a hawk or eagle demanding his attention. Then, out of the edge of the woodland, a small white head peeked out. Oh'Dar squinted and stared. It couldn't be. No, it couldn't be—

When he was a boy, he had rescued a white bobcat kitten that had crawled too far out onto a limb hanging over the Great River and was in danger of falling into the rushing waters below. He had named her Kaishee, and he had seen her off and on during the following years. He suspected too much time had passed for it to be the same cat, but regardless, he knew it was a sign.

They all saddled up, and Oh'Dar led them into the forest, the white bobcat leaving just enough of a glimpse to be followed.

He could hear Storis and Ned behind him, wondering how he knew where to go. Ned surmised that it must be what Oh'Dar and the Chief had been talking about the day before in the conversation he couldn't follow.

He knew it would take a day or two to get to the Chief's village, but from there, he didn't know how far ahead the Chief and his people would be. He believed Khon'Tor was probably right, and the group was no doubt traveling on foot, which would slow them considerably.

They rationed the food that the women had packed for them, saving it in case, at some stage, their hunting wasn't productive as they would have wished. Oh'Dar got to see first-hand how much Ned had learned while away and was proud of him. However, he could see the worry creasing Ned's brow. Ned had grown close to Chief Kotori's people, and Oh'Dar knew all too well the anxiety that accompanied the knowledge that your friends or family needed you.

Ned knew that Oh'Dar could find the Chief's village, but once they left it, Oh'Dar had no idea how he would explain away the fact that he knew where he was going. During the trip, the bobcat had so far been replaced by a wolf, several different deer, and a fox. Once they reached more open land where the sky was not hidden by the canopy of trees, the eagle Oh'Dar had been expecting appeared.

At the Far High Hills, Iella watched through the eagle's eyes and kept Harak'Sar and Urilla Wuti updated. Out of sight but traveling with them were scores of Haan's people.

Ned tossed and turned. It wasn't that he couldn't sleep on the ground; he had learned to do that during the months he had been at the Chief's village. He just could not stop worrying about them. Myrica, Awantia, the Chief, and the others. Young Kele also weighed heavily on his mind. Would the soldiers realize he was different? Would they overlook it, or would it make him a target? He knew the militiamen were simply following orders, but how much humanity lived in their souls?

The next day, they entered the Chief's village. Ned was deeply affected by the empty shelters and the abandoned fire pits. The bright blue winter sky overhead made everything look smaller and lonelier.

They dismounted and looked around. Ned went to the shelter which had been his, pulled the flap aside, and went in. He stood in the center, then fell to his knees and prayed for the villagers' safety and wellbeing and that they might be given a sign that help was on its way. And he buried his burning face in his hands as shame filled him that his people could do this to others.

When Ned reappeared, Oh'Dar was headed into the village center, his hand shielding his eyes as he searched the sky.

Ned walked over to Storis, "This is where I stayed. These people were kind to me. They are good people. They have to be alright; they just have to be."

"There is no way of knowing how far we have to travel yet. And what are we going to do when we find them? The three of us can't sustain a whole village. What if they need medical care?"

"They may not all be in a bad way. The majority are very fit, and they do have a Medicine Woman with them," Ned said. "I have some general medical training, and Grayson studied to be a doctor. We have to hope it will be enough. There are also many things about Grayson we don't know. Not just ordinary things. Peculiar things, not only about his past but how he lives now."

"Such as where Ben and Grayson's grandmother really live?"

"Yes," Ned said. "At first, I assumed it was with another village like this one. And you said that when you came to Chief Is'Taqa's village, Oh'Dar brought Ben there comparatively quickly, so it must be close to there.

"There could be another village close by in another direction. That is the logical conclusion."

"No, I know they are not living with any of the locals. For reasons I can't talk about."

"I suspected there was more than you told us about. Is that why you wanted to live with Grayson?"

"Yes. Something happened, and because of what happened, I know Ben Jenkins and Miss Vivian are not living with any of the locals."

The screech of an eagle broke out overhead, and the two men saw Oh'Dar walking toward them. "Come on, we still have lots of daylight left. There are no supplies here that can help us; we will hunt when we get settled in later today."

CHAPTER 17

Myrica and Awantia sat huddled as close as they could to the fire the soldiers had let them build that evening. They were hungry. They were all hungry. Their elderly were tired and getting weak, and everyone was worried about them. The children were cranky, missing the comfort of home and full bellies. And the temperature was dropping. Soon the heavy snows would fall, and then the trials they were encountering would worsen. The soldiers, weary and anxious to get back to their compound, now kept them moving from first light nearly to dusk, giving little time to hunt and build temporary shelters.

As time went on, the soldiers decided they didn't like even the women talking much among themselves. So the women communicated in Handspeak when they were sure the soldiers could not see them, and when that wasn't possible, they would sneak in conversations when they could, mostly when they were allowed some privacy to relieve themselves.

The women would go together in small groups and keep their voices low. Ever since they had seen the eagle circling and then flying so low overhead, the conversation had reflected their anticipation that help would come.

The two friends sat together clasping hands, leaning against each other, and staring wordlessly into the yellow and orange flames that danced before them. So comforting and reminiscent of many past happy nights sitting together just like this, though in the safety of their village.

Across from them, Kele's parents sat with him sandwiched tightly between them. He asked every day when they would be going home. The whole village worked together to keep him away from the soldiers' attention. It had been a difficult journey, and the strain was showing on the Waschini's faces. Many feared it was merely a matter of time before they took their irritations out on their captives.

Chief Kotori seemed unaffected. He remained calm, which helped everyone else. His expression never changed, and the strength behind his steady gaze restored their confidence that somehow, all would be well. They relied on his great faith and that of Second Chief Tawa to shore up their own. Tiponi, the Medicine Woman, also seemed assured that help would be provided and that it was just a matter of time. And the appearance of the eagle, a messenger of the Great Spirit that represented courage and love, seemed proof that their faith was justified.

"Where do you think Ned Webb is now?" Awantia whispered to her friend.

"No doubt safe with his Waschini family. I wonder; will he ever return, and if he does, what will he think when he finds our village empty? Abandoned. Do you think the Waschini world knows what is happening to our people? And if so, do they care?"

"If they know, they must not care, or surely they would do something to stop it?"

"We should go to sleep, my friend," Myrica whispered, "We must preserve our health as much as we can. We do not know how long we have yet to travel or what the conditions will be like where they are taking us."

Awantia did not answer, but based on how they had been treated so far, she was sure no good future awaited them.

The three men were stretched out around their own evening fire. They had eaten well, thanks to Oh'Dar's hunting skills. The horses were comfortable, and despite the long journey, the men's spirits were good.

Ned was enjoying the warmth of the heat on his face. Beyond the snapping and crackling of the fire, he could hear Storis starting to lightly snore. And soon, he had also dropped off to sleep.

A few hours later, the fire had died down, and as Ned woke up to pull another blanket over himself, he saw that Oh'Dar was missing.

Ned waited, thinking his friend had gone to find some privacy and would be back any moment, but time passed, and Ned started to worry. He carefully got up, wrapped his blanket around his shoulders, grabbed his rifle, and went to look for Oh'Dar.

As he approached the woodline, he heard something that sounded like talking. And it sounded like Oh'Dar's voice, yet he was not speaking English. It sounded something like the Brother's language and yet not quite. At least, not enough that he could make it out. Maybe Oh'Dar was simply praying in another language, asking for help as Ned had repeatedly done on their journey. And then Ned heard what seemed like a reply. His blood ran cold. Oh'Dar was talking to someone in the dark, only the voice that responded was deeper and more guttural than he'd ever heard before. The hair on the back of Ned's neck stood up. He tightened his fist around the stock of the rifle, and waiting to hear more, held his breath as the cold slowly seeped through his clothing.

Who, or what, was Grayson Morgan talking to out there in the wilderness?

Fearing he would be discovered, Ned carefully crept back to his place by the fire, his hands shaking. He rolled over so his back was turned to the direction

Oh'Dar would come. His heart was pounding, and he didn't sleep the rest of the night. Though he trusted Oh'Dar, he couldn't quell his fear. But he knew one thing; this must be to do with what Oh'Dar was hiding. *Only what was he hiding?*

Oh'Dar came back to the fire and slipped into his spot. That Haan's people were traveling with them gave him great reassurance. Though they could not intervene with the regiment accompanying Chief Kotori and his people, they would be able to provide more than enough food for them after the Waschini left. It was up to Oh'Dar to convince the regiment to turn the Brothers over to him.

Ned and Newell seemed to be sleeping soundly, but Oh'Dar was filled with anxiety—the strain of so many problems going on at once. He had not really recovered from the stress of the trial, and now there was this. The routine life he had hoped for as Acise's life-walker and I'Layah's father seemed far out of reach.

Acise. He longed to be lying next to her, talking about the day's events as they often did. Now they had I'Layah's future to mull over. What would her personality be like? What would she want for her own life as she grew older? He was so happy to be a father and longed to be fully able to embrace his place in her life.

He thought about his mother, up at the Far High Hills, with his brother Nootau, and his father, Acaraho, back at Kthama without her.

The full moon lit up a clear night sky. Sparkling stars dotted the black expanse. Occasionally a stray bat, not yet hibernating, would weave a lacy path across the sky. Oh'Dar prayed that the Chief and his people would soon be safely back home, safe from being bothered again by the Waschini.

Before he let sleep overtake him, he looked again at his traveling companions. They had both become his friends, and he realized he needed companions of his own kind. Though it was a strain keeping so much hidden from them, that they were there made the arduous journey so much more bearable. He turned over, rearranged his blanket, and closed his eyes.

The next morning, as they started to leave, two eagles were circling overhead. Oh'Dar took this as a sign that they were getting close. The eagles led them up a higher ridge, and before long, he could see the Waschini regiment and its captives in the distance below. He signaled for the others to bring their mounts up next to his and pointed to the long line of figures trudging slowly forward.

Oh'Dar turned Storm around and led his companions back a short way down the ridge to talk. "Someday, you will have to tell us how you found them," Ned said.

"We can easily catch up with them. Should we

wait until tonight, or tomorrow before they move out again?" Storis asked.

"I say we get this over with now."

"I agree," said Ned, and Storis nodded.

The sound of horses coming up behind them was unmistakable. The Brothers at the back of the line stopped and turned to look, as did the Waschini riders bringing up the rear. As those further up stopped and turned, others nearer the front also did until, eventually, everyone had stopped moving forward, including all the riders.

As Oh'Dar, Ned, and Storis whisked past the long line of Chief Kotori's people, faces relaxed, and some smiles even broke out. Overhead, the two eagles had been joined by a third, and they circled above, not to be missed by the Brothers.

The commander turned his horse around and waited for the riders to get to him, astonishment on his face.

Storm shook his head and pranced as Oh'Dar had him circle the commander, slowly coming to a halt.

"I am Commander Riley of the 14th regiment. Who may I ask, are you?"

"I am Grayson Stone Morgan the Third, owner of the property you are crossing."

"I see." The commander's eyes quickly covered the man's black stallions. Nearly everyone in the area from which he came knew of the Morgan horses. This man was who he said he was.

"There is no record of this land belonging to you, Mr. Morgan."

Oh'Dar reached into his jacket pocket and took out the papers. "This is my attorney, Newell Storis; he can attest to the validity of these."

Commander Riley took the papers, opened them, and briefly looked them over.

"I see. I'm under orders from the Governor to transport these locals to our outpost. They will be relocated from there to an area out west set aside for their kind, so your land will shortly be rid of them."

"These people are my guests. I do not want to be rid of them, as you put it. I need you to leave and return to your outpost. You can send a message to the Governor that this is private land, and he has no right to remove these people from it. And kindly tell him that no other tribes are to be removed from it either."

"What do you propose to do with them now?" the Commander asked.

"We will take them back to their village. I am grateful you did not destroy it."

"We are just following orders, Mr. Morgan. No harm intended."

Oh'Dar clenched his jaw. He did not want a fight, but his blood was boiling. "I fear how many atrocities have been committed by those *just following orders*, sir. As for no harm being intended, ripping people away from their homes and making them walk across country against their will in freezing weather without proper care or provision is harming them."

Then he added, "You may take those papers to the Governor if you wish."

"Thank you. I will get them to him. This is a very large tract of land you have purchased, Mr. Morgan. If the Governor wishes to speak to you, where will he find you?"

Storis spoke up, "I am Attorney Newell Storis; I represent Mr. Morgan, and you can reach me at Wilde Edge."

The commander's eyebrows rose in spite of himself. "You have come a long way to find us. We are only days away from the compound."

Ned spoke up, "These people are our friends. We couldn't stand by and let this be done to them."

By then, the riders from the back of the line had reached the front. The commander addressed them. "We are traveling on to our outpost. These people are being remanded to the custody of Mr. Morgan."

"I trust they are all in good health," Oh'Dar said. "If they are not, you can let the Governor know he won't have to look for me; I will find *him*."

The Brothers closest had been watching with rapt attention what was unfolding. They couldn't understand English, but they saw the exchange of paperwork and could read the body language. Somehow, Oh'Dar had convinced the Waschini to leave.

Oh'Dar waited for the regiment to get out of earshot and then turned and addressed the Brothers.

"The Waschini are gone. You are safe with us. Who will speak for you? Where is Chief Kotori?"

By now, those in the back had started to come forward, the better to see and hear Oh'Dar. Mothers were wiping the tears from their eyes and hugging their children closer. Myrica and Awantia hugged each other, and Kele pointed to Ned, calling out his name.

Chief Kotori stepped out in front of the crowd, and Tiponi and Second Chief Tawa joined him.

The Chief spoke. "The Great Spirit has brought you to us. We are immeasurably grateful." He briefly glanced skyward at the three eagles still circling.

The people nodded their heads, and a murmur of agreement passed through the crowd.

"It will be our honor to escort you and your people back to your homes," Oh'Dar said. "Are any of them hurt or ill? He looked over the crowd. They were dirty and undernourished, clothing was torn, and many looked ill. His countenance fell.

Tiponi said, "Our elderly are very weak. Several have a fever. Some time ago, I used up what medicinals I had with me, and I haven't been allowed to search for more. Our braves have done the best they can, but for many days, no one has had enough food or water. The children are frightened and distraught, as are some of the elderly."

"How far back did you camp last night? And was it in the forest or out here in the open?" Oh'Dar asked.

"Perhaps a half a day back," Second Chief Tawa answered. "It was heavily wooded, and there was a stream nearby."

"Can everyone make it that far?" Oh'Dar asked.

Chief Kotori looked at Tiponi, who nodded. Then the Chief raised his staff. Everyone turned around, and they began the long trek back as the snow started falling.

Kele didn't move; he stood waiting with his parents for Ned to reach him. As Ned brought his ride around, he dismounted and gave Kele a hug. Then he lifted Kele onto his horse and helped his mother join him so they could ride together.

The journey back was made with lifted hearts and heads. Despite their weariness, the Brothers moved a little more quickly, and their voices broke the silence. Some of the elderly were gently carried. Tiponi would be able to look for the plants she needed once they stopped traveling. Oh'Dar took the lead, now following a lone eagle.

Others could ride Storm if Oh'Dar led him, and some took turns doing so, mostly women holding young children. Newell did the same with his horse.

It was obvious when they arrived at the spot, as there were multiple fire beds around. Oh'Dar pulled the horse to a halt and waited for the others to trickle in.

Oh'Dar took care of Storm and the other horses as best he could. He knew the stallion was strong and would most likely be fine, but if anything happened to Storm, he would never forgive himself.

A group of people immediately started gathering materials to build makeshift shelters, while some of the braves set out to hunt. No longer restricted to a limited area, they had some success, but in such a short time, they could not bring back enough meat to sufficiently feed the whole village.

Oh'Dar had tried to keep his worry in check but to no avail. He knew he needed help. They all needed help.

Some of the mothers settled down the children, and other women went to fill the water gourds with snow or find materials for the fires. They would later place the gourds close enough to the fires for the snow to melt. Ned and Storis also helped gather firewood and start fires.

Tiponi took Awantia and Myrica with her to look for the herbs and roots she needed to treat those with fevers. They had luck finding ginseng root and white pine needles, but it was too late in the season for the purple cornflower plant from which she got echinacea.

That evening, even though most were still exhausted, for the moment, the mood around the evening fire was lighter. But they still had a long way to travel, and all were worried about the elderly and sick.

Ned wanted badly to speak to Myrica and Awantia alone, but all the women were busy doing what needed to be done. He did exchange smiles with them each as they all went about their duties. Hopefully, tomorrow he would be able to talk to them.

He had unanswered questions, one about the forest animals that seemed to show Oh'Dar the direction in which to travel and then, later, the eagles that flew overhead as if leading them. The other was the conversation he had heard Oh'Dar having with *something* in the woods.

Ned, Oh'Dar, and Storis slept close to each other. Because of everything on his mind, Ned could only doze. Once again, he was awakened by Oh'Dar getting up in the middle of the night.

He waited, as before, for Oh'Dar's quick return, but he was gone for a while. As much as Ned wanted to follow as he had done before, he was sure that with so many people there, someone would notice and might mention it. So he lay there and did nothing.

That morning, when the people awoke, there were three newly hunted deer lying in a row in the center of their camp.

The Brothers knew who had brought the deer, and so did Oh'Dar, but Ned and Storis were mystified. Oh'Dar hoped they would assume that some of the braves had done some early morning hunting and therefore would not question it. The Brothers, aware of the two Waschini strangers, muttered under their breath in clipped sentences so Ned could not understand what they were saying. But Ned heard one word, which they kept repeating. Oh-Mah. Whatever that meant.

There were so many frail people that they had to stay another night, but the next morning, the Chief decided they were ready to move on. He knew that as short as the days were, they would only get shorter and that much colder weather could move in at any time.

Some of the braves went on ahead each day and hunted as well as they could, but the days strung together until finally, Tiponi went to the Chief and Oh'Dar, who were working together. "It is too much," she said. "Our elderly are losing strength, and I am afraid we will lose many of them before we get back."

Oh'Dar was lost for words. The winter storms would come in full force before too long. It seemed unlikely that they could make it back to the village before the storms hit. He had a cold feeling in the pit of his stomach and was truly afraid things would end in tragedy. Tiponi herself looked exhausted; how could she continue to care for everyone, even with help? Even the men were torn between trying to shore up the temporary shelters, hunting for food, or using their body warmth to try to keep the women and children from freezing to death.

If he hadn't brought Ned and Storis, Oh'Dar could have asked the Sassen to help openly, but he could not ask for anything that might in any way appear obvious. He was caught in a terrible predicament. Reveal the Sassen's existence, or press on and risk people dying.

Off in the distance, they all could see heavy grey storm clouds moving in. The temperature had dropped severely over the past several days, and it was apparent that the clouds would deliver more snow. How much remained to be seen. A heavy snowfall would make it that much harder to travel, especially carrying the ill and infirm.

Oh'Dar let his eyes follow the line of the mountain range in the distance. How he wished it was Kthama's range. He longed for the shelter and the help it would promise.

Overhead a lone eagle circled, and he knew that Iella was still watching and guiding them. He wondered if she realized the trouble they were in. He knew that the eagle's view would show how worn the people were and how many were sick and exhausted. He prayed for a solution.

The storm hit with full force the next morning. The swirling snow was coming down at an alarming rate and was so thick that Oh'Dar could not see very far.

He bundled up and went out in search of Nimraugh, who was in charge of the group of Sassen who were helping him. However, he could only see a few feet in front of him, so was not able to go far. Having no choice, Oh'Dar shouted as loudly as he could in their shared language.

If Ned and Newell heard him speaking, what did it matter? Many were soon going to die out there, unprotected from the elements.

As he was waiting, a black bird alighted on a nearby branch. *How peculiar.* Just then, Nimraugh appeared, accompanied by Yar.

Nimraugh spoke. "Oh'Dar, the Brothers are in trouble, yes?"

"Yes. They are cold and exhausted. We cannot let them die. What can we do?"

"My people and I can build strong shelters for them. We can help take them there; it will not be far. We can hunt, forage, and feed them every day. They need more than the meager warmth their fires and temporary shelters can give."

Just then, the crow cried out.

"Ravu-Bahl has come to us," Yar said. "He reminds us of the sacred laws and of our duty to the Great Spirit."

The Sacred Laws. Oh'Dar knew them so well; he had been raised on them. And he knew that the crow was a messenger of the Great Spirit. "Take care of the sick and helpless." Was this the reminder that Ravu'Bahl brought?

Suddenly, something inside Oh'Dar broke. All the years of trying to keep the secret of the People, the stress of the trial and persecution he had just endured, the worry about Acise and their unborn child, worrying about his grandparents, trying to bridge three worlds. He had done his best to juggle it all, and he had still ended up in failure. The Brothers were going to die if he didn't do something. He had to have help, even if it meant making Ned and Newell aware of the Sassen's existence. He brought his thoughts back to the moment and stared at Nimraugh and Yar, standing in front of him stalwartly waiting on him to speak. So tall, so massive, and totally covered in hair. They were impervious to the cold. And then he realized the answer was literally staring back at him.

"Tell your people to prepare the shelters, please. And hurry. When they are ready, come back and tell me."

Oh'Dar turned and walked back directly the way he had come. He didn't have to travel far, and soon he was back among the others. He sought out Chief Kotori and told him that Oh'Mah was here to help and that there were many of them. The Chief left his shelter and gathered Second Chief Tawas and Tiponi together and told them what was happening, that Oh'Mah would soon join them to care for and protect them, and they set about spreading the word.

Before long, there were sounds coming from the woods surrounding them. Everyone could hear branches snapping and trees cracking. Oh'Dar knew the Brothers would understand, but he also knew Ned and Newell would not. He got up and walked around the perimeter of the circle, straining to see through the wildly whirling snow. He finally found Ned and Storis huddled together.

He leaned over and asked loudly, "Where are your rifles?"

Ned pointed, "Over there behind that tree, if you can see it. What is going on, Grayson? He leaped to his feet. "All this noise; are we about to be attacked by something?"

"No," Oh'Dar answered. Then he retrieved the rifles. Ned watched him and nudged Storis to be sure he also saw what Oh'Dar was doing.

"Why are you taking our rifles?" Storis asked.

"You will understand in a moment."

"Grayson," Storis said, "What is going on?"

"Something has to give. If something doesn't change fast, a great number of these people are going to die. I need help, and I can't straddle all these worlds any longer."

Ned frowned and looked at Storis, who had the same bewildered look on his own face.

"You wanted to know the mystery? The mystery I have been hiding from your world? Well, it's going to be revealed, at least part of it, in just a few moments. There is no way I can prepare you. All I can ask is that you try to control your reaction. Try not to panic."

The swirling snow was starting to calm down a bit, and visibility was increasing. Though most of the people were still huddled together, Kele had slipped away from his parents. He stood looking into the woods and pointing. He smiled profusely and announced, "Oh'Mah! Oh'Mah!"

Just then, Oh'Dar heard the familiar whoot call.

Ned and Storis turned in the direction of the sound and saw Kele pointing. Ned jumped back and fell down, scrambling backward on hands and knees through the snowbank as quickly as he could. Storis looked at Oh'Dar and reached out to take one of the rifles. "No, Newell! No. You don't understand."

"What in the name of—" Newell shouted, pointing at the huge figure of Nimraugh. "What is that—thing?"

"This is Nimraugh. He is not a threat to you. He is a friend; he is a friend to me, and to you, and to the Brothers!"

Just then, Kele laughed again. "Oh'Mah!" Then he ran to embrace Nimraugh, who helped the child scramble up to sit on his shoulder and braced him safely in place.

"Oh! Oh," Ned exclaimed, scrambling to his feet in a panic to save Kele before realizing that the boy was smiling and hugging the giant hairy creature.

Oh'Dar turned to shout to the Brothers, who had been alerted by the noise.

"Oh'Mah is here to help. Not far from here, they have built enough shelters for all of us. You will be able to build fires and get warm. They will lead those who can walk and carry those who cannot. Please, go with them."

Slowly the group rose, bundling up and moving slowly. One by one, they followed Nimraugh. Then several other Sassen appeared. They went to help the men with the stretchers loaded with the elderly and ill.

"This isn't real. This can't be real," Storis was stammering. "How many of these things are there?"

"Grayson," Ned pleaded. "What is going on!"

"I don't have time to tell you all of it," Oh'Dar said, distracted by the activity in front of them. "You have to trust me. The reason I took your rifles is that I knew you would be panicked, and panicked people are dangerous and act reflexively. But these are not creatures; they are people like you, me, and the Brothers. They have an organized culture, they speak a sophisticated language, they love their families and are true to their mates. They are called the Sassen, or Oh'Mah, which means Masters of the Forest."

Ned squeezed his eyes open and shut several times. "I— I don't know what to say. I think I am in shock. I knew you were hiding something, but I never expected—"

Newell continued to stare at the Sassen, who were moving among the Brothers and offering help. Several of them bent down and gently lifted the very sick with giant hands, cradling them carefully against their bodies to keep them warm and carrying them to the shelters. Led by Nimraugh and his people, the crowd slowly disappeared into the woods.

"We need to go with them," Oh'Dar said, breaking them out of their stupor. "Grab your horses and satchels."

Oh'Dar headed off and turned back to see both Ned and Newell standing where he had left them.

"Do you trust me or not?" Now Oh'Dar was shouting. Time was of the essence in getting the Brothers settled. "I need your help; the Sassen and the Brothers need your help. Are you coming or not?"

Ned and Newell stared briefly at each other and went to fetch the horses.

It was not far at all. The moment Ned and Newell saw what the Sassen had constructed, they understood the meaning of the noises they had heard. In front of them were twenty or thirty small shelters. The frames were pieced together from tree trunks and branches and were covered with a thick layer of fir boughs. Most of the Brothers had already entered.

To the side was a large structure with a single tall opening at one end. Its top and sides were also covered in fir branches. Ned realized it was for the horses and was touched by the concern for their welfare.

When each shelter was full, a Sassen entered it, blocking the door.

"What are they doing?" Newell asked.

"They are blocking the entrances," Oh'Dar explained. "Their body heat will warm the shelter. They are protectors of Etera, and long ago, their

Ancestors were charged with the care and protection of the Brothers. That is what they are doing now."

Oh'Dar was chilled to the bone, but he took care of the horses, making sure they were settled into the makeshift stable. He found it contained a long log, with a deep well clawed out from the middle, filled with melted snow. Once he was assured the horses were as comfortable as possible, he went from shelter to shelter, looking for the Chief and Tiponi. He found them together.

"The Great Spirit has provided," the Chief said after hearing that his people were all safely inside the shelters now.

"In the morning, we will deal with food and other needs. I also need to get the other Waschini inside."

Oh'Dar left to find Ned and Newell and get them inside too. All three were covered in snow and shivering.

"Nimraugh just told me there is a shelter over there that has room," Oh'Dar said.

"I didn't hear anything," said Ned.

"He didn't speak; he used a hand language."

Ned just stared at him. "So they use a hand language as the Brothers do." It seemed he was still trying to process it all.

Oh'Dar motioned for them to come with him to the shelter. As they approached, one of the Sassen came out of the entrance, barely squeezing through, to let them enter. As they did so, Ned and Newell looked away, apparently still afraid and trying not to make it worse.

Once they were inside, the Sassen re-entered and took her place, blocking the door. Oh'Dar asked her name, and the others paused when she spoke.

Ned recognized the language as the same he had heard before when he had followed Oh'Dar and heard him talking in the dark. He realized now that this must be the same creature to whom Oh'Dar had been talking. Ned was so cold and longed to be wrapped up in his blanket but was still afraid and feeling vulnerable. He tried reasoning with himself that if the Sassen had wanted to hurt anyone, they could easily have done it before now. Why go to all the trouble of making these shelters if they meant harm? And then he remembered that they were helping the Brothers. But what of him and Newell? Did the Sassen blame them, as Waschini, for the harm that had come to the Brothers?

The conversation between Oh'Dar and the Sassen ended, and Oh'Dar explained, "This is Ensata. She said that in the morning, they will help find food for all of us. They cannot help with water as our water vessels are very small and hard for them to handle, so we will fill them with snow and set them by the fires to melt, as usual."

Ned found the courage to look at the creature. He

knew he shouldn't think of her as a creature, but he couldn't help it. Obviously, it was as Grayson had said. They had a language, and a sophisticated one at that. No, they were not creatures, and Ned had a lot of thinking to do.

Ensata was huge and completely blocked the opening. And Grayson was right; the shelter was already getting warm. Except for her face, hands, and the bottoms of her feet, which he could see from the way she was sitting, she was covered in hair or fur—in the dim lighting, he wasn't sure which. He was grateful for the warmth, and his heart rate was starting to slow. He realized he was staring but couldn't stop himself. When she looked at him, he saw intelligence in the dark, deep-set eyes. Finally, he garnered enough self-control to lie down and wrap himself in his blanket. It was only then he realized that the floor of the shelter had also been covered with a deep layer of fir branches. They were soft and thick, and they served not only as a mattress but also as insulation from the cold ground.

Before he fell asleep, Ned lifted his head and said to Oh'Dar. "Please tell her; tell Ensata, thank you."

Newell was also in shock and was having a hard time coming to grips with the reality of what he was seeing. Oh, it explained so much. Why Oh'Dar had refused to fetch his grandparents. Why he had refused to reveal where they were living. Why he had even said that he would hang before he would tell anyone where they were. Newell had always believed that Oh'Dar was protecting Ben and Miss Vivian's interests, but now he knew there was an additional element.

Oh'Dar had been right to hide the truth. Newell shuddered to think what would happen if the existence of these—people—became known.

When light broke, Oh'Dar awoke. He took a moment to cherish the feeling of being warm; it had been so long. He looked over and saw that Ned and Newell were still asleep, as were most of the others in the shelter, though, as he was getting up, he saw some open their eyes and then close them again.

Ensata moved enough for him to squeeze by.

The cold air hit Oh'Dar like a hammer. The Sassen had already gathered bundles of dry branches and kindling and set them in piles, ready for the morning fires. He walked over to Nimraugh, who had stood watch during the night.

"Greetings, Nimraugh. You have been busy."

"Others are out tracking deer. When the Brothers start waking, we will get the fires blazing."

"You saved our lives. I pray that everyone survived the night. But know that any losses would have been greater had you not built the shelters and brought everyone to them."

Oh'Dar looked over to where the horses were under their shelter with the heavy roof of fir boughs. "I need to check on the horses."

"They are fine. Their blankets are dry, and we are sending them calming vibrations, so they are eating well and drinking. How are your—friends?" Nimraugh asked.

"They will not betray you. They were frightened at first, but they will be fine."

"We are not offended. We realize that our appearance would frighten any Waschini.

"Ravu-Bahl returns," Nimraugh said, gesturing.

Oh'Dar looked at the black bird once more perched not far from them. The storm had lessened, and he was strikingly visible against the snow. There was no sight of the eagle, but Oh'Dar was not surprised, considering how volatile the high winds were.

"We cannot stay here forever," he said to Nimraugh. "Do you know how far it is to their village?"

"Many, many days. More than you want to hear."

Oh'Dar fell silent. How long could they live here? And even if they could stay the winter, there was not enough medicine. Nor were enough of the Brothers well enough to hunt or to help care for the rest and prepare meals. They had been traveling for almost two months, and all were suffering from exposure, malnourishment, and exhaustion. The Sassen were incredibly strong, but they were not built to deliver the comparatively delicate care the Brothers needed.

Then Oh'Dar remembered the mountain range in the distance. It wasn't Kthama, but could it be the Far High Hills? What was he thinking? Could the Brothers be taken there with the Sassen's help? But there were nearly a hundred of the Brothers; how long would it take? And what of Ned and Newell? It would mean exposing the People to them.

It fell to him to make the decision. The care they needed was at the Far High Hills, at the hands of Urilla Wuti and Iella. And the countless other volunteers who could help tend to the sick. But it meant revealing the People's existence to Outsiders.

"How long would it take us to get to the Far High Hills?"

Nimraugh thought a moment. "If those in the worst shape will allow us to carry them, and if we go quickly, we can make it in half a day. It will take longer for those healthy and strong enough to walk. How much longer, I do not know. But it is still many days closer than their village."

"How many of you are here?" Oh'Dar asked.

"More than you realize. And we can call others if this is what you want to do. They can cloak themselves and be here within a day; the storm will not slow them down," he explained.

Oh'Dar knew Iella had been watching their journey through other eyes. He looked across at the crow. It was close enough to hear their conversation. Was it possible she could also hear them? Either way, she would understand when the People's watchers said the Sassen were bringing the Brothers. She would have time to arrange immediate help for them. As for Ned and Newell, well, there was no other choice. They would have to be trusted even further, and they would also have to open their minds even further. Oh'Dar knew he had to prepare them for this next revelation, the existence of the People.

He turned his attention back to Nimraugh. "Tell the other Sassen our plan. I will confer with the Chief and their Healer, but I believe the Brothers will need another day here, a chance to stay warm, eat, and gain some strength. It will also give you time to get the others here to help."

CHAPTER 18

Luckily, the swirling, biting squalls that had made moving and seeing so difficult had died down.

Oh'Dar returned to find the Chief and Tiponi awake and gathered around one of the fires. It was not as warm as being in the shelter warmed by the Sassen's body heat, but it was still comforting. The delicious smell from the skewers of meat roasting over the fires was starting to draw others out from their shelters.

Oh'Dar explained what he proposed.

"They need at least another day," Tiponi said.

"What of your friends?" Chief Kotori asked.

"I will do my best to prepare them, but they are already reeling over the Sassen. I hope they are strong enough to handle it. Speaking of which, have you seen them?"

"I believe they are still in their shelter," Tiponi answered, pointing.

Oh'Dar realized that Ensata was still blocking the exit. He wondered if they were still asleep or trapped.

He greeted Ensata as he approached, and she moved so he could enter. Once inside, he saw Ned and Newell still under their blankets.

"There's breakfast cooking. Don't you smell it?" Oh'Dar asked.

"Yes," Ned said, "But we weren't sure how to —leave."

"If you get up, Ensata will realize you want to leave and move for you. There are branches stacked to the side of the shelter, so the last people to leave can cover the opening. It won't keep the heat in, but it will cut down the cold air entering."

Oh'Dar waited for Ned and Newell and then led them outside to one of the fires. Not long after they were seated, Awantia and Myrica found them.

"I am glad to see you both," Ned greeted them. Newell stared at hearing Ned speak the foreign language.

Both women were glad to see him too, and they listened as Oh'Dar explained who Newell was and how he had helped his grandparents. Then Oh'Dar explained to Newell who the women were and what they had just been talking about.

"Tiponi explained to us that in a day or so, we are going to the Far High Hills," Myrica said. "We are going around telling the others about it and that I have been there. That, and the shelters the Sasquatch built and the food they are providing, is giving everyone great hope."

Soon, the two women excused themselves and went about their task.

"What is the Far High Hills?" Ned asked.

"I will explain shortly. For now, just eat and get some strength back. We will rest here for a day or so."

Newell looked around, "Where are they?"

"The Sassen? They are close by. You cannot see them if they do not wish to be seen."

"I know you said they are peaceful, and I can see how they are helping the locals. But I am still— unnerved by them," Newell added. "And now they can just disappear if they wish?"

"These are the people who raised you then?" Ned asked.

"No. These are friends of the people who raised me," Oh'Dar reluctantly answered. He didn't want to get into it now, but Myrica's mention of the Far High Hills had precipitated the conversation.

"If you weren't raised by the locals, and you weren't raised by the—Sassen—then who raised you?" Ned asked. "Don't tell me you were raised by wolves?"

Oh'Dar was relieved that Ned was able to joke. "No, not wolves. But I did have a wolf as a pet when I was growing up. He now lives at the Far High Hills, the place we are going. There are people there who will tend to the Brothers. It is the best chance that everyone will survive."

Then he added, "But, it means exposing you to another revelation. I can't leave you here by yourselves, which means we have to take you with us."

The three of them sat together at one of the fires. Oh'Dar's concern had made Ned think of his mother. No doubt she and Grace were worried. He wished he had kept track of the days because now he wasn't sure how long they'd been gone. When he started to eat some of the meat, he realized just how hungry he was and looked around to make sure that he wasn't taking more than his fair share. He was glad to see more than enough meat for everyone, so he ate a good portion and enjoyed the feeling of a full belly.

Newell was also almost finished. Ned assumed that he was just as anxious to hear about this place, the Far High Hills. From the little Grayson had said, if there was a Healer and others ready to help, it must be some type of established village. But if not the locals and not these Sassen people, who was left? Then it occurred to Ned that it might be a group of their own kind—the Waschini. Immediately, he felt relieved, though now even more intrigued at how this might have come about. It would make sense, of course. So Ben and Miss Vivian were living among other Waschini. The muscles in his shoulders relaxed, and the uneasiness that had taken up residence in his stomach for the past few days was letting up.

He wondered what Newell was thinking and wanted to share what he had figured out, but before he could say anything, Oh'Dar started talking.

"Let me tell you more about the Sassen. You already know that they are friendly and that they have a language and a culture. They do everything we do; they plan for the future, provide for their families, love their children. But what they do not do is squander Etera's resources and harm others needlessly as we Waschini do."

Ned realized he was holding his breath in rapt attention and let it go.

"If you were to learn to speak their language, you would see for yourselves that everything I'm saying is true. But they are not the people who raised me. They are, as I said, friends of the people who raised me."

Newell asked, "Then who raised you, Grayson? I'm tired and exhausted and worried about Grace, and this suspense is more than I can bear."

"We are going to the Far High Hills, which is a cave system that stretches far back into the mountain range you can see in the distance. It is a community of the People. My people. They have lived in peace for thousands of years. Like the Sassen, they have an organized culture. They plant, harvest, hunt, and fish. They fall in love and pair—marry. The men provide for their families, the women raise the children—at least until the boys are around maybe five, then the fathers get more involved with their sons."

Ned controlled his reaction. That was where they had taken him and Grace. That *was* where Ben and Vivian were living. Among these people.

Ned could contain his excitement no longer. "So that is who Ben and Miss Vivian are living with? Somehow this community was separated from the rest of us and has lived like this for centuries? It makes sense now, Grayson, why you want to protect them from discovery. This is amazing!"

"Not centuries, Ned. Thousands and thousands of years. Back further than we can imagine. But they are not just like us. They are different."

Newell sat up straighter. "Different how?"

"What are you saying? That these people are not us?" Ned asked. "Not white people? A branch of the locals, is that what you are saying? But still like us, only darker-skinned?"

"No, Ned. Not like us or the Brothers. Similar, but not the same. For one thing, they are taller. Much taller."

Pause.

"And broader, stronger. More muscular. And hairier. Though it is not noticeable from a distance, when you get close, you can see they have a fine, downy coat on most of their torso, arms, and legs."

"Are they a branch of these others, these Sassen?"

"In a way, yes. A long time ago, their ancestors

bred with the Brothers. And they are the result," Oh'Dar explained.

Ned knew he was staring at Oh'Dar, but he couldn't help it. "How would that be possible? And, well, I'm sorry to speak so boldly, but I can't imagine wanting to be intimate with any of them."

"We don't exactly know how it happened," Oh'Dar went on to explain. "But somehow it did. And my people are the result. They are called the Akassa."

Newell rubbed his hands over his face and over his head. Then he stood up.

"I believe you, Grayson," he said. "But I also can't believe it. Does that make sense?" He wrapped his blanket tightly around him and started to pace.

"It does. You're not going through anything different than my grandmother and Ben did. Just under different circumstances. This is being forced on you, whereas for them, it was a choice. A choice they made, knowing how it would rock the foundation of what they were sure they *knew* to be true. I am sorry it happened this way. It wouldn't have happened at all if the Brothers' lives were not at risk, but I had to choose. In order to save them, I had to trust you with this or let many of them perish."

"No, you chose correctly," Newell said. "I am just having trouble with it all."

"That is understandable. It is different for me; I was raised among them and the Brothers. It is as natural for me to be around them as it is for you to be around the people at Wilde Edge or Millgrove."

"That is why you had the Morgan Trust formed and bought all the land. To protect them?"

"And the Brothers, yes."

"I would say the Governor didn't know that you owned this land when he dispatched the regiment to collect them," Newell added. "When this is over, I hope you will pay the Governor a visit. The Morgan name still carries a lot of weight. You need to show him a copy of the deed, so he doesn't try to remove any of the other Brothers from their villages."

"So, Grayson," Ned had to ask. "What is this plan that Myrica and Awantia were talking about?"

"The Sassen will take those who are the sickest and the weakest and start transporting them to the Far High Hills," Oh'Dar explained. "They will cut a path through the snow as they go for us to follow later. Those of us who can travel by ourselves will set out when we are able. The People at the Far High Hills will see they are coming and will have made arrangements for emergency care. The Far High Hills is much closer than the Chief's village and is really the only hope many of the Brothers have at this point."

"I will be glad to see Miss Vivian and Ben," Newell said.

Ned heard Oh'Dar sigh.

"My grandmother and Ben are not at the Far High Hills. That is only one community. They are at another, the one I was raised at. It is not far from Chief Is'Taqa's village, where you tracked me to, Newell."

"There is more than one?" Ned asked. "How many?"

"I think you have enough to take in as it is. We are among those in the best shape, so spend part of the day seeing how you can help the others. Then eat heartily tonight and get some rest. And do the same the next day. No doubt the Sassen will start transporting the weakest Brothers tomorrow."

Oh'Dar excused himself and left Ned and Newell alone.

"I can't believe this," Ned said. "It was enough to find out about the Sassen, and now this? Another race of people totally unknown to us?"

"We can't blame them for hiding their existence. Look at what we are doing to the Brothers, or at least, starting to do. They have every right to fear us. It's men like Constable Riggs and others in power who are planning on stealing the Brothers' land and driving them from their homes. I am ashamed of my people."

Ned answered softly, "You are right. No wonder they call us the White Wasters."

"That is what they call us?"

"Yes, Waschini. It means the White Wasters. Because we take and take and don't appreciate it. And now we're also going to take everything the Brothers have. It makes me sick."

Ned stood up to work off his agitation. "We can't let this happen. We have to stop it somehow. I don't want to be a part of this!"

"Grayson's buying the land was a great first step. But it won't help the other villages that aren't on his property."

"It's an abomination. I can't believe anyone would do this to them."

"You have gotten to know these people, Ned. That's why you feel that way. They are real to you. Unfortunately, most people are caught up in their own lives. I wonder if the majority of white people even know this is going on? As slow as news travels, it's hard to say. I would like to believe that the average person would see it as we do. As a terrible wrong."

"You may or may not be right, but that doesn't help them now." Ned fell silent for a moment. "At last I understand. Why the months of testing. Grayson didn't want to see if I could learn how to live more simply, though that was part of it. He was waiting to see if I was truly committed to this. He had to know that before he could reveal the rest of the truth to me. And I failed."

"You didn't fail in learning the basics of living among the Brothers."

"No, I failed at the most important part. How committed I was to this change. But now I know differently. It is bigger and more important than I realized. I saw it as an adventure, not for what it is. It isn't an adventure. It's a cause. There's an important cause here, and that is to protect innocent people from a terrible injustice being done to them by immoral men in power. That's what it is. And to think Grayson could have been hanged—would have gone to his death—to protect the existence of these people. Not just the Sassen but also those who raised him, the Akassa. He couldn't prove Ben and Miss Vivian were alive and well without betraying them."

Ned was pacing rapidly in front of the fire that still burned next to them. "This changes everything." He turned to look at Newell. "My calling was right, only not for the reasons I thought it was. I belong here, with Grayson. Fighting for these people. For their right to live their lives in peace."

"What are you saying?"

"That I'm not going back. Whenever we get out of this, I won't be going back with you. I will have to find a way to write a letter or something explaining it all. You have to make my parents understand. I hope I will be back someday, but it will not be anytime soon. I could never rest again, any more than I could live a normal life, knowing what I now know."

After a moment, he asked, "Do you think I'm crazy?"

"No," Newell smiled. "I think you are a man who just figured out where his place in life lies."

One by one, the giant Sassen bent down to pick up their precious charges. Elderly and ill were wrapped as snugly in blankets as possible, the edges tucked in around them after they were each placed safely in the arms of one of the Sassen. Mothers were lifted, and their children handed up to them. The mothers cradled their little ones between their own body heat and that of the Sassen carrying them.

With their charges, the Sassen made their way to the Far High Hills. They traveled as quickly as they safely could. Front runners cleared a way through the snowdrifts, and those following tamped them down further as they went. It made a clear trail to the Far High Hills, but no Waschini would be in the area in this weather, and the coming snows would soon cover it. A lone eagle circled overhead, now and then letting out a piercing cry.

"They are almost here," High Protector Dreth called out. Harak'Sar, Urilla Wuti, Iella, Nootau, and a host of others were gathered, waiting to help the Brothers the moment they came in. The community had been told what was happening. Many had not attended any High Council meetings so had not had the benefit of seeing the Sassen up close.

A large sick room had been set up, prepared with thick mats and extra hides—all they could find—and

Nootau stood with a group of males ready to help settle those who couldn't walk.

The Sassen entered one by one, stomping the snow from their feet and legs as well as they could. Urilla Wuti and Iella immediately began assessing the condition of each Brother and directing those waiting to help. They had made plans for the worst affected to be placed together to make caring for them more efficient.

It seemed the line would not stop. "How many are there?" High Protector Dreth remarked. "And where are the others?"

"These are the sickest and most helpless. The able-bodied will arrive next," Iella said. "Oh'Dar will be with them, but there are others—"

Khon'Tor nodded. "There are two Waschini with Oh'Dar. He can't leave them behind, so he is forced to bring them here."

"It cannot be helped," Harak'Sar said. "He made the right choice."

"Since they are friends of his," Khon'Tor said, "we can count on them being of good character."

Nootau's heart was warmed at hearing Khon'Tor stand up for Oh'Dar, the Outsider he had rejected and wanted destroyed from the moment he discovered his existence. Khon'Tor had come a long way, and for Nootau, it eased the sting of having learned that this male was his seed father.

Suddenly Pan's words came back to him. "You come from greatness, and you have greatness in you." He realized that he had not *only* come from Acaraho but from Khon'Tor too. It gave him pause. Could she have meant Khon'Tor?

As soon as a Sassen handed over who they were carrying, he or she turned around to fetch another.

Nootau went to his mate and gently rubbed her back as she was examining one of the Brothers, still held in a Sassen embrace. He had seen the growing look of shock on her face as they kept coming and coming and coming, one after another. "Are you alright?"

"Yes," she took a quick moment to reply. "Just overwhelmed at how many there truly are in such bad shape."

Iella stayed in the entrance and continued to sort out the Brothers as they were brought in. Urilla Wuti had gone back to help Adia attend to those who had already arrived. The room was nearly full, and other females were aiding the Healers by hurrying from one to another, doing the best they could to administer what medicinals had been ordered.

"It is still too cold in here. What can we do?" Adia asked Urilla Wuti.

A voice spoke up, "The Sasquatch built us shelters from the storm. Then one stayed inside each shelter with us, blocking the entrance. They warmed us with their body heat."

"Perhaps we can ask them to stay when they are done," Adia said. She assessed the size of the room and did a quick calculation. Luckily it had a low ceiling compared to some they could have chosen and would warm relatively quickly.

Adia turned to one of the females who was helping and asked her to quickly run to Harak'Sar and ask him to get a message to Nimraugh. She didn't know how many they really needed, so it would be better to fit in as many as they could. They had no mats thick enough for the Sassen to sleep on, though, and she felt badly for that.

Harak'Sar asked the next Sassen who was ready to leave to ask Nimraugh if they could help out as they had in the shelters.

Though it seemed like it would never end, finally, the last Brother was settled into the sick room. They had been divided into three groups; those who were in greatest need of care, the mothers and their children, and then those who seemed strong enough to survive without much intervention, many of whom were just undernourished and dehydrated.

Then, slowly, one by one, the Sassen arrived. Harak'Sar introduced himself to the Leader, Nimraugh, and thanked him for what he had done while Urilla Wuti directed them until they were evenly spaced around the room between the sleeping mats. They had to slide some of the mats over to make wider aisles, and it was comforting but also frightening. Even when the Sassen sat, as most did, they were just so huge. But it was a great relief when, before long, the room began to get warmer. Those who were not needed stayed a while standing near the doorway just to block a few drafts.

Eventually, the Sassen's deep rhythmic breathing became a comfort to the Brothers.

"How are we going to feed the Sassen?" Urilla Wuti asked Adia.

The Sassen closest to them spoke. It was Nimraugh. "We will take care of that. We will provide for our own, as well as the Brothers, and will alternate places with each other. We will stay until you no longer need us."

"Thank you," Adia said.

"I am going to return to your son and his two Waschini friends," Nimraugh assured her. "They should be ready to head here tomorrow."

Only Oh'Dar, Ned, and Newell, along with several Sassen, remained in the camp. The Sassen had stayed behind to provide for them so they could rest and recuperate. They were safely huddled in the warm shelter, heated by Ensata, who was one of those who had remained. The horses outside were covered with many blankets and were well fed and watered, also thanks to the Sassen.

Ned and Newell still had not gotten used to seeing Oh'Dar engaged in conversation with a creature such as Ensata. It was a guttural language, and every time they spoke together, it was a reminder that these were intelligent beings despite their frightening appearance.

While Oh'Dar and Ensata were conversing, Ned asked Newell, "Do you realize how powerful these people are?"

"Don't remind me," Newell said. "Instead, tell me again how peaceful they are."

"You don't believe Oh'Dar?" Ned whispered.

"Oh, I do; I was just joking. But it is hard not to be unnerved by their size and appearance. It helps to hear Ensata and Oh'Dar talking."

"It helps me too. Tomorrow we set out for the Far High Hills?"

"That is what Oh'Dar said. If we are up to it. I am; are you?"

"Yes," Ned kept his voice low. "I think I am ready."

"Yes, you look well rested," Newell observed.

"I meant emotionally."

It was time. The three men gathered up their belongings, wrapped themselves in some of the remaining blankets, and mounted the horses. The path had been well-flattened, and the sun was just starting to break through the winter clouds. They were glad for the overnight cloud cover, which had kept the temperatures a little warmer.

Despite the cleared path, it was arduous. There were stretches of open ground and then stands of forest. They went as fast as they could and stopped in the wooded areas when they needed to rest. Oh'Dar searched the skies for the eagle, and each time he found it, he took comfort that those at the Far High Hills knew how their trek was going.

The Sassen made it as easy on them as possible, providing food and water along the way for them and the horses as well. Oh'Dar believed that their care and protection were reassuring to both Ned and Newell.

Ned was left alone with his thoughts for much of the trip. It was a mindless task guiding his horse along the path. Slowly, he was starting to feel comforted by the presence of these gigantic creatures. He knew they weren't creatures but still had trouble not thinking of them as such. He tried to imagine Oh'Dar's life when he was growing up among these people they were about to meet and with those of Chief Is'Taqa's village. How different it had been from his own. If he had been in Oh'Dar's place, would he have fared as well? There was no way of knowing, but his respect for Oh'Dar had quadrupled after learning about his past.

As for how Newell really felt, Ned didn't know. Newell had not said much, and Ned didn't know if it was disapproval because he had decided to stay or if Newell was simply also turning over and over in his own mind the revelations of the past few days.

Ned remembered the letter Miss Vivian had written that had freed Oh'Dar. So there must be paper, quills, and ink somewhere. He would ask if he could write a letter to his family to be delivered by Newell, explaining his reasoning and telling them he would return to visit as soon as possible, most likely in the spring. His parents had understood before, and though they would be disappointed he had changed his mind again, he was confident they would find it in their hearts to understand once more. But who would he be when he went home again? How would this experience change him? How long would it be before he felt life had returned to normal.

He was glad for Myrica and Awantia's friendship and for learning at least enough of their language to get by. And then he realized that he might have another language to learn. He put that thought out of his mind. *If I let my thoughts wander too far ahead, I will be overwhelmed.* He must take this day by day and let it unfold as it would.

The mountainside that enfolded the Far High Hills loomed larger and larger. They were on the last leg of their journey. He looked over at Newell, whose face was expressionless.

The horses stepped into the massive entrance, their hooves clopping on the rock floor. Ahead of them was a small crowd of—giants. There was no other word to describe them. Not as large as the Sassen, but more human-like, so their size was as awe-inspiring as that of the Sassen had been.

There were three men and two women. One of the women was considerably older than the others. The men were larger than the women, hairy, and quite muscular, though the women also looked strong and fit. Ned's immediate impression, other than their size, was that they were a very attractive people. They seemed to glow with health. It was only when he got closer that he noticed the soft undercoat covering their arms and legs. It hit him then that these were not just larger people of his own kind; they were—something else.

The three dismounted, and others came forward to take care of the horses. Before releasing him to their care, Oh'Dar hugged and patted Storm, telling the horse he would be there soon.

One of the women ran over and embraced Oh'Dar. She had tears in her eyes and, after they separated, put her hand on the side of his face in a loving gesture. This must be his mother. Then the older woman and the two men greeted him.

When they were done, Oh'Dar introduced Ned and Newell. Ned felt small as he had to tilt his head back to look up at them.

"This is Harak'Sar, Leader of the People of the Far High Hills. This is his second in command, called the High Protector, and this is his son, Brondin'Sar."

"You are welcome," said Harak'Sar.

"This is my mother, Adia. She and Urilla Wuti here are Healers." As Oh'Dar was speaking, two others entered the chamber. "That is my brother, Nootau, and his wife, Iella. Iella is also a Healer."

There was some conversation, some of which Ned could follow, and then Oh'Dar continued, "Everyone says you are welcome here and to try to calm your fears. You are safe; no harm will come to you. They realize this is a shock, that it will take time for you to feel comfortable, and they understand that."

Ned and Newell both thanked him and tried to look grateful.

"Come, they have places prepared for us to stay; I will explain the system as we walk. We will have the remainder of the day to settle in, and they will let us know when it is time to eat."

One of the women said something else too quickly for Ned to catch, and Oh'Dar explained, "There are new clothes waiting for you. They will fit you loosely, so if you are cold, let me know, and they will add more layers for you or find something better fitting now that they can see your sizes."

Ned looked over at Newell and, for the first time, could clearly see the strain in his face. His lips were tight, and he frankly looked pushed to his limit. Ned felt an urgent need to talk to him and hoped he would be able to very shortly.

Oh'Dar walked on ahead, then turned to wait for

them to follow. They crossed the rock floor of the entrance and headed down a tunnel. The tunnel was spacious, which relieved Ned as he was somewhat claustrophobic. It became darker the further they went, and Ned wondered how they would navigate these in the dark. He wanted to run his hand alongside one wall to keep his bearings but didn't. Thankfully they soon stopped, and Oh'Dar indicated an opening.

He led them into a room that had slightly lighter walls. Then he showed them hanging gourds, which he said had water in them, and other lidded baskets along a shelf, which he said contained nuts and dried fruit. Enough sunlight was coming in through an overhead break in the ceiling, so they could see their surroundings easily enough. Oh'Dar explained that the fluorite stones would need to be recharged whenever there was enough daylight coming in.

After the tour was over, Oh'Dar left them together, reminding them that they could close the wooden door if they wished and that no one would enter the room without first announcing themselves by clacking a rock against the wall.

Once they were alone, Ned blurted out, "Newell, you look like you are about to jump out of your skin. Are you alright?"

Newell ran his hand over his face, then wiped it across his chin. He looked around for something to sit on.

"This should be a dream, but I know it is not. I

don't know what to say, what to think, other than how can this be, and what would happen to these people if they were known to exist? Everything is so clear to me now. The secrecy, Grayson's willingness to take the blame for his grandparents' deaths rather than let the constable and others poke around the area. I am having a difficult time accepting all this, yet I can see it is real and that I am not hallucinating. My mind is just struggling to grasp it all."

"I understand," Ned said. "Having seen what our people would do to the Brothers, who are just like us only with darker skin, what would they do to these people? Or the Sassen?"

"How can they stay hidden forever, though? Grayson was right to buy up as much land as he could, and I wonder if their kind is isolated to only this area."

"Good question. If they are not, he can't buy up all the land everywhere."

"I want a hot bath," Newell said, "though I know that is not possible. I will settle for a cloth wash. I am going to do that and then try to sleep. Maybe when I wake up, this will all have been a dream."

Ned thought otherwise and hoped it was not a dream. He could hardly contain his excitement to learn more about these people.

CHAPTER 19

Moart'Tor had come to a decision about his future. Though he had thought he would not return home, he had now decided he would. He sought out Haan to explain.

"Though I thought different before, I have decided to return to Zuenerth."

Haan said nothing, so Moart'Tor continued. "I will not betray you or your people, nor the Guardian. I appreciate your offer to stay among you, but I need to return home."

"What will you tell your father?" Haan said.

"Simply that I failed. That I could not find Kayerm. He will rejoice at my return. I am ashamed for my deceit, and I must make amends to you. I will not betray you, I promise. I will stay until the Guardian returns, as I wish to explain this to her myself and not simply have her return to find me gone."

Haan was certain that the Guardian had somehow heard everything Moart'Tor had said but did not comment. "I will tell the others you will be leaving soon. It will give them time to say their goodbyes."

Over the next few days, many of the Sassen who had returned to Kayerm to give Moart'Tor a chance to get to know them sought him out. The Mothoc spoke with each one for some time, expressing his regret for his behavior. The kindness and understanding in their eyes and words touched him deeply, which made him even more ashamed of how wrong his people were about them. He noticed that Eitel hung back and wondered if perhaps she would not say goodbye to him. He had rebuked her offer of friendship, and perhaps that still stung.

Finally, he went to her instead. "I will be leaving Kayerm and wanted to say goodbye now in case there is no opportunity later. Thank you for extending your friendship to me. I am sorry I did not accept it and get to know you better."

Moart'Tor's regret deepened as he looked into her soft eyes that were filled with kindness. She was beautiful, inside and out, but his prejudice had kept him from seeing that.

"I wish you would not go. You could make a life here with us," she said quietly.

"For a time, I thought I might. But I know now I must return home."

"No doubt I will never see you again," Eitel said sadly. "I have to go. Please take care of yourself," and she turned away from him.

Moart'Tor watched her walk away. Her brother had been watching from a distance and put his arm around her when she reached him. She leaned into his shoulder as they walked, and Naahb gave Moart'Tor a backward glance, but that was all.

In her brother's position, Moart'Tor thought he would perhaps have acted the same. He had hurt Eitel and totally unnecessarily.

He felt a heaviness in his heart that he could not name.

Life went on at Kayerm while everyone waited for Pan to return. The Sassen had told Haan they would stay until Moart'Tor left. Moart'Tor did not know how to summon the Guardian, so he simply waited, confident that when the time was right, she would show herself, and he could explain in person why he was returning to Zuenerth.

Days passed, and the Brothers at the Far High Hills started recovering. The Sassen's body heat had helped immensely. Caring for the sickly Brothers and the Sassen taking turns at their posts or going out to forage or hunt had become a routine. Everyone moved with synchronicity. Tiponi had recovered enough to start helping care for her own people. Though she was amazed at the existence of the Far High Hills, she put it out of her mind to be mulled over later. For now, there was work to do.

Tiponi watched the People's Healers go about their ways. As she had been at the High Council meeting at the High Rocks, she was fascinated at how they applied many of the same medicinals she used. She asked questions only now and then, not wanting to interrupt. She found she was drawing closer to Iella, the one who spoke with the forest creatures. Iella was kind-hearted and patient, and the two soon developed an affinity for each other.

The Brothers were recovering and would soon be able to leave, so Urilla Wuti decided it was time to hold a High Council meeting after all. To keep commotion away from Kthama, she declared that it would take place here at the Far High Hills. It was not as large and accommodating as the High Rocks, but they would have to make do.

Harak'Sar sent messages to the other communities as well as the Brothers' Chiefs.

That being settled, Urilla Wuti went to Tiponi and Chief Kotori and explained that the High Council meeting would be held there and would take place at the next new moon.

"My people are well enough to return home," the Chief said. "Once we are settled, Tiponi and I will return for the meeting. We have learned much here, and I wish to express gratitude to the entire brother-hood for your care and help. Both to your people as well as to Oh'Mah.

"I also wish to tell the other communities of my people about the good will of these three Waschini," Chief Kotori added. "We must all fight prejudice against others. They have shown that it is as wrong for me to believe they are all evil as it is for the Waschini to see us as only an enemy. Yet, the threat the Waschini pose is still very real."

Urilla Wuti knew that the Chief was also speaking of the Waschini threat to the People's exis-tence, as well as that of the Sassen, should the Waschini find out about them. In the back of her mind was a concern about whether the two Waschini, Ned and Newell, would be able to keep their existence secret forever.

The village was nearly in sight. The trip home had been bittersweet. The children were excited, and the mothers were happy to see them so. Kele rode most of the way on Nimraugh's shoulders, enjoying the warmth and comfort of the shaggy Sassen, inter-twining his fingers in the thick coat to steady himself. Nimraugh kept one hand resting gently against Kele, making sure he didn't tumble off somehow. Kele kept pointing to this and that along the way. The young boy's innocent joy lifted everyone's spirits.

Myrica and Awantia held hands and stepped in union the last part of the way, laughing at each other for their silliness. The children who were close saw them and did the same, enjoying the levity.

When they arrived, tears came to the eyes of many at seeing how some of the Sassen had gone on ahead and prepared the village for their homecoming. Weeks of work already taken care of for them. The large stacks of kindling and wood, the cleaned-out fire pits. The shelters had been reinforced and more branches added to the outsides. The Sassen had gathered up dried grasses and made plentiful beds in the shelters, which would soon be covered with the Brothers' blankets and hide coverings. The Sassen had collected a mountain of kindling and branches for their fires. Others had returned to Kthama Minor and had brought back medicinal supplies from their own stores. For a while, the Sassen would hunt for them to give them time to re-establish their way of life.

The families returned to their shelters, again with many tears. Some were tears of joy, and some were tears of relief. Some were just tears of exhaustion. They were home, but because of their abduction, it would never be the same.

Tiponi marveled at the abundant supplies the Sassen had brought. They had even built separate shelters to store everything. Sitting down in the midst of the piles of goldenseal, dried cornflower, wild onion, acorns, and potatoes, she bowed her head and thanked the Great Spirit for the provision and the kindness of the Sassen in doing this for her and her people.

That evening, they all had a hearty meal of roasted venison and potatoes. Instead of individual family fires, everyone gathered around a huge village fire.

The children basked in the waves of heat coming off the flames. The pungent smell of burning wood comforted them. Sparks drifted upward, symbolizing their prayers of gratitude and thanks. The snow, which had besieged them so greatly not so long ago, now fell lightly, and this time its great fluffy flakes seemed to add a magical quality to the scene.

Ensata had stayed with the Brothers along with Nimraugh. But soon, they would return home themselves, though, by agreement with Chief Kotori, who had now accepted Haan's offer of help, many would stay and live in the area as watchers. The Brothers would never again be surprised by the Waschini, though Oh'Dar had assured them that he would visit the one he called the Governor to do all he could to make sure they were never bothered again.

"Were you not happy to see Ned Webb again?" Awantia asked Myrica.

Myrica licked the rest of the meal off her fingers. "I, like everyone else, am grateful for their help. Are you going to eat the rest of that?" She pointed to the stick Awantia was hanging on to. It was a little rude to ask so directly, but they were friends, so Awantia just laughed and handed Myrica her unfinished portion.

"You did not answer my question," Awantia said.

"Of course, I was happy, but not in the way you are hinting at!" Myrica said, tearing off a piece of meat with her teeth. After she had chewed and swallowed, she added, "Why are you trying to pair me off with him? What do I need with a Waschini life-walker?"

"You discourage all the other men. It just seems like you are waiting for—someone else."

"I am waiting for someone, and I will know him when I meet him—and it is not the Waschini, I can tell you that. Now tell the other women to stop whispering about it behind my back. Or better yet, I will."

"Do not be harsh. Everyone just wants to see you happy. As I do."

"You all think Ned Webb is interested in me, but the truth is, Awantia, my friend, you were the one he spent the most time with."

"Pffft. You suggested I teach him. That is all there is to that."

"You two would be a good fit; he respects you and he sees your value. And I have often overheard you laughing together. He is not useless like he was when he came here. He would be a good provider for you."

"All that is good, but I want more than that."

"What is there more than that?"

"I want love. I want my life-walker to love me," Awantia said. "It is what you want, too; admit it!"

"Then both you and I want too much. A good provider, a strong, brave man to protect us and our children. One whose aim is as true as he is wise. That is the best any woman can ask for. Where did you get this notion of love?"

"Too many children's tales, I imagine. But that is what I want. That is what we all deserve. To love and be loved by someone who can see no other but us."

Myrica fell silent. "I suppose you are right, and I do not mean to be disparaging. But for most of us, that will never come. We will be lucky to find a mate at all. There is no one here either of us is interested in. But with the tribes coming together more frequently now, and if we attend the High Council meetings, perhaps we will meet the right one that way."

Awantia thought to herself, *I have already met that someone.* But despite what Myrica said, he does not seem to know she was alive.

Knowing the High Council assembly was not long off, Oh'Dar went to check in on Ned and Newell. He found them both together, chatting.

"I am astounded by what we have seen," Ned said. "There is no other word for it. Grayson, you probably do not believe me as I said this once before and then backed out, but I want to stay with you. I can tell you I will not change my mind this time. I can't go back to everyday life, not after seeing what I have. I want to help you. I want to help protect the Brothers. I know that this is where I belong."

Oh'Dar wasn't sure if he was surprised by this or not. Ned's excitement had hinted at it, and his staying would present no threat as long as he remained hidden from any other Waschini. He already knew too much, and anything else he learned would probably only bind him to this new life further. So something good had come out of it; Ned had found his place in the world.

Newell finally spoke. "I have no words to describe what I've experienced. For the first few days, I truly considered whether this might be a dream—a very real, very detailed dream. I am past that now, though. As Ned said, it is beyond believability, yet it is real. I know you have noticed how quiet I have been. I am consumed with terrible imaginings of what our kind would do if they discovered the existence of either the People or the Sassen. Though I have gone over and over it a hundred times, I am at a loss about what to do to protect them."

A tight knot Oh'Dar hadn't known was there undid itself at hearing Newell's words. Now he could let his fears go. He could trust Newell.

"I understand your drive to help them," Newell said to Ned. "And I support your staying here. For myself, I can best help as who I am. As a lawyer. Your idea to buy up the land was genius, Grayson. Though, how long it will stand up to protect those living on the Morgan Trust property, we cannot know."

"Thank you both," Oh'Dar said. "A great meeting is about to take place. At this meeting will be the Chiefs and Healers from many villages, as well as many of the Akassa Leaders and Healers, and the same for the Sassen. Yet others will visit with them. You are welcome to stay in your quarters if you find it overwhelming."

"No," Ned almost shouted. "I want to experience it all, no matter if it is overwhelming!"

"I agree," Newell added. "I don't want to miss anything while I am here, but I want to get home to Grace as soon as I can." He absentmindedly patted the satchel he had brought with him, the one carrying his Waschini clothes.

Oh'Dar explained the purpose of the High Council meeting and how everyone was coming together to try and find solutions to their shared and their localized challenges.

"Just as there are differences among our kind— my grandmother has red hair, my eyes are blue, Newell's are hazel, some are taller, some stouter, so you will see individual variations at the gathering."

"Your people seem homogenous, though," Newell observed.

"You are probably mostly right, yet there are

some which display greater variation. But among the Sassen, there are those that are silver-white. They hold a special position within our culture. They are called Guardians, and they are stronger and have greater abilities than the rest of the Sassen. There are twelve in total. And then there is The Guardian of Etera. Her name is Pan. At this stage, we do not know if she or any of the Sassen Guardians will attend."

"She is one of the Sassen?" Ned asked.

"Similar, but she is actually one of the Ancients." Oh'Dar then went into the history of the Mothoc and how they chose to introduce the Brothers' bloodline into theirs rather than become extinct. He did his best to convey the desperation of the times and the link of the Mothoc to the life of the planet itself. When he had finished, both men were silent for a long time. Only the night sounds in the background broke the stillness.

Finally, Newell spoke, "This all took place thousands of years ago? And this Guardian is still alive?"

"Yes. Thousands, as in multiples. The Sassen and Mothoc live far longer than we do. Guardians are said to be practically immortal."

Before continuing, Oh'Dar gave them a moment to process what he had just told them. "After this meeting, we will travel to my home, and you can see Ben and my grandmother. It will look much like where we just were, with the same way of life."

"I can only imagine what your grandparents went

through at first," said Ned. "So much to learn, so many unimagined possibilities."

When he reached the Far High Hills, Acaraho was greatly relieved to see Adia and their offspring again. He held her for a very long time and relished how she surrendered to his embrace and how her body molded to his. "I have missed you so, Saraste'," he whispered into her luxurious hair as he nuzzled her ear.

"Me too. My heart aches to be home with you. Do you have any idea how much longer we must stay here?"

"No, we have not heard from Pan in a long time, and Haan's people are still at Kayerm. That is why the High Council meeting was moved here, I was told. Too much coming and going might have drawn Moart'Tor's attention to Kthama. So far as we know, he has not wandered past the boundaries set for him, but that could change at any moment. We just have no way of knowing."

Then Acaraho turned his attention to their offspring. An'Kru was playing on the floor with some pine cones and sticks. He had built little structures in which he moved little stones in and out in a hopping motion, no doubt pretending they were rabbits. The twins were lying wrapped up next to him, their little heads turned as if fascinated with what their older brother was doing.

"What are your plans for them at the assembly?" he asked.

"I prefer to keep them out of it. There will be so much going on, and with the two Waschini here, I still do not want to reveal An'Kru to them."

"I agree with your decision. It is possible, though unlikely, that someone would mention An'Kru to them, but it is another element to explain, and they do not yet have a solid understanding of our culture or our past. It can come later. If anyone asks where he is, I will explain that you have chosen to keep him away from the commotion."

Finally, the first day of the assembly came. By the time Oh'Dar, Ned, and Newell arrived in the large meeting room, nearly everyone else had as well. Ned and Newell waited off to the side, taking it all in before going to sit down. Then from behind a group of people, Ned saw a young woman rushing toward Oh'Dar. They caught each other up in a warm and enthusiastic embrace, and then Oh'Dar lifted her up till her feet left the floor. Ned smiled broadly at the reunion. Honovi was there too, carrying a bundle in her arms.

They chatted amongst themselves for a moment,

then Oh'Dar brought Acise and Honovi over to greet the men.

"How are you faring with all of this?" Honovi asked them.

"Better with each passing day," Ned answered. Newell said he was managing but still struggling with some things.

Oh'Dar motioned to the bundle Honovi was holding. "This is our daughter, I'Layah."

Honovi pulled back the blanket so the men could see her.

"Gracious," Newell exclaimed, looking from the red-headed baby over to Oh'Dar.

"I know. It complicates matters, does it not?" Oh'Dar remarked. "She will be raised, as I was, here among the People and the Brothers. Due to her coloring, we must just be judicious with our visits to Chief Is'Taqa's village. Hopefully, however, the constable has learned his lesson."

"This further reinforces my position, Grayson." Newell straightened up, standing taller. "You must visit the Governor. You must impress upon him that he has no jurisdiction on the Morgan Trust property. I will go with you if you wish."

Oh'Dar let out a long breath. "I am so tired of traveling. I wish only to settle down and live my life. But I know what you are saying is what I must do."

Before long, Tiponi joined their group. "I admit, I am glad to be among others of our size," she said.

Ned smiled.

Then Tiponi saw that Honovi was holding a baby, she peered in at her as the others had and had the same reaction to her coloring. "We have gotten used to Oh'Dar's eyes, but the color of her hair is unprecedented!"

"Will all your people make a full recovery?" Honovi translated Newell's question to Tiponi.

"I believe so. We nearly lost several of our elders, but the Sassen's body heat made the difference. We are told they will stay until our winter food stores are sufficient. Some will remain in the area, though, as watchers."

"I will be going back to my own home after this meeting," the attorney said. "I promise I will do whatever I can to help you, as well as the others here."

"As for you," she said to Ned, "I hear you are staying here with Oh'Dar?"

"Yes. I, too, must do my part to help, and my heart is here."

◎

Moart'Tor waited patiently, though keeping some distance from the Sassen. He had made up his mind to leave, and he did not want to get any more friendly with the people there. He did his best to insulate his heart as he was already feeling the pain of leaving them.

He was both relieved and saddened when Pan

finally appeared to him one morning.

"I have been waiting for you," Moart'Tor said.

"I know. The time was not right for my return. You have decided to go home?"

"Yes. It is for the best. I hope you trust me not to betray the Sassen to my father?"

"I do, but before you go, there is something I want to show you."

Acaraho, Haan, and Urilla Wuti stood at the front with Harak'Sar as he opened the assembly. The Leader took a moment to welcome the new attendees, this time even asking them to stand.

In preparing for the event, Harak'Sar had asked Acaraho to explain the presence of the two new Waschini among them. He took the floor and briefly outlined the abduction of Chief Kotori and his people. He went on to describe how Oh'Dar, Ned Webb, and Newell Storis had helped free them, and with the immense help of the Sassen, taken them to the Far High Hills for care.

As arranged, Chief Kotori stood. He described the devastation of being taken from their homes with few supplies and made to walk for days on end. He described the children's distress, that of the adults, and the horrors all his people had suffered. He said how blessed they were to have been rescued just when a terrible death was staring in the face of so many. He thanked the Sassen and the three Waschini and declared it to be proof that not all Waschini were evil and that they should not all be judged as such. He commented on how it had greatly lifted his people's spirits to know that Oh'Mah was with them in such robust numbers.

When he mentioned the Waschini's help, heads turned to look at Ned Webb and Newell Storis, sitting in the back with Oh'Dar and his family. Some faces were smiling, and others remained stoic.

Oh'Dar was sitting with Ned and Newell on one side of him and his wife and daughter on the other. Behind him were Nootau and Iella. When the Chief finished speaking, Oh'Dar turned back to Iella. "Thank you for sending the crow. It gave me the strength to make the decision I must, to take the Brothers and the Waschini to the Far High Hills."

Iella looked at her mate, then back at Oh'Dar. "I sent the forest animals and the eagles. I did not send a crow."

Oh'Dar realized that at the time of his greatest despair and need, his prayers had been heard. It was the Great Spirit who had sent the crow.

Over the next few days, even deeper connections formed. Hearing Chief Kotori's tragic story had reinforced the importance of what lay before them to do.

In the Healer's Group, Apricoria told them of the

latest vision she had experienced of the destruction the Waschini would bring to Etera. Urilla Wuti asked her to share it with the entire assembly on the final day.

During their free time, members of the individual groups started to mingle more with the others. Many, Brothers and Sassen alike, gathered around I'Layah to marvel at her distinctive coloring.

Ned and Newell kept to themselves much of the time. Though Ned could understand some of the Brothers' language, there were so many speaking at once and so quickly that he could not process much of what was being said. The Sassen and the People towered over the Brothers and the Waschini, and it sometimes became too much. They found they did periodically have to retreat to their room in order to handle it.

Eventually, the final day of the assembly arrived. Urilla Wuti, as Overseer, was to close the session. Standing at the front with her were Harak'Sar, Acaraho, Haan, and Apricoria.

Urilla Wuti explained that Apricoria was among the Healers and Helpers who, at the previous High Council meeting, had been granted in person a special gift by the Guardian, Pan. The Overseer then asked Apricoria to speak about her gift.

The young healer looked tentatively at Urilla

Wuti and then found the courage to speak. She took a few steps forward. "I have been given the ability to see events before they happen. It is not a gift I control; it comes to me unbidden, and I do not know the source. The visions appear in my mind, complete with sights, sounds, smells, and emotions. So it is with great concern and humility that I share what I was recently shown."

Apricoria cleared her throat. "We all know of the Waschini threat to the Brothers. Chief Kotori has told us about the cruel treatment he and his people received at their hands. But the persecution of the Brothers has only begun. In the upcoming years, more and more of the Brothers will be removed from their homes. They will be taken far away, to other places. Barren places. Places without the resources and blessings of where they now live. But in time, the Waschini's self-serving motives will harm more than the Brothers.

"We have heard it said that the Waschini are among the most inventive of all who live on Etera. This inventiveness will, in part, be channeled to good, but not always. In time, they will discover a power hidden within Etera, an amazing secret force that will allow them to develop many different contraptions. The spread of it will be slow, and in the beginning, this will seem only to be a good thing, making their lives easier. But eventually, these artificial creations will move to the forefront of all they do.

"These inventions will start to dominate their way of life. They will not only lighten the burden of their labor, but they will entertain them, capturing their attention with their vivid flashing colors and loud sounds. The devices will distract them from how hollow their lives are becoming, lives lived only to acquire more ease, more conveniences, greater entertainment for themselves.

"They will push their appreciation for Etera and her gifts into the background, trampling her under their rush for more and more of these artificial distractions. Their hearts will grow silent, deafened to the longing of their souls for connection to the Great Spirit."

The room was dead silent.

"The voice of Etera calling to them to commune with her will fade from their awareness, lost in the din of their inventions which will mimic the joys of life but give none of the satisfaction. As their greed multiplies, they will strip Etera of her resources—whatever it takes to supply bigger, better, more mesmerizing tools. And competition between the Waschini and other similar groups of people will escalate. In time, they will develop powerful weapons on a scale far more devastating than the few we already know about. These weapons will have the power to destroy all of Etera, to make it entirely uninhabitable for a length of time I could not see the end of."

The audience remained entirely silent.

"There is no doubt in my mind, my heart, and my soul. If the Waschini and the other lost ones are not turned from their present path and brought back into harmony with each other and the Great Spirit, they will end up destroying Etera along with all other life on her."

Urilla Wuti moved quietly to stand beside Apricoria. "We have no time to lose. Apricoria could not tell how far off this possible future is. And I do say possible because, as we all do, the Waschini have free will. The future is not set. This terrible future may be the path they are headed down, but it can be averted. I do not know how, but I know that we cannot assume we are powerless to change it."

Acaraho spoke. "The Guardian, Pan, said that the Brothers are the key to saving Etera. Therefore, we must do all we can to help prepare you to become the teacher of the White Wasters. You must learn to speak their language, not only so you are not at a disadvantage if the Waschini come to your village, but also so you can communicate with them under other circumstances. Every change we make, every inroad into convincing them to listen to you, to learn to live in harmony with the Great Spirit, is one more step toward heading off the future that Apricoria has seen.

"You have heard me speak of a brotherhood. Our brotherhood, which I see becoming stronger each time we come together; this is the unity that will save Etera if that is possible. And I believe it is. We have heard of the atrocities of the Waschini, but I must remind you, as Chief Kotori has, that not every Waschini is evil. You know of my son, Oh'Dar, rescued as a tiny offspring by my mate Adia and raised among us and the Brothers. His grandparents live among us at the High Rocks, and they are committed to helping us, just as Oh'Dar is. I am sure you have noticed that Oh'Dar is here with two other Waschini. They will come to the front now."

Oh'Dar had warned Ned and Newell of this, and they were prepared.

The three walked to the front, and Oh'Dar spoke first. "You know my story and that of my grandparents, Ben and Miss Vivian. Many of you have met my life-walker, Acise, first daughter of Chief Is'Taqa.

"Standing with me now are two friends of mine, the two Chief Kotori spoke of who came with me to return him and his people to their homes. Their names are Ned Webb and Newell Storis. Newell Storis has helped me in the past. He has made it possible for me to limit where the Waschini will now be allowed to travel. As a result, all your villages are protected from the Waschini, but how long that protection will be honored, even though it is based on Waschini laws, remains to be seen. Newell Storis will be returning to the Waschini world to help us further, but Ned Webb will be staying here. He wishes to join forces directly with us to help protect the Brothers and defend them from those of his kind who would harm them."

Ned had not planned on speaking, but he was so moved that he turned to Oh'Dar and asked if he might address the council and if Oh'Dar would help him if he said anything incorrectly.

He took an awkward step forward and looked into the sea of varied faces staring back at him. He almost lost his nerve but steeled himself to speak in the language he had started learning so many months ago.

"I am Ned Webb. I am Waschini, as you can see, but I stand with you. I came with Oh'Dar to stop the wrongful abduction by my people of Chief Kotori and his people. I am choosing to remain with Oh'Dar and his grandparents and immediate family, who are already living among the People of the High Rocks. This is because I see the honor and decency of all of you, and I am ashamed to my core of what my people are doing. I must help. I am not sure how, but, as you can hear, I am learning to speak your language. Perhaps, one day, I could go into the Brothers' villages and teach those willing to learn how to speak Whitespeak."

Chief Kotori stood. "I welcome your help. It is a good plan, Ned Webb. But it is not good that you should travel alone. I will send one of my braves to accompany you when it is time." Then he sat back down.

Other Chiefs murmured their agreement, as did many of the Medicine Men and Medicine Women present.

Ned clasped his hands in front of himself and said, "Thank you. Thank you. That is all I wanted to say." Somewhat awkwardly, he stepped back to stand again with Newell.

Harak'Sar made a few closing remarks, and then the assembly was officially over. The room became a sea of motion as some sought out their new friends to say goodbye. Chiefs conferred with each other, and some came forward to encourage Ned Webb and Newell Storis, telling them they would welcome their help however it came. The Healers and Helpers exchanged last words. There were embraces, smiles, laughter, and some sadness. The chamber was filled with different voices, and different tones, all beautifully blending together to create a pleasant clamor. And the energy that filled the room was one of friendship, love, and unity.

CHAPTER 20

Pan turned to Moart'Tor, whom she had brought with her to watch the last day of the High Council meeting. They were unseen by the others as Pan's powers allowed them to be present yet unnoticed.

"So those are the Akassa. They are not that different from the Brothers. You brought me here to witness this before I left. Why?"

"I wanted you to see for yourself the Akassa, the Sassen, and the Brothers working together in harmony. In brotherhood. I wanted you to witness the good will and even the love between them. This. This is what your father would destroy. Tell me, Moart'Tor, what you have learned by coming here?"

He answered her, "That the Sassen are very much like us and the Akassa are very much like the Brothers, our wards. If the Sassen and Akassa come from the Fathers-of-Us-All, how can they be evil? Why would our protection not extend to them both, as it does the Brothers, when it is our blood and the Brothers' blood that flows in their veins."

Pan waited while Moart'Tor collected his thoughts. He finally looked up, and she saw deep compassion and sadness in his eyes.

"They are just like us," he said. "They love, they care for their offling. They protect them. They provide for them. They laugh together, and they praise the Great Spirit. Why would the Great Spirit consider them an abomination when they are no different from us, other than some physical differences? How does that make them an abomination? If they are an abomination, then it would show in their deeds, and yet I see none of that. I see no reason for either the Akassa or the Sassen to be destroyed, no reason to think the Great Spirit would want them to be wiped from the face of Etera."

Then Pan asked, "So answer me one last question. Where is the abomination?"

Moart'Tor lowered his head. "The only abomination I know of is the hatred in my father's heart."

Pan reached out and touched his face gently, so he would lift it again and her silver eyes could meet his.

"Look at me, Moart'Tor, son of Dak'Tor, son of Moc'Tor and E'ranale and kin to Straf'Tor from the time of The Fathers-of-Us-All. I need your help. Not only to save the Akassa and Sassen but, if there is any way, also to save those at Zuenerth.

"Will you stand with me?"

Newell was ready to leave as soon as possible. He had his Waschini clothes clean and ready to pack. Though he did not think he would ever need them again, he would keep the Brothers' clothing he had been given. He did not intend to return, and in the end, his mind had reached the limit of what it could handle. He was anxious to get back to the familiar and the routine and into the arms of his loving wife.

Oh'Dar, Ned, and Newell traveled to Kthama on horseback by taking the route above ground. Oh'Dar purposefully took them on a roundabout path, obscure, with few notable landmarks. He was still cautious. Newell was hard to read, seeming to keep tight control of himself. It gave Oh'Dar pause as he could not tell what the lawyer was thinking.

Finally, they came up the steep path to Kthama's Great Entrance. The fact that this new system looked very much like the other gave both men some relief. There was the same huge cavern, though this one seemed larger and had moisture dripping from the ceiling. Ned realized this explained the dampness he had felt when he was brought to see Ben and Miss Vivian. He could see that the Great Entrance was much like the one at the Far High Hills, only the moisture raining gently down in places from the high ceiling overhead answered the question of where the dripping sound had come from. The whole system was more humid than the Far High Hills, which Oh'Dar explained was coming from an underground river that snaked through Kthama's lowest levels.

Miss Vivian looked up from her sewing when she heard the announcement clack. "Oh, they're here!" she exclaimed to Ben.

He rose and hobbled over on his crutch to join her at the wooden door. It was pushed open, and there stood Oh'Dar along with Ned and Newell Storis.

"Oh my!" Miss Vivian exclaimed, embracing her grandson and smiling warmly at the others. "I can't imagine what you have all been through."

"I will tell you all about it, I promise," Oh'Dar said.

Ned looked around the room. "Yes, this is the same room Grace and I were in," he said absentmindedly.

"Grayson did his best to make us comfortable," said Miss Vivian.

"You both look as if you have been through a lot," Ben remarked. "I see you are all wearing the Brothers' clothing."

Newell looked down at the hide wraps covering him. "They are comfortable. I will regret having to go back to Waschini clothing." It wasn't strictly true, but he meant it in the spirit given.

Miss Vivian smiled, perhaps at Storis' use of the term Waschini.

"Learning that there are other kinds of people on Etera changes the perspective, doesn't it?" she said.

"In so many ways," Newell answered. "However, I am anxious to get home. Grace moved in with her parents, which was a great relief for me, but they must all be worried by now."

"That is one of the main drawbacks of living here. There's no way to get a message through," she commented.

Ned spoke up. "Miss Vivian, I have decided to stay here with you, Ben, and Oh'Dar. This will be my life now, and if you can spare the materials, I would like to write letters for Newell to take back to my parents and Grace. I want to explain my decision as carefully as possible without revealing anything critical and assure them I will be back to visit as soon as I am able. As we agreed before, they will have to tell people who ask that I am helping out a friend's elderly relatives."

Then Ned added. "This underscores the need for the ruse about your deaths. Goodness, do I understand that even more clearly now."

The next day, Oh'Dar and Ned took Newell to Chief Is'Taqa's village and helped him make ready to leave.

Newell was ready for the return trip with the map

he had made, the same one that had brought Ned and Grace there. He was glad to be wearing familiar clothing. It reminded him who he was and helped brush away some of the confusion his mind was still struggling to handle. He admired Ned for his decision to follow his passion, but Newell needed the structure and order of the life he knew. Perhaps that was why he became a lawyer. It gave him the means to exert some control, to bring life back into line when it got out of sorts.

As Newell was about to leave, Ned held out several sealed letters, which the lawyer took and tucked into his jacket pocket. He would deliver them to Ned's parents and his sister, Grace.

"I will do my best to help them understand your decision and what changed your mind," Newell said to Ned. Then he turned to Oh'Dar. "I will choose my words carefully when I tell them of our experiences. If there is anything I can do to help, let me know."

Oh'Dar nodded. "Take care. I have to see the Governor, and depending on the outcome, I may see you sooner than we both think."

Newell shook Oh'Dar's hand and then Ned's.

"Don't forget to tell my family I will be back next spring. Somehow!" Ned added, just as the lawyer flicked the reins.

CHAPTER 21

It had been months since Moart'Tor had left what was known to the People as the rebel camp. Formed thousands of years ago at the time of the great division when the followers of Moc'Tor and Straf'Tor went their separate ways, the community had lived in exile, waiting for the day when they could eliminate the Akassa and Sassen from Etera.

Their first Leader, Laborn, had been killed, replaced by one named Kaisak.

Visha paced around the evening fire outside their personal dwelling at Zuenerth. As it was situated away from the rest of the community, she did not have to contain her agitation. Her arms waved around as she ranted.

"Where is Moart'Tor? Why has he not returned? Have the Sassen captured him? Perhaps killed him?

Maybe you were wrong; maybe the Mothoc did not accept him? Did not give him sanctuary?"

Her mate, Kaisak, sat watching her, knowing he would be wise not to say anything that would add to her emotion. He wondered if they were indeed far enough away that her raised voice would not reach the others. "Moart'Tor is fine. Do you not believe that if he were dead, you would feel it. You are his mother."

"I do not know; I just do not know." She continued to pace as she lamented her son's possible fate. Then she stopped and faced her mate. "You must send someone after him. You must."

"That would not be wise. Please, try to calm down and listen to me." The moment the words were out of his mouth, he knew they were wrong.

Visha sent him a look that would have killed a lesser male.

"There are two possibilities," he tried again. "Perhaps it is as you have said, that they have captured and killed him, but that is not likely. He has done nothing wrong, and they would have no cause to do so. Mothoc will not rise against Mothoc, nor would they let the Sassen harm him. The more likely possibility is that he is busy gathering the information we sent him there to find. He will be back soon enough, and we will know how many Sassen and Akassa there are living with the Mothoc at Kayerm and Kthama. And we will know more about the Promised One and when he might be born if he has not already been. Remember, we cannot move against them without knowing their numbers and strengths."

Kaisak waited for a reaction and, seeing that what he had said at least hadn't inflamed his mate further, continued. "In either case, sending others there would not improve the situation. If he is alive, and I truly believe he is, they have accepted the story we gave him about sneaking away and going there to seek sanctuary. And more of our people showing up would only contradict what he was to tell them."

"You should not have sent him to Kayerm with the Sassen," Visha barked. "You should have sent him to the High Rocks. There is no way the puny Akassa could have kept him there against his will. The plan was to send him to Kthama!"

Kaisak held his tongue. He was tired of her bringing up that point. Yes, they had originally planned to send him to the High Rocks, but she kept forgetting that they no longer knew how to find it. The memory had somehow been erased. And there were just as many Mothoc at Kthama as at Kayerm, no doubt. So if she really believed the Mothoc would have harmed him at Kayerm, there was no reason to believe they wouldn't equally have done so at the High Rocks. But his mate was high-tempered even on a good day, and he knew that in her present emotional state, his logic would only make matters worse.

"Saraste', we must wait. We must be patient."

"How long?" Visha demanded, angrily stomping her foot. Even from a distance, the vibration sent embers flying high into the night. "How much longer must we be patient?

Kaisak let out a long breath. "As long as it takes. As long as it takes."

All offling at Zuenerth were raised with the Leader's belief that their cause to correct the mistakes of the Ancients by removing the Akassa and Sassen from Etera was just. And from the beginning of their union, Kaisak had gotten Visha to agree that her offling, Moart'Tor, who had been seeded by the Guardian's brother, would play a critical role in bringing their plans to fruition.

The Guardian had visited Zuenerth once, though she had known it only as the rebel camp. At that time, she had talked of the Promised One, but only briefly. Her brother, Dak'Tor, professed to know no more than the little she had shared, and he had never changed his position through the centuries since he arrived.

And they had been long centuries.

Though the community had grown in numbers, they were still faced with a limited number of safe breeding combinations. It was a long time since any new offling had been born. And the population was aging. Kaisak still had a while to finish his mission, but he did not have forever.

So Moart'Tor had been sent to learn what he could and bring that information back to them.

Visha, possibly exhausted by her own uncontrolled outburst, plopped down on the ground across from Kaisak. She leaned forward, resting her elbows on her knees and her head in her hands. Kaisak prayed she was not crying. He did love her, and even as difficult as she was to live with, he could not bear to see her hurt. He would rather have her furious with him than see tears in her eyes.

Kaisak said as gently as he could, "The longer he stays, the more he learns about their culture, their routines, and potential weaknesses. We must trust that he will return when he feels the time is right. No matter how long it takes. We only have one chance at this. Moart'Tor, son of the Guardian's brother, was the only one we could send. He will not fail us."

Kaisak could not explain to his mate that if by some wild chance she was right and the Mothoc had killed her son, sending others to their deaths was not a choice he would make. Moart'Tor was *her* son, not his, though when he had asked Visha to pair with him, he had vowed to raise and treat him as his own. But each time he looked at him, he saw the father in the son.

And in the end, Kaisak had never been able to set aside that it was Dak'Tor, brother to the Guardian, who had sired Moart'Tor.

And for that reason, Moart'Tor was expendable.

EPILOGUE

The Far High Hills had returned to normal. Adia had said goodbye to her beloved, and with their three youngest offspring all resting peacefully was hoping she would soon be able to return to Kthama.

Her thoughts returned to the conversation with Nadiwani about how she considered herself to have been greatly blessed, despite the challenges of her life.

It seemed centuries ago, not decades since she had lifted Oh'Dar from his box on the Waschini wagon, where he had miraculously missed detection by the Waschini who had been hired to murder him and his parents.

In the time that had passed, Adia had found a way to prevent the destruction of the Peoples' culture by thwarting the High Council's plan to reveal Khon'-Tor's grievous crime against her. She had made the terrible choice to send her newborn daughter, Nimida, away to safety, and she had survived Hakani's attempt at killing herself and Nimida's brother, Nootau.

She had experienced a new level of Healership and connection to the Great Mother, opened up by her friendship with Urilla Wuti. She had been brought to the Corridor by E'ranale and even been reunited with her father, the great Apenimon'Mok, former Leader of the People of the Deep Valley.

Adia had fallen in love and paired with the most wonderful mate anyone could ask for and had raised two offspring to adulthood. She had lived to see Nootau and Oh'Dar paired and Oh'Dar now with an offspring of his own. She had experienced the birth of An'Kru, and recently, their twins. The shameful secret she had lived with regarding Nootau and Nimida's true birthright was now out in the open.

Proving that it is never too late, she had watched the redemption of Khon'Tor and his discovery of the true blessings in life.

She had witnessed the events leading up to the opening of Kht'shWea and the creation of the twelve Sassen Guardians. Waschini now lived among the People, and a new brotherhood was forming between the Brothers, the People, and the Sassen.

There were moments when her faith had wavered and times when she had not been sure she would find it again, but her connection to the Great

Spirit had expanded and deepened with each challenge she had been presented.

Adia's thoughts returned to the moment when Pan had announced that she would be taking An'Kru with her when he turned seven years old. And that same time, when Nootau had said he would be going with An'Kru to wherever Pan was taking him.

And through all that has happened to me, I think the most important lesson I have learned is that hard times cannot be prevented; all we can do is trust that somehow we will find the strength within ourselves to get through them.

Adia had weathered everything life had thrown her way, and each victory had reassured her that she was not alone. That she was never alone. The love of her friends, family, and the Great Spirit had been there for her through it all and would be there for her through whatever lay ahead.

But how fortunate for Adia that a Healer's vision of her own future was often blocked, and she was free to celebrate in peace the blessings and the challenges she had already experienced.

Because a storm was coming.

AN INTERVIEW WITH THE CHARACTERS, WHO WERE SITTING AROUND WAITING TO SPEAK WITH ME.

Ned: That was amazing. And exhausting. I will be glad for a break while you are writing Series Three.

Storis: I agree. I am still reeling. Whatever is coming next, it can't be more alarming than what we just went through.

Ned: Why are you smiling like that, Leigh?

LR: We never know what is around the corner, do we? Well, that's life. Sometimes we are embraced and gently led along the path. Other times we are dragged kicking and screaming. What matters is to remember that, despite how it may appear, we are never really lost. And though each one's path looks different, we are all headed to the same place. Home into the arms of the Great Spirit.

Adia: Frankly, I was glad to sit most of this one out. I am exhausted. But I am grateful that Iella and Nootau will be returning with me to Kthama— whenever that happens.

Acaraho: It has been difficult for us to be apart. I, too, will be grateful when our family is reunited.

LR: Eitel, this is your first time here with us; how are you faring?

Eitel: I am glad to be here, but my heart is heavy. I am afraid I am in love with Moart'Tor.

Naahb: Do not say that; you cannot be. You do not even know him. And it is too dangerous!

Eitel: Brother, I appreciate your concern for me. But despite his size, he is not dangerous; I know this in my heart.

Naahb: That is not what I mean by dangerous. Your size difference. You cannot possibly bear his offling. Do you not remember hearing the story of what happened to Hakani, Haan's Akassa female, when she was carrying Kalli?

Eitel: The Mothoc and Sassen are not as different as Hakani and Haan. It is not the same. Oh, stop glaring at me, Naahb.

LR: I hate to see you two at odds with each other. Just take it one step at a time and see what happens. Eitel, you and Moart'Tor barely know each other, and he has said he isn't staying at Kayerm. So it is all up in the air, isn't it?

Eitel: I know. I just like him so much.

(Naahb leaned over and put an arm around his sister, which I was very happy to see.)

Chief Kotori: I am grateful that my people are safe and sound back in their homes, though the scars of what they endured will not heal quickly. We will take refuge in knowing we are now part of a larger brotherhood, working together to save Etera.

Oh'Dar: Leigh. My grandparents, Ben and Miss Vivian. They are getting older. And so is Kweeuu.

LR: I know, Oh'Dar. I know your heart is heavy. It is the heartbreak of our lives that our paths and those of the people we love so dearly do not continue together until the end of our days here. But, perhaps it is merciful that we do not live forever on this side. When we have carried the burdens of this life too long, our hearts weary, and our bodies worn and tired out, how sweet the relief must be to cast it all off and step through the veil to be made whole and vital again. Think of the joy at the moment of our reunion.

Ned: I miss Buster dreadfully.

LR: Okay, everyone, lighten up! It is the end of Series One, not the end of everything. You are going to have me crying here in a moment!

Ned: I want to bring Buster back with me.

LR: Do you think Buster would like that?

Ned: No. You're right. I'm being selfish. Buster deserves to stay at home with my parents. It's the only life he's known.

Oh'Dar: Goats.

LR: Pardon?

Oh'Dar: My grandmother's goats. I think they are at Grace's. Drat. Another trip with the wagon. It seems all I do anymore is go back and forth between places. Is that going to end?

Ned: We should get them in the spring. I wrote in my letters that I hoped we would be back in the spring.

LR: You have a few more trips to make, Oh'Dar, but it will settle down at some point. You have a daughter to raise, after all. And more children coming—

(At overhearing that, Acise just popped in.)

Acise: As you would say in your world, Leigh—*wait, what*?

LR: Yes, of course you will have more children, Acise. And your sister will have children, too.

(Acise and Oh'Dar just hugged each other, by the way!)

Acaraho: Why is Pan never here, Leigh?

LR: It is just her way. She keeps to herself. She bears many burdens.

Adia: We know so little about the Guardians. Even Haan and his people do not seem to know much. Who was the first? How many have there been? We know of Moc'Tor and Pan. There must have been others. And why are their lives always so tragic?

LR: The mantle of Guardianship seems to ask everything of its wearer. But that is an interesting thought, Adia. Maybe I will write a story about the origins and lives of the Guardians of Etera. I am sure there are also unanswered questions in the minds of the readers. Of course, Series Two tells the story of the Guardian Moc'Tor, the events that led up to The Great Division, and the creation of the Sassen and Akassa.

Thank you, everyone, for speaking with me. I bid you goodbye until we meet again—

Come with me, and we will see what was, what is, and what might be.

PLEASE READ

This is a work of fiction, but many of you will recognize storyline threads reminiscent of the dark period in US history brought on by Andrew Jackson's 1830 Indian Removal Act, which resulted in the forced eviction of hundreds of thousands of First Nations People from the land they had lived on for generations. The resultant suffering was truly an abomination and, in my opinion, remains one of the deepest stains on our history. No words can truly convey the travesty and injustice of this act, which nothing can make right.

You can read about it here: https://www.history.com/topics/native-american-history/trail-of-tears

This is the end of Series One. You have come the complete journey with me. And I have one last favor to ask. Please, if you would, find your way back to the Amazon order page for each of the 13 books in this series, and if you have not, please leave a 4 or 5-star rating for each book. You do not have to write anything if you do not wish, but a rating would help me immensely. Of course, 5-stars are the best.

I know I ask you to do this in each book, but that is because ratings are important to an author and also to potential readers. Ratings on Goodreads are also very appreciated.

Thank you so much.

Blessings - Leigh

ACKNOWLEDGMENTS

My mother, who took me on journeys of wonder through the stories she would tell my brother and me. She didn't live a charmed life. She married a man whom she loved more than he loved her. It was painful for all of us. But she loved us the best she could, trying to keep her pain from us, trying to keep the peace in the household. I lost her when I was only 35, but I will see her again, in a place where there are no more tears and no goodbyes and where we are loved more than we can imagine.

My best friend, Carolene Blain, has been my stalwart supporter throughout this journey. My world is happier, less lonely because she is in it.

And my beloved brother Richard, whom I am blessed to have still continuing on this journey with me.